The Antique Hunter's Murder at the Castle

ALSO BY C. L. MILLER

The Antique Hunter's Guide to Murder
The Antique Hunter's Death on the Red Sea

The Antique Hunter's Murder at the Castle

⋟ A NOVEL ⋞

C. L. Miller

ATRIA BOOKS

NEW YORK ⚜ AMSTERDAM/ANTWERP ⚜ LONDON ⚜ TORONTO
SYDNEY/MELBOURNE ⚜ NEW DELHI

An Imprint of Simon & Schuster, LLC
1230 Avenue of the Americas
New York, NY 10020

For more than 100 years, Simon & Schuster has championed authors and the stories they create. By respecting the copyright of an author's intellectual property, you enable Simon & Schuster and the author to continue publishing exceptional books for years to come. We thank you for supporting the author's copyright by purchasing an authorized edition of this book.

No amount of this book may be reproduced or stored in any format, nor may it be uploaded to any website, database, language-learning model, or other repository, retrieval, or artificial intelligence system without express permission. All rights reserved. Inquiries may be directed to Simon & Schuster, 1230 Avenue of the Americas, New York, NY 10020 or permissions@simonandschuster.com.

This book is a work of fiction. Any references to historical events, real people, or real places are used fictitiously. Other names, characters, places, and events are products of the author's imagination, and any resemblance to actual events or places or persons, living or dead, is entirely coincidental.

Copyright © 2026 by BWL Management
Originally published in Great Britain in 2026 by Macmillan, an imprint of Pan Macmillan

All rights reserved, including the right to reproduce this book or portions thereof in any form whatsoever. For information, address Atria Books Subsidiary Rights Department, 1230 Avenue of the Americas, New York, NY 10020.

First Atria Books hardcover edition March 2026

ATRIA BOOKS and colophon are registered trademarks of Simon & Schuster, LLC

Simon & Schuster strongly believes in freedom of expression and stands against censorship in all its forms. For more information, visit BooksBelong.com.

For information about special discounts for bulk purchases, please contact Simon & Schuster Special Sales at 1-866-506-1949 or business@simonandschuster.com.

The Simon & Schuster Speakers Bureau can bring authors to your live event. For more information or to book an event, contact the Simon & Schuster Speakers Bureau at 1-866-248-3049 or visit our website at www.simonspeakers.com.

Manufactured in the United States of America

3 5 7 9 10 8 6 4 2

Library of Congress Cataloging-in-Publication Data has been applied for.

ISBN 978-1-6680-3206-0
ISBN 978-1-6680-3208-4 (ebook)

Let's stay in touch! Scan here to get book recommendations, exclusive offers, and more delivered to your inbox.

To Billy, Aria, and Leo

Sooner or later we have all to pay for what we do.

—Oscar Wilde

1

Bella
Wednesday, February 7, 5 p.m.

The snow was descending in sheets as Bella turned her rental car down the long drive to Fawside Castle. It blanketed the world around her. The tires slushed on the gritted tarmac and the headlights lit up snow-covered evergreen trees lining the drive, creating an eerie avenue. It was deathly quiet—too quiet.

A few moments later, the car lights illuminated the castle: a large, square building with turrets on each corner. It would have made Disney proud. The battlements, windowsills, and gargoyles were all partially hidden beneath the snow, and it made Bella wonder what else was hidden in plain sight. Craning her neck, she studied the row upon row of windows rising up in an almost never-ending procession, as far as the eye could see. Not one interior light glowed against the coal-black night. It was as if the darkness had leached into the castle walls—it looked cold inside and out. Bella shivered.

She took a fortifying breath and parked near the entrance, knowing she would need to make this meeting quick. There was no way she was turning back now. It had taken her years to get to this point.

After tugging her bobble hat over her ears and pulling on her large puffer jacket, she reached into her bag for the lip gloss Carole had given her. She swept the cherry-colored wand over her lips and checked her makeup in the mirror before tugging at the tips of her gray wig. She looked old, really old, but that was the point of going undercover as a new but experienced auctioneer from the local auction house. It was imperative that the owner of the castle did not recognize her.

Bella knew the role she needed to play. Act professional. Convince him that she only wanted to look around, determine the rough value of the castle's contents, and take some photos—all the while learning as much as she could about him, and keeping an eye out for any of the paintings or antiques that Arthur Crockleford had listed in the third of his six journals.

Snowflakes settled on her eyelashes, clouding her vision as she reached for the cord on the old-fashioned pull doorbell. It clanged inside, but still no lights came on.

Bella took a step back, her boots crunching on the recently settled snow. "Hello?" she called, scanning the windows above her. "I'm Emma Page. I have an appointment with Euan."

Her neck prickled, which was normally a sign she was being watched. *Turn around and go*, her senses screamed. But she wouldn't allow fear to control her actions—that was for amateurs.

"Euan? I'm from Griffin & Thompson, the auctioneers. We have an appointment."

In her pocket she had a fake Griffin & Thompson business card matching the one she had swiped from the desk of their employee Alexandra Pattern. She hoped Euan didn't know the auction house and its employees intimately, because she had also used a copy of Alexandra's outfit and overall look as inspiration while putting together her disguise. Bella often found it useful to assume real identities when out hunting; if she was spotted, it made people—particularly the law—look in the wrong direction.

"... I believe you were friends with Arthur Crockleford?"

Darkened silence echoed in the icy air around her.

It had taken every ounce of her skill and determination to get to this point, and now she stood outside in the freezing cold, at a loss. Maybe she was wrong, and the answers she had spent years searching for wouldn't be found inside this spooky old castle tonight. The snow was falling more heavily now; before long, the roads would be impassable without snow chains. Her time was running out. Soon she would be trapped.

Bella twisted the handle.

The door didn't budge.

Everyone in the countryside knows that the front door is never used, so she pulled up the fur-trimmed hood of her coat and followed an ice-covered path around the side of the castle. A flurry of fresh snowflakes settled on the bushes and vines that climbed up the side of the building, clinging to the gray stone.

Bella turned the corner and stopped. The castle's back door stood wide open. Instinctively her fists clenched, her stance widened, and her core straightened, ready to fight if needed. In the summer, an open door was a welcome—in the winter, it could mean something far worse.

The only sound came from her boots compacting the snow as she approached the open door and peered inside. Should she cross the threshold? Would it be safe?

Before her she could just make out a large room with a tall ceiling supported by black beams. To her right was a long row of coats with welly boots below, and beyond that a pitch-black hallway. A whirl of freezing wind rushed over the gardens and passed the open door, making it thunder against the wall. Bella shuddered and pulled out her phone.

"Hello? . . . Is anyone here?" Her voice sounded commanding, even if her racing heart was telling her to flee.

This can't be a dead end, can it?

She pressed the only phone number on her favorites list, and it wasn't lost on her that this was the first time she had ever had anyone to call when a hunt didn't feel right. The number rang twice, then beeped as the signal went out.

"Euan?" she called again.

He had insisted that she come at 5 p.m. on the dot.

Curiosity tingled in her veins and began to silence her pounding heart.

"Euan?"

Maybe she should step inside and search for him. If he wasn't there, she would leave.

The moment she passed the threshold, she noticed an accumulation of snow along with pools of water. It looked as if the door had been standing open for quite some time, perhaps hours. The wind howled down the empty corridors and it was as if the shadows were whispering a warning of impending danger. Bella shuddered again but forced herself to stand up straight. There would be no cowering. She never backed down, especially not when a hunt was as personal as this one.

"Is anyone here?" she called, forcing her legs to move forward. Even though she was inside now, her breath fogged out in the frosted air.

Last time she'd called the castle's landline, she recalled, there had been dogs barking in the background. So where were the dogs now?

The phone vibrated in her hand and she relaxed when she saw the name.

"Bella?" Carole sounded worried. "You called, are you all right? The signal is terrible."

"Carole." She didn't like the relief that rushed through her when she heard her friend's voice. "I thought this was the place I was looking for, but the back door was wide open. There isn't anyone here. I'm going to look around, but it feels wrong... Carole, this could be a..." She paused—she didn't want to voice her stupidity out loud, but if she was going to admit her fear to anyone, it would be Carole. "A trap. I think I need..."

"What? Well, don't go in there, darling. Wait until we come to Scotland next week—" The phone went silent.

"Carole, are you there? I thought I was so close, but..."

The line beeped again, then went dead.

Bella berated herself for almost asking for help. She had always done fine on her own, and a quick scout-around wouldn't hurt. She told herself it was just an empty castle. It might creak and rattle with age, but there was no such thing as ghosts.

She hurried to the first door she found and pushed it open.

"I have an appointment," she called into the room.

After finding the light switch, Bella studied the large kitchen before her. She flinched as a tabby cat, its hackles high, hissed at her from the kitchen island. Another shiver ran through her. She preferred dogs.

"There, there... nice kitty. Don't attack." She backed out into the corridor again and shut the kitchen door, turning and calling out again, "Hello?"

This wasn't going to plan at all. The warm excitement that had filled her during the drive over here had given way to cold, hard disappointment. It was clear that she wasn't going to meet Euan tonight, but she drew in a long, deep breath and consoled herself with the thought of looking around the castle unsupervised. It was an easy decision to make a quick scan of the downstairs rooms before leaving. She had made this appointment in order to meet Euan face-to-face, but she'd also wanted a good look at the place, so that was a consolation prize she could live with. Her hand shook as she reached for a door handle on the opposite side of the corridor. Freezing fingers, she told herself firmly, even though her hands were covered in cashmere-lined leather gloves. Absolutely nothing to do with the nerves that swept around her stomach.

Where was Euan?

Turning the handle quickly, as if she were ripping off a bandage, Bella pushed the door open harder than she intended. It swung in easily and banged against the wall. Her phone's light came to rest on a large mahogany desk in the center of the room and she palmed the wall for a light switch. When the room lit up, she smiled. She was in a study or library. Leather-bound books lined the walls from floor to ceiling to her left, and an illuminated central cabinet was filled with row upon row of silver.

A pair of silver candlesticks had pride of place in the middle of a shelf at eye level, and Bella stepped toward them to take a closer look. They were antique Scottish sterling silver, modeled in the form of cobra snakes. She had seen ones exactly like them in Arthur's third journal— the snake candlesticks were rare enough that her smile widened as she scanned the other silver pieces. A row of silver beakers above the candlesticks was yet another indication that Bella was in the right place. She reached out with her gloved hands and tried the little brass handles, but the cabinet wouldn't open.

Bella might not have met Euan McGovern, laird of Fawside Castle, that night, but she had found a few of the items that were catalogued in Arthur's journal. It was almost a win—almost. She wondered how many of the other items he had listed, such as paintings by Sir Henry Raeburn or valuable pieces of Wemyss and Mauchline Ware, might be hidden in the castle. She and her friends believed that most of the items recorded in Arthur's journals had either been stolen or bought on the black market over the years and now resided in private collections.

Did this castle house one such collection? Bella intended to find out. If some of the Scottish silver was here, perhaps she was getting close to finding other items. And on top of that, the Lockwood Antique Hunter's Agency had been contracted to work on a case for the FBI's Art Crime Team: the hunt for the origin of the so-called Boston paintings, three paintings that were listed in Arthur's journal and had been discovered at a Boston auction house a few months back.

Was that a coincidence, or was it all linked?

A hum of satisfaction escaped her lips as the realization settled over her. It was either an overly bold or sloppy move to put the silver collection on display—an indication that the castle's owner believed the theft of the silver had taken place so long ago that people had stopped looking for it. What else was the castle hiding? The Boston paintings were believed to have been sent from Scotland. Could they have been sent from here?

Weeks earlier, Bella had been sent an article regarding the paintings. She had reread it earlier today, curled up in a tartan armchair by the fireside in the Kelmore House Hotel sitting room.

The Boston Chronicle

Three paintings previously attributed to the eighteenth-century Scottish artist Sir Henry Raeburn have been identified as forgeries while on display at Boston's Hayward Auction House. The FBI's Art Crime Team has been brought in to hunt down a suspected international forgery ring.

According to an anonymous source, the investigation began over a month ago when the auction house was contacted by Scottish specialists who believed that the Boston paintings were forgeries. Curators at Glasgow's Kelvingrove Art Gallery and Museum had found while putting together an exhibition that they held the same paintings, which they verified as originals.

The forged paintings are believed to have been sent to Boston with false provenances and verification from an Edinburgh-based collector.

The FBI is working with UK consultants to trace this individual. Our source suggests the forger may be part of a larger ring specializing in selling British and Scottish works to US collectors. The three paintings found in Boston may be only the tip of the iceberg.

The biting winter air coiled round Bella's bare fingertips as she turned to step back out into the corridor and search the rest of the castle.

The creak of a floorboard behind her made the muscles in her shoulders lock, and she reached into her pocket for her flick knife. Her gaze swept the room. In an ornate gilt mirror she saw the reflection of someone raising a bronze candlestick behind her head, ready to strike.

2

Freya
Wednesday, February 7, 5:30 p.m.

In Little Meddington, ice clung to the windows of Crockleford Antiques and freezing February air seeped in through the shop's warped door, because I was still unable to bring myself to have a replacement fitted. Arthur Crockleford, my antique-hunting mentor and former owner of the shop, had installed new windows and a new door decades ago. Part of me wanted to modernize the place now that I was establishing my own antique-hunting business; but then, everything about it reminded me of Arthur, and that made me want to keep it exactly as it was. I was stuck in a strange limbo between past and present.

Sitting behind Arthur's antique partners desk, I reached for a Victorian lock and placed it back in the old box with the others I had been practicing on. Sky Stevens, our twenty-five-year-old assistant, who now lived above the shop, had found the box tucked away in a cupboard in Arthur's former bedroom. It was filled with salvaged locks and the tool kit. Arthur had shown me how to pick them decades ago. I had started teaching Sky, but this afternoon Owen had arrived to take her out on a date.

The first lock I'd picked up had taken me longer than expected to open and it was clear that my skills were rusty. The second one had opened easily, but the third had defeated me. I threw them all back in the box and closed it just as the Georgian longcase clock chimed five thirty. Time had slipped by while I had been caught up in my own thoughts. It wasn't surprising, considering we hadn't seen a customer in two days and opening and closing the shop had become a formality.

I was flipping the *Open* sign to *Closed* when the electric went out.

"Carole?" I called instinctively before remembering she had hurried to the post office some time ago and not returned. I fumbled in my pocket for my phone to call her, but the signal was down, so I switched on the torch instead. It wasn't unusual for our electricity to cut out in a winter storm, but ever since the Copthorn Manor case last spring, it always made me uneasy. Where was Carole?

In about three hours, or whenever my phone signal and the power came back on, I would receive a useless text message from the electricity board informing me that they were aware of the situation and were trying to fix it.

Carole would have followed the local tradition and headed to the Crown—the only place in the vicinity that could offer a warm welcome, the company of locals, and a generator.

I locked up the shop and made my way down the street, waving to Agatha, who was closing the Teapot Tearooms. "Everything okay?" I said, nodding in the direction of her shop. This was the standard question one asked in such a situation.

She grabbed hold of the silver torch she'd had clenched between her teeth and smiled. "Always happens, doesn't it? A little bit of wind, rain, or snow and the whole county comes to a standstill. My cousin lives in Calgary, Canada, and she's always laughing at us. Bet the trains to Colchester are all canceled now."

I chuckled. She wasn't wrong. "Be careful as you go. It's getting icy."

"Oh, I'm not driving home in this, dear." Agatha looked up at the three snowflakes making their way to the ground. "No, no! I'm going to the Crown to get a hot toddy like the rest of the village, and Simon can get us home in his tractor." She waved at someone behind me. "Clive, save me a seat, won't you?" she called to the young farmer on the other side of the road, then added to me, "I saw your aunt heading that way an hour ago."

"Let me help you. I know you're still on the waiting list to replace that knee of yours . . ." I stepped toward her and she smiled as we linked arms. "Can't have you falling over, can we?"

"You're such a valuable part of this community, Freya. You do know that, don't you? Even if you're not very Suffolk."

I tutted and nudged her. "I arrived here when I was twelve."

Agatha patted my arm. "And we're glad you did. Now, your Aunt Carole, on the other hand, has a proper country nose for a storm coming. I'm quite sure she'll be in prime position by the pub fire."

The Crown was overflowing with villagers, so much so that the tables had been given over to children having their tea while the adults had an early glass of wine in the bar. I found Carole in pride of place beside the roaring fire at the center of the pub. She had reserved the empty chair next to her by slinging her coat and bag over it.

"Yoo-hoo!" She waved frantically when she saw me.

I squeezed though the throng of people toward her. Agatha had waved me on and headed for her husband, Simon, at the back. Carole stood and swept me into the vacant seat. "It's taken you quite a while to get here, darling. That chair was almost snatched away a thousand times over!"

"The electric's only just gone out, and by the look of this . . ." I motioned at the packed pub. "You would've thought it went out hours ago."

Carole patted my knee, but there was a tension in her shoulders that told me something was wrong—and it had nothing to do with the snow. "When you've been living on this Suffolk hill as long as we have, you get a sense of these things and plan accordingly." She handed me a large glass of wine and before I could refuse said, "It's nearly six p.m., darling, and we're in the eye of the storm." She winked, because we all knew that we were not actually in a real storm.

"Thank you." I tapped my glass to hers as we smiled at each other, and I took a small sip. "What's the matter?"

Carole wouldn't look at me.

"Better if you just tell me, isn't it?" I soothed.

"Were you all right when the electric went out?" She looked concerned, but she was also changing the subject. "I know you get a bit . . . anxious, after Bella locked you in the Copthorn Manor vault. And then when those criminals kidnapped you, and . . . Well, we got out of it all okay."

"I'm fine. Really." It almost wasn't a lie.

Carole continued. "I've been talking to Bella. She is sorry and *really* does want to make up for it. She has a good heart, but she's had no one to show her the right way. Arthur was beginning to get through to her, but he . . ."

Was murdered before he could, and now it's down to us. That was what Carole was trying to say.

"Honestly, I'm not worried about anything to do with Bella. I'm fine." Which was mostly true. But the way Carole anxiously tapped her finger on the stem of her wineglass and the small crease in her forehead made me believe that something was troubling her. "What's going on? What's wrong?"

She put her glass down and ran a hand over her blond hair. "It's . . . well . . . Bella, she called me, but . . ." Carole reached for her glass again and lifted it to her lips—her hand gave a little tremor and her frown deepened. "Her phone cut out. I tried to call her back but I couldn't hear a lot of what she was saying. I'm quite sure she was about to ask for help."

Our eyes locked. Carole knew I had my issues with Bella, but I admired her fierce, stubborn independence. Never in all the time we'd known her had she asked others for help. "She was in a deserted castle, but it could be a trap. Now I can't get through to her."

After we'd first met Bella at Copthorn Manor, our paths had crossed again while she was undercover on a specialist antiques cruise heading to Jordan. I was officially there as an onboard antiques expert, but I was also hunting down a mysterious figure known as the Collector. Bella clearly possessed a wealth of knowledge on the art and antiques underworld and its various players, but she wasn't always entirely forthcoming with the rest of us at the Lockwood Antique Hunter's Agency. Still, Arthur had trusted and mentored Bella before his murder, and that made me want to give her the benefit of the doubt.

"Freya, are you listening? I'm thinking we might have to go to Scotland. See if she's all right."

I leaned forward. "Are you sure she was asking for help? Where exactly was she when your phone cut out?"

I hadn't heard much from Bella since early December. Phil, the FBI agent we were now working with, had emailed to let us know that a Boston auction house had called the FBI's Art Crime Team to inspect three paintings they believed to be forgeries. One of the discoveries made by Phil and his colleagues was that the three paintings were not only forgeries but had been trafficked from the UK. Agent Sloane, Phil's new partner, had looked into it, and all the leads pointed to Scotland, but the seller's identification was fake. That stopped the case at a dead end—until the Lockwood Agency was called in, and we recognized that the paintings were the same ones listed in Arthur's journal. But we had no way of knowing if it was a list of original or forged paintings.

The moment we found the connection, it was as if we had handed Bella the map and keys to the Crown Jewels. Her excitement was palpable. When I questioned her about her interest in Arthur's journal and how she knew about it in the first place, she simply shut down. Going by our previous cases, I believed that Bella could contribute a huge amount to the agency with her black-market knowledge, but it was hard to make her a colleague when being a team player wasn't in her skill set. Carole thought differently. From her point of view, Arthur had wanted Bella involved, so that meant she was now part of the family and could be treated as another wayward niece.

It was clear Bella knew a lot more about the Boston paintings case than she had told any of us. Did she know who had sent the paintings from Scotland to Boston? Had she uncovered any of the other paintings listed, and were they all forgeries? Or had she grown too close to the art underworld and been discovered?

Questions whirled in my mind. "We should go home and pack."

Carole nodded. "I thought you'd come around. We can check at the hotel where she was staying first, and if she's not there we'll head to the castle."

Leaving our wineglasses still full, we hurried out into the frosty evening.

3

Wednesday, February 7, 6 p.m.

It always amazed me how quickly Carole could get ready when she really wanted to. Within twenty minutes, we were packed and on the road.

As the lights of oncoming traffic flickered by, Carole held Arthur's third journal on her lap and we mulled over what we knew of the case so far. The journal held photographs of twenty-three paintings, mostly Scottish masters. The three paintings that had been found in Boston were forgeries; the originals had been accounted for in private collections by the Scottish art expert putting together the exhibition in Glasgow. But the question remained: Were all the paintings catalogued in Arthur's journal forgeries, or were some originals?

Sky had managed to track down a further four of the paintings in Arthur's journal to private collections, and she had sent emails requesting viewings. Those collectors believed their paintings were authentic, but without verification by an expert it was hard to know for certain. I had a sneaking suspicion that Sky and Bella had been looking into the owners of the paintings on the sly, but I trusted Sky enough to believe that if she found something, I would be the first to know.

There were three other sections in Arthur's journal. One contained details of a large collection of Scottish silver that had been stolen from a manor in the Highlands twelve years ago. Three years ago, six pairs of candlesticks from that collection had been recovered after a private house in the same region was raided by police looking for a drug-smuggling ring. The insurance company still had a reward out for the rest of the collection's recovery, and this had initially made us focus more on the Scottish silver. If we found it, we would get some much-needed income for the agency on top of our consultancy fee from the FBI.

Arthur's other two lists focused on Wemyss Ware and Mauchline Ware, collectibles with Scottish associations dating back to the nineteenth century. Wemyss Ware pottery is named after the aristocratic Wemyss family of Fife; Mauchline Ware isn't pottery but wooden souvenirs decorated with little pictures, originally aimed at tourists. It's named after a town in Ayrshire where much of it was manufactured. All of our research into Wemyss Ware had come to a dead end, as many of the pieces were not rare or hugely valuable. This journal was different in that sense from the others we had researched—there was no single big-ticket item.

As soon as Bella had learned about the Boston paintings, she'd volunteered to go to Scotland to start looking into where the three forged paintings might have originated. Knowing her as I did, I strongly suspected there was more to her interest than she was letting on. Bella was a wild card of a person—I had hoped that after our adventures on the Red Sea together, when she'd been undercover searching for her missing boyfriend, she would come in from the cold and become part of the team. Instead, she had done the opposite. Now here we were, chasing her to the Scottish Borders after she'd decided to go it alone and put herself in danger. It wasn't out of character, but it was disappointing.

And it seemed as if I was the one Bella had really shut out—Carole had been her first call when she was in trouble. Why had she chosen my aunt over me? Deep down, I knew the answer. Carole had a way with people that I wished I had. She was open and warm with everyone she met—there was never a moment's hesitation to trust. She saw the bright side. People like Bella and me were far more wary. It took someone with Carole's personality to draw us in, and before we knew it, we had told her everything.

Back in Jordan, Bella and I had come to an understanding. She knew that Arthur had kept journals, which he'd left to me, and that one of them had listed Scottish antiques. In return for her help on the Red Sea case, she wanted to see that particular journal when we got back to Suffolk. I agreed, and after we returned the whole agency started looking into where the Scottish art and antiques in that journal might be hidden.

At first, Bella had joined the weekly team calls where everyone updated their progress and Carole extracted relationship gossip and imparted cocktail recipes. During one call, I remember seeing the light dim in Bella's face when Sky told us that she'd failed to uncover anything important about the Scottish collections.

The identification of the Boston paintings felt like the break we had been hoping for. But once Phil assigned everyone an area to focus on, rifts started to grow. When he suggested during a meeting that Bella could share the names of her "friends" in the art-and-antiques-trafficking world as a "sign of good faith," the temperature dropped to match the winter storm outside the shop window. After that, she rarely showed up.

"When Bella called yesterday, she said she had narrowed it down to two Scottish castles outside of Edinburgh," Carole said. "But the main problem, darling, is that she never told me how she found that out . . . I've been sitting here wracking my brain, wondering how it's all connected. Bella has been a bit . . . secretive." She gripped my arm, and her forehead furrowed. "Freya, I've been trying to call her since the phone went dead an hour ago, but it goes straight to voicemail. What if something really bad has happened? Could she be lying in a ditch somewhere? Could she be stuck in a dungeon?"

I had steered Carole's nautical-blue vintage Mercedes down the narrow country lanes and we were now, at last, on the motorway heading north to Scotland.

"Bella's one of the strongest and most self-sufficient women I've ever met. It's hard to imagine her being unable to handle any situation."

Carole hummed in agreement, but I knew that didn't stop her worrying, because I felt the same.

I sometimes wondered if it was just a protective layer that Bella had built around herself—as if experience had taught her that the only way to not get hurt was to try and control every situation. People were hard to control, so she distanced herself from them. I recognized that desire to be an island, to survive without anyone's help, but I had learned during the Red Sea case that I didn't need to do things on my own anymore.

Somewhere along the line, between our collective lack of progress and Phil's mistrust, Bella had decided she was better off researching this case on her own.

"If something has happened, then I feel like I'm partly to blame for showing her Arthur's journal." I glanced across the console and caught Carole's eye, and she shook her head.

"This is Bella we're talking about . . . there's never any stopping her. All we know is that Arthur told her he had written down the paintings that she was interested in, and that's why she struck the deal with you to look at Arthur's journal when we returned to Suffolk. But you and I have both asked her repeatedly why, and she never says. Arthur and Bella had an agreement, but she doesn't trust us enough to tell us what that was."

"Do you think she's working for someone else?" I asked, not taking my focus off the road.

"Um . . . well . . ."

I snapped my head around. "Out with it."

"Now, I don't want you to get angry, but she *might* have mentioned she was trying to get into a castle . . . And when she told me the name of it, Fawside Castle, I remembered that I had met the residents once, with Arthur. So we came up with a rather marvelous plan of Bella pretending to be a valuer from an auction house. It was all going so well, but then the phone cut out . . ."

I gripped the steering wheel so hard that my knuckles turned white. "Phil said no one was to act. When did you and Bella discuss this plan?" Bella wouldn't think twice about doing whatever it took to get the answers she was looking for. Her moral code was gray at best.

"When you put it like that it sounds *criminal*, darling." My aunt kept her gaze fixed on the lights outside the window. "But you know Bella and I don't like following orders from men. If *you* had asked us, it might have been different, but you seemed to defer to Phil, and we weren't keen . . ."

"Weren't keen!" I tried to keep my voice low. "This isn't, *would you like a side salad with your steak?* This is an active Lockwood Agency case, and that *man* is an FBI agent who's our boss!" I sighed. "What else have you two been up to behind my back?"

"I absolutely refute the charges of being deceitful. We had a few chats and decided to get the information first before bothering Phil and the FBI. And you do seem very . . ." She paused. "*Fond* of him. We concluded that you might take the opportunity to call him before we were ready."

"I'm no such thing . . . I wouldn't just call him up." Although I might have done. "We were given a clear way of working." Although working with Carole and Bella was anything but clear.

Carole tutted. "Unfortunately, Bella and I are impatient by nature. Phil's way was too slow for us."

I'm not sure why, but the phrase "Bella and I" stung ever so slightly. "And now Bella has gone storming into a castle in the dark and hasn't been heard from since?" I glared at her. "We're meant to be a team." And how did Carole always know everything before I did?

Carole sighed. "Then our team needs a new leader. One whose orders we'll follow."

I hoped it wasn't going to be on my shoulders to tell Phil about this. He really did like being in charge and having people do what he told them, and now Carole and Bella had done the opposite. I, on the other hand, didn't feel like I had enough experience to lead the full investigation, so happily followed his lead. Before we opened the Lockwood Agency, I had spent over twenty years away from antique hunting while I raised my daughter, Jade. Throughout all that time, Phil had been in the field hunting down members of the art and antiquities black market.

Phil was as passionate as I was about stopping the black-market trade in antiques, and about helping repatriate items of cultural significance to their original countries. We had grown close over the last couple of cases and I wanted everyone I cared about to get on well together. Now it seemed Carole and Bella had decided on mutiny before this case was even fully underway. I had a feeling it was all going to be a lot harder than I'd initially thought.

I suspected that what Carole really wanted was an adventure—and now she had an excuse to hightail it to Scotland. Despite my frustration, a part of me knew it was exactly what we needed. Antique hunting was in my blood, and it was a hard call to turn away from.

4

Wednesday, February 7, night

Somewhere in the Midlands, around midnight, we stopped at a service station for coffee. Worry itched at the very edge of my senses. We had tried ringing Bella repeatedly throughout the evening, but all our calls went to voicemail. We'd called the Kelmore House Hotel, where she was staying, but they hadn't seen her either and her in-room phone just rang out.

There was only one other person I could call for help: Phil. But I didn't want to get him involved just yet. Not after what Carole had said.

My chest tightened. I didn't want to admit that two—or perhaps even three, depending on where Sky stood in all of this—of the four "members" of the Lockwood Antique Hunter's Agency had gone rogue. The agency's role as an FBI consultant had only just been formalized; our first case had only recently been assigned. It made me worry that I had already failed. Phil would be deeply unimpressed that Bella had gone off on her own, especially since he'd warned me last month that this would happen after she didn't show up for yet another team meeting. Perhaps he was right. Bella wasn't going to be a team member just because I wanted her to be one; she had to want it too. And it was clear that she didn't.

After staring out the service station café window for another fifteen minutes, I conceded that I had to call Phil. I couldn't make this about my pride—Bella might be in trouble.

"Hi, it's Freya." My heartbeat picked up, but I told myself this was a professional relationship now. One that I couldn't mess up with memories of his warm hand on my lower back as we danced at the Halloween Ball on the cruise ship back in October.

"I see that, and it's the reason I'm answering." Phil's deep Southern drawl always seemed more pronounced over the phone. "Is everything all right?"

I took a long breath and Carole leaned closer to me while gripping her coffee cup.

"Freya?" He said my name in that tight way of his that demanded an answer.

"Um, it's fine . . ." This was more awkward than I'd expected, and I wondered if Phil was thinking about October too. I sighed. "There is something."

"Oh, really? What sort of something?" His voice dipped lower and I sensed he was smiling. I wondered if this was getting dangerously close to flirting.

Just tell him and then deal with his "I told you so." I let out the air in my lungs as a truck blared its horn at another driver. "We can't get hold of Bella."

"Okay, and . . ." He paused, clearly waiting for me to fill him in, but I couldn't find the words; I had closed my eyes, trying to black out the truth. So he continued: "She has a habit of disappearing and resurfacing. Her nature is worryingly predictable. She reminds me of that fable about the scorpion and the frog trying to cross the stream."

I sighed. Was he telling me I was the frog? Clearly he was going to make this difficult.

"She was looking into the paintings . . ." I waited for him to catch up so that I wouldn't have to say it out loud.

"And . . . ?" His tone had darkened.

I started indenting the top of my disposable coffee cup with my nail. "She took what you told us about the Boston paintings being sent from Scotland and headed up there. I think she has contacts . . ."

"The contacts she wouldn't share?"

"Yes . . . Well, she was visiting a Scottish castle earlier. Carole tells me that Arthur knew the owner of the castle, and Bella must have found out . . . something." I almost whispered the last bit. "And now we can't get hold of her."

Silence.

Carole leaned over the small metal table, trying to hear what Phil was saying. "What did he say? Give me the phone."

I covered the phone and mouthed, *Nothing, yet*.

"Oh dear." Carole's eyes were lit with mischief.

I knew Phil well enough to understand that his silence meant he was livid. And if he was angry now, he might totally lose it when he found out we were halfway to Scotland already.

"Phil, are you still there?"

"Let me guess. She was on her way to meet someone alone, without telling anyone all the details, therefore placing herself in danger?"

I rubbed my free hand down my jeans. "It might be a bit worse than that." This was like cold-water therapy. Plunging myself into freezing water and trying to remember how to breathe.

"We all agreed," he barked. "We were going to keep looking for evidence and leads, and then we would all go to Scotland together."

"Well, actually, Bella didn't agree to that . . . because she wasn't in that exact meeting." I gripped my coffee cup and lifted it to my lips, only to discover there was no coffee left.

Another horn blasted outside.

"What time is it there? Where are you?" He didn't wait for an answer. "No. You. Are. Not."

Carole grabbed the phone from me. "Now, darling, this is an emergency. Our friend could be in trouble. You wouldn't expect us to sit on our hands, would you?"

I could hear him groan, and Carole smiled at me. We had him.

"I've no doubt you aren't one hundred percent thrilled, but we are going to save her. This is actually my forte—I saved Freya from that vault, remember? And I'm quite sure I got us out of that trouble in Petra!"

My mouth made a large O, as she was taking a huge liberty with the truth—or one could say it was utter fiction. But she gave me one of her dazzling smiles, and all I could do was shake my head.

Carole held the phone away from her ear and covered the mouthpiece. "He is *really* not happy with you." She listened again. "Phil, the signal is about to cut out, so if you could, just use your contacts and see what you can dig up on Fawside Castle and the Kelmore House Hotel, where she was staying. I'll email over anything else she told me. Lovely chatting to you."

She ended the call and handed me the phone. "He says you're walking headfirst into danger, *again*. He might have used the word 'again' excessively. Oh, and 'reckless.' He seems to like that word a lot."

"Me! You're here too. You're the one who disobeyed his 'ways of working' and your allotted areas of investigation."

"Ah yes. I don't like rules." She shrugged in a "what can I do?" way. "But, you see, he doesn't want to jump my bones, so I don't get the brunt of all this darkly good-looking moodiness."

Phil was our point of contact at the FBI Art Crime Team, but he was more than that. We had been through a lot together over the last two cases, and he always seemed protective of us.

". . . Do you think he's annoyed enough to get on a plane?" Carole added. "Because we could do with his help if Bella is in danger, or if she's found the items. He has a gun and knows how to use it." She winked at me, and I tutted. "Wouldn't it be nice for you to spend some time together again? And he has an FBI badge and everything. That's very useful when we find ourselves in scrapes."

"You're jumping to conclusions," I told her firmly. I didn't want Phil to fly all the way from Washington to Scotland only for Bella to show up tomorrow morning safe and well, having uncovered nothing of any use. My mind conjured the image of his scathing look, and I grimaced.

Carole shook her head, her blond hair swishing over her shoulders. "I have a deep-in-my-bones feeling that something is very wrong. And my bones never lie."

I agreed with her. Something wasn't right. It was easy to pretend all we were doing was moving up the date of our trip to Scotland and looking into the case, as we had already planned.

"We need to get back on the road. I'll drive and you can get some sleep." As we headed back to the car, I remembered something. "Do you know the name of that antique-dealer contact of Bella's? The one she told us about after Jordan? I think she had Sky look into someone . . . a dealer, or maybe it was a collector, in Edinburgh."

"She messaged me about someone she was meeting a week or so ago. Here we are: Alexandra Pattern. She works for Griffin & Thompson auctioneers in Edinburgh. When Bella showed Alexandra the photos of some of the paintings, she said she didn't recognize anything, but Bella thought she was lying. She'd heard from a friend that there had been paintings like the ones from Arthur's journal taken to the auction house and valued by Alexandra but those paintings were never listed for sale by the auction house. It's possible that the auction house found out they were stolen or forged and refused to list them. Bella told me it was a dead end, but . . ."

We frowned at each other. We both knew that Bella was adept in the art of deception.

"I've booked into the same place where Bella was staying, the

Kelmore House Hotel outside St Abbs. That's where we'll start. Then on to Fawside Castle, which is also close," said Carole.

"I've never been to St Abbs," I mumbled while berating myself for not keeping a closer watch on what Bella was up to.

Carole tapped on her phone.

"It's very beautiful, right on the coast, but I'm sure the wind will whip at us this time of year. I hope you've brought your gloves." I frowned; in our hurry, I hadn't even thought about what I was packing. "Don't worry. We'll get a tartan hat, scarf, and gloves and you'll look right at home."

"I'll look like a tourist."

"And everyone will think you're so cute! Especially . . ."

I glared at her but didn't reply. Continuing the conversation would probably end in Carole buying Phil and me matching kilts as a sign of encouragement. And she, of course, would look fabulous in anything tartan.

My phone pinged, saving me from more relationship and fashion advice.

Phil: *I'm on my way. I'll be there by tomorrow evening. Don't do anything until then.*

Carole scoffed after she read it. "He wants to see you, doesn't he? Soon he'll understand that even if we've signed up as consultants, it doesn't mean he's in charge."

I hadn't really expected anything less after calling him, but I wasn't sure who Carole believed was in charge if not Phil. I needed the consultancy position to work out, as it was one of the only ways we could keep paying the bills and build a reputation for the agency. Working with the FBI could bring us a lot of clout if I could only keep everyone together—although it wasn't looking like I could. We hadn't even got through our first case and Bella was in the wind.

The wind howled, and sleet pelted the windscreen so hard that the wipers were having trouble keeping our view of the road ahead clear. Motorway warning signs flashed up messages about dangerous driving conditions, and I couldn't help but wonder if it was an omen of something to come.

An hour later, our headlights illuminated a large sign telling us we were crossing the border into Scotland.

5

Dolores
Thursday, February 8, 7 a.m.

Dolores Fraser hurried into Fawside Castle as fast as her arthritic ankles would carry her. The alarm was switched off and the back door stood wide open. There were puddles all over the hallway, likely melted snow someone had brought in on their boots.

"Hello?" she called, anxiety fluttering in her stomach.

She'd had a text the previous night from Jane—the glamorous and much younger girlfriend of the laird, Euan McGovern—saying that since the storm was getting worse, she was going to stay with a friend. Dolores knew that this meant her "bit on the side" in Edinburgh.

"... India? Are you here?"

She was fond of the laird's daughter. India possessed a quiet strength and was a lot cleverer than she let people see—but Dolores was in a position to see more than others. The young and the old sometimes went unnoticed, and that could be used to their advantage at times.

The corridor was steeped in darkness and the icy chill seeped into her old bones, making her finger joints stiff. She shivered and pulled her coat around her shoulders, taking out her handkerchief to dab her nose.

"Is anyone here?" She tutted at the floor and mumbled, "Such a mess."

You're paid to clean, not to complain. Her mantra popped into her head reflexively. For decades she'd said the same thing to herself every day before work, but there was a quietness about the castle this morning that told her today was different. Perhaps it was because she didn't normally work on Saturdays and therefore wasn't used to the weekend atmosphere. But she had ignored the twinge in her gut—the storm was over, and a sunlit blanket of snow dazzled the lands around the castle. The rugged beauty never ceased to please her.

She got ready to start her cleaning routine, toeing off her wellies and pulling on slippers before heading to the large kitchen down the hallway. "Mouser, where are you?" she called down the corridor to the castle's resident tabby cat as she opened the kitchen door. Jane had taken the dachshunds with her as usual, but the old scraggy tabby cat was still around somewhere.

She reached up to the stately Victorian Welsh dresser for a jar of cat biscuits and shook it to rattle them. "I don't have all day, Mouser. There's too much cleaning to get done."

It wasn't true. She did have all day, and Mouser knew it. Fridays were normally dedicated to the upper floors of the castle, but she hadn't finished yesterday's work. Hoover and dust the master bedroom; open the curtains and windows in nine of the guest rooms to air the place out if the weather was agreeable. By the time she was done, there wouldn't be a fingerprint or smudge on any surface.

Dolores Fraser had a process, and nothing could get in the way of it. She had been that way from the moment her second son was born, recognizing that the only way to get through the days would be to have a strict routine. He was a wild child, never sleeping, always on the hunt for some adventure—something his older brother couldn't stand. But with the structure Dolores put in place, the three of them muddled along quite well. Until her wild child went truly off the rails and his reckless spirit led him to an early grave...

She stopped the cutting grief with a sharp intake of breath before it overtook her heart.

For years she had taken care of Fawside Castle, and it was the best job she'd ever had. The castle had fourteen spacious bedrooms, although a few weren't furnished, and eight bathrooms spread evenly over the two upper floors, but one floor was never used. On the ground floor, the front door opened to a large entrance hallway leading onto a library, a dining room that could easily seat thirty for dinner, and an enormous drawing room with family portraits adorning the walls, hung over elaborate William Morris Strawberry Thief wallpaper on a light blue background. Dolores loved that wallpaper, with its swirling flowers, leaves, and birds—so much so that when she'd found a spare roll of it after Jane had insisted on redecorating the room, she had taken it home. A section of the design was now framed and hanging in her bedroom.

The kitchen was as grand as they came, and yet it was all but abandoned. Not one person who lived in the house—Euan, Jane, or India—knew how to cook a good hearty meal.

A loud meow came from a corner of the kitchen. Mouser wandered toward her and headbutted her leg.

"When will Jane be back from Edinburgh, do you think?" she asked the cat as it licked its white-tipped paw. "Wonder if she's up to no good again." She winked at Mouser. It was their little secret.

Dolores, being part of the household, believed she was the only village resident entitled to speculate about the laird and his family. The local gossips were stuck in a loop when it came to Euan McGovern and Jane, and she was growing very tired of everyone's questions. They asked if she saw the bruises on Jane, but Dolores did not gossip about her employers—not ever. It was another of her rules. Getting side-tracked into gossip wasn't professional. She liked to stick to the facts. Euan McGovern arrived back from New Zealand six or so years ago, with young India following six months after that when her mother died, and had settled into running the castle, farm, and farm shop with ease. The castle was still standing and that was what mattered most.

Dolores fed Mouser, collected her cleaning basket from the hall cupboard, and headed for the central staircase. She allowed herself to daydream, as she often did when cleaning . . . she liked to play queen of the castle while she was dusting, imagining what it would have been like a hundred years ago in the rooms that were now unused and unloved. She lived in a warm modernized cottage on the estate looking out toward the North Sea and was glad of it. But it never hurt to dream, did it?

The muddy footprints in the corridor led from the library all the way outside, which made her tut and put her basket down again. From what she saw, it was clear this wasn't going to be a normal cleaning day.

6

Freya
Thursday, February 8, 7 a.m.

The Scottish Borders was a winter wonderland. Drifts of snow blanketed any signs of life, glittering in the early sunlight as dawn broke.

According to Carole, who had become our tour guide on the drive, St Abbs was a historic fishing village in the Scottish Borders. "A seventh-century Northumbrian princess struggled ashore here after being shipwrecked and promptly founded a nunnery," she read aloud from a website as I drove. "St Abb's Head National Nature Reserve comprises 200 acres of wild and rugged coastline with sheer, seabird-nesting cliffs rising 300 feet above the water . . . The Berwickshire coastline consists of high cliffs over deep clear water with sandy coves and a picturesque harbor." She gripped my arm as I changed gears; we were approaching a bridge over a river. "Maybe that's what happened to poor defenseless Bella? She fell into the sea! Put your foot down. We must get there faster."

With the bridge behind us, I took my eyes from the undulating road and raised an eyebrow at my aunt. "This is Bella we're talking about. A beautiful twentysomething woman who can disguise herself as almost anyone, who locked me in a vault last May in Copthorn Manor because she thought I might slow her down, and then went on a revenge mission on an antiques cruise. 'Defenseless' isn't the word I would use." I sighed. "But . . . I am worried. Let's hope that what we fear isn't real and that she's tucked up in her hotel room when we get there. I'd love to know what she's found out, and maybe she'll finally understand that if we all work together, we might find the answers faster."

"If Bella was lured into a trap . . ."

I put a hand on Carole's arm. I wanted to believe Bella could get herself out of any situation, but everyone's luck runs out eventually, doesn't it? And I was concerned that following a lead on the Boston paintings might have put her in the path of some dangerous black-market players. My aunt and I had followed clues laid down in the first two journals Arthur had left for us before his untimely death, and on both occasions—at Copthorn Manor and on the Red Sea cruise—we had found ourselves in grave danger. Before Arthur was murdered in his eighties, he had swum undercover in the dark underbelly of the art and antiques market for decades. His dying wish was for those he met to be brought to justice, and his journals were his way of doing this. Now it was down to the Lockwood Agency—to me—to carry on his legacy.

Worry twisted in the pit of my stomach. The question remained: What exactly had Bella thought was lurking behind the castle door? And why hadn't she told us about it first? What had happened in her past to make her so radically independent and suspicious of others?

I had come to suspect that Arthur had taken Bella under his wing in much the same way he'd done for me back in my early twenties. I wondered if there was more to it than teaching her the antiques trade. Arthur had strong protective instincts, which raised the question . . . what had he been trying to protect her from?

We turned off the main road and drove down a small country lane that wove up and down small hills and through farmland. Thanks to Hadrian's Wall, the Romans never had the chance to build their straight roads this far north. Carole made me pull over to take a photograph of the snow, which had washed the landscape with one perfect brushstroke, sweeping up and over the hedgerows and drystone walls. A robin ruffled his feathers on a nearby branch.

"You look concerned," said Carole.

I pulled myself away from the Hallmark scene and realized I was frowning. "Maybe we shouldn't have shown Bella that journal."

Carole shook her head. "I think Arthur told her about his records. She wouldn't say what her connection to all this is, but the way she talks about it is *personal*." I agreed. "When he left us the journals, they were his way of making amends for crimes he knew about but couldn't get justice for while working as a spy in the antiques underworld."

The first journal had enabled me to hunt down an antiquities forgery ring. In doing so, I had discovered the real reason Arthur and I originally became estranged so many years earlier. The second journal had not only given Phil answers about the murder of his late FBI partner but helped bring down an international trafficking ring.

"I'm beginning to think Arthur's third journal could mean something to Bella. That he was trying to help her in some way, more than just hunting down a valuable antique." I rubbed my eyes; the long drive was beginning to take its toll. "If she'd told us what it was, perhaps we could have helped her find answers sooner."

"I'm not sure that's what Bella wants . . ." Carole offered me a mint. "But don't take it to heart. Bella's never trusted the law, so naturally she doesn't trust Phil, and now we're working with him. We'll ask her when we find her." Her tone was upbeat, but as she popped a mint into her mouth and stared out the window, I noticed her fingers playing anxiously with the tassels of her scarf.

Carole and I arrived at Kelmore House Hotel in the early morning, tired to our bones. As we trudged up to the entrance, lifting our bags high to keep them from dragging in the snow, I ran through the two things we had to go on: Bella had stayed here, at this countryside hotel, and she had visited nearby Fawside Castle. It was a good bet that if she were anywhere at 7 a.m., she would be asleep in bed.

The hotel was not what I'd expected it to be. It was a huge, L-shaped historic tower house that wouldn't have looked out of place in a period drama. Its gray stone walls blended into the snowy landscape as if designed for winter camouflage. One tall central turret reached for the clouded sky, the Scottish flag fluttering from its top. The house had numerous pitched roofs, all covered in snow, and leaded windows. It was magnificent.

"This looks expensive," I said, scanning the building. When my gaze came back to Carole, she was beaming from ear to ear.

"I'm spending your inheritance on a glorious Scottish adventure. I moved our booking and got a winter discount, because I don't think many people stay here this time of year."

With the early morning sun catching the snow, the whole place looked as if it had been created in a fairy tale. My aunt marched up to the large wooden front door, over which hung an elaborate coat of arms, with the air of a lady of the manor.

"Let's hope Bella left the castle safe and sound and is tucked up in bed. Perhaps her phone just lost battery or is turned off," she said, pushing the door open. "If she's here, we'll find out what she uncovered last night."

Inside, a roaring fire warmed my frozen cheeks and the gleaming wooden floors and deep green-and-gold wallpaper filled me with wonder. A substantial mahogany reception desk stood to one side beneath two wall-mounted stags' heads. Behind the desk was a young woman, immaculate in a crisp white shirt.

"Hello," Carole said brightly. "We're here to meet a friend..." She paused and looked back at me. Both of us knew that Bella wouldn't have checked in under her own surname—I wasn't even sure if we knew it. Just one more indication that we really didn't know who we were working with.

I stepped forward and improvised. "We have a room booked, but we're also here for a meeting with another guest. Her name is Bella. She's tall and slim, with..." And then I came unstuck again, as I had no idea what type of wig Bella would be wearing. "Short dark brown hair, brown eyes..."

"She's beautiful," added Carole. "Hard to miss."

The woman's face lit up, and I knew that she recognized the description. Relief rushed through me until she said, "Yes, she was here... although I didn't see her yesterday... But I was only on in the evening, so maybe I missed her."

Carole sighed.

"I'm afraid I can't give out room numbers or guest names," the young woman said apologetically. "Could you call her and say you're here? Or if you'd like to leave a note?"

"We'll do both. Do you have a pen and paper?"

It didn't take long to write a note and check in.

"How about we get some breakfast before we go to our room? I'm sure this lovely lady will keep our bags?"

The receptionist nodded. "I can have the bags taken to your rooms. Breakfast is served down the hall and to the left."

Carole linked her arm through mine. "We need to find out what room Bella was in, and I know a way," she whispered.

I was about to ask how breakfast would help us with that, but she was pulling me down the hall and saying good morning to everyone we passed on the way. Although we were both hungry after our long journey, there was a skip in Carole's step that meant she was up to something.

The dining room was grand, with windows sweeping along one wall, gorgeous tartan carpet, and crisp white tablecloths. We approached a young man standing behind a desk.

"May I take your room number?" His Scottish accent was soft and welcoming.

"Oh my—we've only just checked in, and I've forgotten my room number already." Carole stepped close to him. "Please don't think of me as a silly old lady!" She gripped his arm and he almost jumped out of his skin.

"I would never think that..."

I could see Carole directing her eyes toward the paperwork on his desk and I angled my head to follow her gaze. A smile began to tip up the corners of my lips before I wrestled it into submission, because I had an idea of what she was doing.

I stepped closer, taking Carole's arm and reading the young man's name tag—Jack. Arthur once told me that the best way to make an instant connection was to use someone's first name. "Jack, could you possibly show my elderly aunt to a table while I retrace our steps to see if she's dropped her room key?"

Carole side-eyed me for calling her elderly. "Needs must," I murmured and then said loudly, "Go with the nice young man, Aunt Carole, and he will find us a table." I smiled politely at Jack. "An out-of-the-way, quiet one, please, as she does get overwhelmed by strangers."

"I do..." Carole saw my look that said "play along" and hunched her shoulders. Jack offered her his arm. "Your granny must be very proud of you." She beamed at him as she took it. "Let me tell you about the time I went to the Galápagos and saw a shark..."

As soon as Jack was distracted, I scanned the list of guests who had included breakfast in their stay. It took only a moment to find the name Bella White, with "Room 18" written next to it. Everyone who had been down to breakfast was highlighted, but Bella's name was not. Which meant she hadn't appeared so far.

We had to get to room 18 immediately and hope there were some answers inside.

7

Thursday, February 8, 10 a.m.

Carole was determined that nothing would stand in our way. After discovering what room Bella was in, she returned to reception and had us moved so that we now occupied the room opposite. We knocked on the door to room 18, but predictably, no one answered. Now I had a plan, which involved waiting with my face pressed to the spyhole of our door while Carole, not known for her patience, paced our twin bedroom, which wasn't big enough for pacing.

An hour into this stakeout, a young woman in a housekeeping uniform knocked on Bella's door. When she got no reply, she opened the door and called, "Housekeeping—may I come in?"

I gripped Carole's arm to stop her wrenching our door open and diving across the corridor. "Wait a few minutes. I have a plan, okay?"

I cracked our door open a little. Behind me, Carole huffed restlessly.

The housekeeper had wedged Bella's door open and gone in, leaving her supply cart in the corridor. We stepped out; Carole plucked a pillow chocolate from a jar on the cart and popped it into her mouth. Noticing my disapproval, she muttered, "It's stress eating, darling."

I straightened my shirt and walked into Bella's room, calling softly, "Hello?"

The maid was over by the window, reaching up to open the curtains. The room was dark, the air stale. As I glanced around the space, my stomach clenched. The bed hadn't been slept in—there was no sign of Bella. Carole shook her head. We now had visual confirmation that Bella was missing.

I corrected my posture and tried to look relaxed, channeling Bella's confidence. "I'm sorry, my aunt here has just checked in across the hall, and I was making sure she was all right."

The housekeeper glanced at the untouched bed.

". . . I like to keep everything very tidy. I was just going to get into my gym gear. Would there be any chance you could come back in a few minutes?"

"Sure, no problem." She left, closing the door behind her.

Carole hurried to the curtains and pulled them back, letting the low winter sun light the room. "Freya, this is bad. All her things are still here, but she isn't."

She was right; it really wasn't a good sign. "Let's look around and see if we can find any clues. We might get an idea of the type of trouble she's in." I noticed a notebook and scraps of paper on the desk by the window. I took out my phone and started taking photos, being careful to capture each piece of paper, and then took a video to be extra sure.

The room had to be one of the best in the hotel. Large windows stretched to the ceiling and the bed was a reproduction mahogany four-poster. Navy-and-red tartan curtains hung from each post, and there were oversize gold bedside lamps with red tartan shades. A dark green tartan armchair stood by the window with a coat thrown over the arm.

"There's a *lot* of tartan in here. Perhaps Bella got overwhelmed and ran," I murmured.

The wardrobe doors were open; three dresses and a couple of

designer jackets hung inside. "She didn't run. There is no way she'd just disappear without taking her expensive clothes," Carole said, picking up one of the pieces of paper on the desk. "There's a letter here from the hotel, welcoming Bella to the honeymoon suite. Do you think she was here with someone?"

I reached for the notebook and flicked through it.

"There's no sign of anyone else, but they could have come and cleared out their things. We can ask around the hotel and see if anyone remembers seeing Bella with someone else." I came to stand next to Carole. "Why does Bella have the details of Edinburgh prison in here?"

"Do you think she's in prison?" Carole grabbed the book from my hands.

"I hope not. Here it says the visiting hours, so maybe she was trying to find an inmate?" I pulled Carole into a hug. "I know you're concerned. I am too. When Phil gets here, he can help us get information from the local police."

"Bella wouldn't like the police in her business." Carole shook her head. "She won't thank us for it if she was getting answers." Over my shoulder, she scanned the notebook. "Look at this." She pointed to the page and I handed the book to her. There were the details of three Boston portrait paintings Phil had sent over.

Lady Montgomery, née Helen Graham (d. 1828), Bella had written, followed by text that seemed to come from the museum's description:

A portrait by Raeburn from his late period depicts the recently wed Helen Montgomery (born Graham). She wears a simple, high-waisted dress, typical of elegant Regency fashions. Inspired by the eighteenth century's Grand Manner, Raeburn's painting depicts a young woman's new life and celebrates her marriage. Lady Montgomery died in 1828 while giving birth to her fifth child.

Colonel Alastair Ranaldson Macdonell of Glengarry (1773–1828)—and another descriptive extract:

> Macdonell of Glengarry is shown in this portrait as the embodiment of a highland chief, clad in tartan. Nevertheless, Macdonell's love of Gaelic culture did not prevent him from removing his tenants to make way for sheep farming.

And finally, *John Stuart Hepburn Forbes, later 8th Baronet of Monymusk, and of Fettercairn and Pitsligo, 1804–1866*:

> The painting features eight-year-old John Forbes, son of Sir William Forbes, a notable Scottish banker and supporter of the arts. The boy is lovingly posing with a dog, maybe a mixed Dalmatian–Pointer, wearing a padlocked collar. Raeburn's painting perfectly captures John's playful nature. John became an important member of society and was elected to the Royal Society of Edinburgh.

Carole flipped over another page. At the top was written "Fawside Castle" and below that was a hand-sketched map of the site, with several outbuildings marked and what looked like a path leading down to the sea. And the words "Man Alive."

"'Man Alive'—isn't that what Arthur wrote at the top of some of the pages in his journal? We never worked out what it meant, but it seems to me that Bella knew all along, or at least had some idea. It must be connected to the castle..." Confusion furrowed Carole's brow. "So, did Bella go to the castle to find the other paintings in the journal? Or did she think the castle was connected to trafficking of the three Boston paintings?"

"I don't know, but it's a good bet it's one of the two. It's where she called you from yesterday, isn't it? Let's not waste time."

We closed the door to Bella's room and headed for the car. We only had two clues to go on—Alexandra Pattern and Fawside Castle—and although we had made some progress, I was getting increasingly worried. I decided that if there were no clues at the castle, I would have to resort to calling the police, no matter what Bella might have to say about it.

8

Thursday, February 8, noon

Fawside Castle was on the other side of St Abbs from our hotel, perched on a snow-covered cliff with the freezing North Sea crashing over the rocks below. The castle was as impressive as it was intimidating: a large foursquare limestone tower, three stories high, complete with battlements at each corner. Everything about it looked to be in such good repair, despite parts of it dating from the fifteenth century, that there was a hint of winter magic to the scene. Whoever lived here must be enormously wealthy.

The long drive ended in a parking area in front of the house. We parked, and I climbed out of the car; the sound of my door slamming shut echoed around the courtyard. When it died away, the remote landscape around us was so hushed that only the crashing waves pounding the rocks below the castle could be heard.

Until Carole's boots crunched on the snow as she came to stand next to me. "I'm sure this is where Bella called me from," she said, scanning the area. "She told me she hired a car but it's not on the drive and there are no other cars here. Doesn't seem like anyone is home, does it?"

We both hurried to the front door and pulled the cord to ring the bell, then stood straining our necks to look for movement in the surrounding windows.

A humming or an electrical buzzing sound came from somewhere above. "Is that a vacuum?"

Carole tilted her head. "I think so. Someone must be there."

I pulled the bell cord again and the sound stopped. Carole gave it another yank, then another. Four rings was an excessive amount, but before I could stop her she gave the cord yet another pull and the bell started jangling again.

"What?" she asked innocently, as if I were the one constantly tugging on the door handle. Even though the buzzing sound had ceased, no one had come to the door.

"If there's no one coming, we could have a quick look around," said Carole, linking her arm through mine and pulling me toward a window. "Just a little peek . . . not really breaking and entering."

"Isn't it that attitude that got Bella into a mess in the first place? Wandering around a castle . . ."

"Oh, do you think she takes after me? How flattering!" Carole let me go and scrubbed her gloved hand over the window to peer through.

"No. That's not . . ." My words dried up. There was just no reasoning with Carole's overly positive outlook on life.

"Come on, darling. When in Rome, and all that." She pulled back from the window, frowning with disappointment, and headed to another a few meters along without waiting for me.

"We're not tourists visiting the Colosseum. Are you really . . ." Yes, Carole really was going to start looking through every window. She brushed away snow and stood with her hands cupped to the glass.

I was just about to join her when she pulled away. "It's dark in those two rooms." She stepped back and started walking around to the other side of the castle. "I think that the back door is over . . ." She took a few more steps and craned her neck. "There it is." She almost skipped her way down the path.

The snow was already trodden down to reveal the path toward the back door, and there was a fainter path leading away from the castle and down the garden. "Carole, do you remember when it stopped snowing?"

Her hand was already on the back door when she stopped and looked down at her feet and the track she had just followed, understanding what I was asking. "Sometime in the night, I would guess. This path had been walked after it stopped, and that one was made while it was still snowing. Is that what you're thinking?"

I nodded.

"Well, we crossed the border around four a.m., and it wasn't snowing then. And I talked to Bella around five p.m. yesterday."

"Why would someone be walking that way in a snowstorm? And for it to be indented so much, it may have been more than one person." I studied the path. "Doesn't that seem strange to you?"

Carole beamed at me as she knocked on the back door. As we waited, I shielded my face from the midday sun and looked around the grounds again.

We had passed through a large opening in a wall, which made me think this must once have been the castle's kitchen garden. The ground rose in stepped levels toward the back wall, with fruit trees along the far right wall, which met the back of the castle—protecting the produce from the biting sea winds. I had started down the indented path. To my left and right, everything was covered in untouched snow, but as I rounded one of the raised beds there was an area in the back right-hand corner that looked out of place. Snow-covered footsteps—as if someone had walked back and forth from the back door while the storm raged. They led toward an oddly positioned mound of snow.

When appraising antiques, antiquities, or art, you look for the details. The quality of a well-made piece stands out just as much as the lack of craftsmanship found in the small intricacies a forger can overlook. Perhaps that's why I started walking—the scene didn't make sense, just like a forgery sometimes doesn't. The truth can often be found in the smallest inconsistencies.

"Where are you going? I think I hear someone coming," called Carole, still standing by the back door.

"I just need to . . ." My boots slipped on compacted ice under the snow, and it took a second to right myself. Nearby, an overturned wheelbarrow lay on its side. Behind it was another mound of snow.

A hand squeezed my shoulder and spun me around. "What's going on?" asked Carole, her cheeks touched red by the biting cold. "What have you . . . Oh no!" Her hand flew to her mouth.

I looked at the wheelbarrow, but that wasn't what Carole had seen. ". . . Are those fingers?" she whispered.

Taking a few tentative steps, I peered closer. She was right. The mound of snow was about the size of a body, and there were bluish, snow-tipped fingertips emerging from it.

Neither of us moved.

Neither of us spoke.

I reached out and linked my fingers through hers to give us both some comfort. The truth of what we were seeing was slowly sinking in.

"It's not . . . ?" Carole's voice cracked. *Bella* was what she wanted to say. I couldn't voice the horror either.

I sank to my knees and reached out, but I couldn't bring myself to touch the icy hand.

"Hello?" a woman's voice called from somewhere behind us. "Can I help you? What are you doing over there?"

I couldn't stop staring at the little finger and the glint of a golden ring catching the morning light. The knees of my jeans were wet through and my flesh beneath was burning cold, but I had frozen in place.

"What are you doing?" I looked up to see a woman in her seventies coming up behind us, looking between me and Carole.

It took her a moment to notice what we had found.

She staggered back, her shaking hand finding her lips, but it couldn't stifle the guttural scream that came out of her as she began to topple sideways.

9

Thursday, February 8, 1 p.m.

The elderly woman had snow-covered slippers on her feet. She swayed on unsteady legs, her face suddenly pale. I rushed to her side and got an arm around her waist, catching her before she hit the ground... I could smell bleach. Carole ran round to her other side and placed an arm under her elbow.

"I'm sorry... I don't know..." She stared at the hand in the snow. "That's Euan's ring." Her legs gave out; I took her weight.

"Let's get you back inside and out of the cold. We'll call the police."

As I helped the woman back toward the castle, Carole was introducing us. "I'm Carole Lockwood and this is my niece, Freya. How about a mug of sweet tea for the shock?" She was rubbing the woman's arm.

The woman slipped on the ice, and we all swayed before righting ourselves again.

"What's your name, darling? We need to get you warm," Carole soothed.

"I'm... Dolores... and I think that's..." She shuddered as we guided her toward the back door.

We entered the castle via the boot room, which was about as large as a London flat. Dolores pointed to the first door on the right and we found ourselves in the kitchen, which was the size of a country cottage.

"Wow," Carole murmured. "How the other half lives."

Worn flagstones covered the floor and a couple of wrought-iron chandeliers hung from the heavy black beams of the ceiling. The wooden kitchen cabinets looked as if they'd been there for decades, but they were spotless.

At the far end of the room was a kitchen table surrounded by mismatched Victorian pine chairs. Beyond it, a long stretch of windows overlooked the cliffs and the frothing sea beyond.

"Come and sit," I said to Dolores.

"I'll pop the kettle on," Carole said, sweeping around the kitchen and opening cupboards.

I settled Dolores into a chair. She was as white as the snow that dusted the windows.

"How are you feeling?" I asked. "Can I call anyone for you?"

"I'm just..." She took in a deep, shaky breath. "It's not something..."

"No, it's not."

It was clear that she knew who the dead person was, but I didn't want to distress her further by asking too many questions. My feet itched to go back out there and investigate—I was sure this had to be connected to Bella in some way. I squeezed Dolores's shoulder and realized she was shivering. A couple of decades ago, I had walked into the kitchen at an Egyptian café and found my boyfriend's body, his unseeing eyes locked on the ceiling. "Can I get you something warmer to wear from your room?"

Dolores ran a hand down her face. "This isn't my home, dear, I'm just the housekeeper. I wasn't even meant to be here this morning..." She placed her arms on the table and rested her forehead on them.

Conversation over.

Carole set down a steaming mug of tea in front of her. "We're going to call the police. You get that tea down you." She hovered over us and gave me a quick nod, her chin motioning to the kitchen door. One of us needed to go back outside and make sure it wasn't Bella lying there in the snow.

When I hesitated, Carole said, "Off you go. We're fine here, aren't we, Dolores?" She took out her mobile.

"I'll go and . . ." I didn't want to say I was going to look around. "Make sure the back door is closed."

Dolores didn't appear as if she was listening, so I stood and Carole took my seat beside her, gripping my arm as she passed me. Trying to give me the strength to go back outside.

The icy air seemed to cut deeper as I walked toward the back of the garden and the frozen body hidden there. I wasn't going to disturb a crime scene, but I also wasn't going back to Carole without the answer to our question.

It took a few seconds to see details I hadn't before: the hand was much larger than Bella's, and male. There was a signet ring on the little finger, as Dolores had mentioned, and I could just see the edge of a navy shirtsleeve with dark hair poking out from it. This definitely wasn't Bella. From the angle of the arm, the man was face down, and as I stepped cautiously around to the other side of the mounded snow, I found a frozen puddle of deep-red blood. I backed away as my stomach churned.

I had no idea who the dead man was. But it had to be linked to Bella being missing, and my pulse picked up as I ran through different scenarios in my mind. My desire to find Bella had increased to a burning necessity.

Back inside, I beckoned Carole over. "It's not Bella," I murmured into her ear.

"But then where is she?" She hugged her arms around her chest. "I've called the police. They're on their way."

"He was meant to have been home alone last night . . ." Dolores said from the table. She was sitting up now, her hands wrapped round the mug. She sniffed. "Why was he out in the garden? Why would he go out in that storm?"

"Can you tell us who the man is?" I asked.

"It's the laird . . . my employer, Euan McGovern."

Carole went pale when she heard the name, as if she recognized it. I started to ask her, but she glared at me and muttered, "Not now."

My mind shifted back to the snow-covered garden and the overturned wheelbarrow, which had had a rust-colored stain along its back. Maybe the laird hadn't gone outside alive. I didn't mention the pool of blood that reddened the snow underneath his head, making me suspect he had been hit over the head with something and moved soon afterward. Dolores was in no state to hear the details.

"What time did you arrive this morning?" I asked her gently.

"Around seven, I think. I was under the weather for a few days, so I needed to catch up on the cleaning."

"And did you see anything out of place inside the castle?" I wanted to ask if she had seen any blood, but I thought that might have been taking things too far.

"No, nothing. Actually, the back door was open, and . . ." She straightened up. "Do you think we had a robbery? Are all the valuable antiques still here?" She was on her feet, heading for the kitchen door. "We need to check the study . . . That's where his collection is."

Carole and I hurried after her as she crossed the hall and opened the opposite door—and gasped. We all stood in the doorway. I scanned the four empty shelves in the middle of the display cabinet, where I presumed the silver had once resided. There were twelve pieces of antique silverware remaining—perhaps the robber ran out of time. On the opposite side of the room hung an image of Jesus on the cross, with bookshelves on either side and a large Bible on a shelf below. Dolores was stepping into the room when I grabbed her arm. "We shouldn't touch anything."

"But . . . what happened?" Her voice was strained and her hands were gripped tightly together. "The silver . . . where is the silver?"

There was a moment when I wondered if she was going to collapse again, but Carole placed a supportive arm around her. "Let's find somewhere to wait for the police. They said they would be as fast as they could, but some of the roads are closed due to the storm."

"Do you think they'll move him soon? . . . He must be cold . . . Will they find the thief?"

Carole's worry tightened her lips. Dolores was in shock, and we needed to stay and help. We found our way to a drawing room with a large fireplace, the fire already laid; I lit it while Carole helped Dolores settle onto a sofa.

As the blaze sprang up, Dolores's nerves seemed to steady. She mentioned that an intruder might have tried to use the front door. If so, he would have been captured on the castle's security camera. Before long, Carole was offering to bring the house laptop through from the kitchen so that we could phone Sky and get her to talk us through how to access the footage.

After what seemed like hours but was probably minutes, we had the camera footage downloaded on the laptop and Carole pressed play. My stomach dropped as we watched a grainy image of Bella walking up to the door and ringing the bell. She might have been in a gray bob wig and clothes far too dated for her style, but her striking eyes and delicate features were the same. I held my breath as she silently called out, looking up at the house, and then followed the same route Carole and I had taken toward the back door.

Carole gave me a look, but we didn't say anything.

"Who do you think that was?" asked Dolores, sitting between us.

"That's the friend we're looking for. The one we can't find," Carole said, biting her bottom lip. "I'm ever so worried after what we've seen here."

Where are you, Bella?

Leaving Dolores with Carole, I slipped away, saying I needed the bathroom. Dolores seemed to be too shocked to take in much of what we were saying, and Carole was doing a wonderful job at calming her. With Carole's driving gloves on, being careful not to disturb anything, I searched the downstairs rooms of the castle in the vain hope of finding a clue to Bella's whereabouts. But I ended up back in the study again, staring at the silver cabinet. As far as I could see, Bella wasn't here, so I pulled out the photos I had taken of Arthur's third journal. Had Bella been in the castle because she had uncovered where the silver collection Arthur had catalogued resided? I scanned through the images on my phone, hoping to match them with the remaining twelve Scottish silver pieces on the bottom shelf of the cabinet, but when I tried the door, it was locked. Why had the robber gone to the trouble of locking the cabinet back up again?

The research I'd done on the journal so far had shown me there wasn't a massive market value to the items catalogued there. Collectively, the Scottish provincial paintings, silver, Wemyss and Mauchline Ware could amount to a nice sum; however, it was evident the items in this third journal were different from the other six journals we had discovered hidden in Arthur's shop. The others detailed just a few big-ticket items, while this one had numerous smaller-ticket items. A few were on the Art Loss Register, but not many. Why had Arthur recorded them all?

When Bella had asked to see the journal back in Jordan, I'd been eager to make a deal with her, for there was no clue as to what Arthur was pointing toward. I'd had a strong suspicion then that Bella knew more than I did. Now, perhaps, that very knowledge had put her life in danger.

I took a picture of the room and the remaining Scottish silver, and as many of the other rooms as possible without Dolores getting suspicious. Then I sent everything to Sky, asking her to find out whatever she could about the property and its dead laird.

~

From the moment the police arrived, everything seemed to move at rocket speed. The castle was secured. Statements were taken and our details recorded; the CCTV footage was viewed again. At some point the detective assigned to the case arrived and we were asked the same questions again. Detective Rodgers was far more interested in Euan McGovern's murder, the missing silver, our agency, and our work for the FBI than in Bella's disappearance.

Detective Rodgers was nearing retirement age. His shirt and suit trousers were frayed at the cuffs and hems, and there was what looked like a ketchup stain on his tie. His scruffy stubble told me he needed a shave, and the slight tinge of gray to his skin indicated he needed sleep, but his blue eyes were sharp and watchful.

"And what evidence do you have that stolen antiques are in this castle or belonged to the occupier?" he asked.

I was sitting opposite him at the kitchen table. It was clear he was experienced enough to believe that whatever we were looking into could be linked to the death of the laird, but I hadn't jumped to that conclusion, because in truth we knew very little. We needed to find Bella to get more answers, and I told him as much, hoping that he would help in the search.

"We don't have any evidence. As I keep saying, it was our associate who was following this lead, and we haven't been able to contact her since last night . . . I'm worried. Look what happened out there. If we hadn't come looking for her then the laird's body could have been out there until the snow thawed."

"Ah yes, Miss Bella. We'll put out a missing person's report once it has been twenty-four hours. And you'll be staying at the hotel for a few days?" His Scottish accent was broad and deep.

I nodded. "The FBI agent..."

"What is going on?" a woman's voice shrilled from the direction of the back door. "Why are you here?" A couple of dogs started yapping. "What are those people doing in the garden? What in heaven's name do you mean, a *body*?"

The female police officer stationed at the back door must have been trying to calm the woman, but it didn't work; the next thing we heard was a loud wail.

"I don't understand," the woman cried.

Detective Rodgers stood up and hurried to the door, and I followed him.

"I'm sorry, but we have some distressing news. Are you a resident of the castle?"

The woman was in her forties, immaculately dressed in chinos, shirt, and blazer, with blond hair cascading down to her shoulders. "Yes, I live here. What is she saying about Euan?"

"Was the laird your husband? May I ask your name?"

"Well, no—he's my partner. I'm Jane Campbell. *Was?*" She placed a hand over her mouth and her bright pink nails trembled against her lips. The commotion had drawn Dolores and Carole from the drawing room.

"Jane, perhaps you want to sit down," said Dolores.

"I'm sorry to inform you that the laird, Euan McGovern, was found this morning," Rodgers began. "He was in the garden, and I'm afraid he..."

"He's dead?" Her features creased as she tried to process the news. Her hand reached for the wall as grief came crashing down on her.

I turned to Carole, but she wasn't looking at me. She was focusing on Jane.

Jane must have sensed the attention as she turned and saw us. "Carole Lockwood... Is that really you? What are *you* doing here? I'm so glad to see a friendly face."

"Jane?" My aunt stepped toward her, her expression utterly confused.

Two chocolate-colored dachshunds stood beside Jane as she watched Carole approach. I would have expected my aunt to show her usual warmth toward an old friend, even in such awful circumstances, but there was a forced smile on her face and a tightness to her lips. I took a step closer to her. "Friend" or not, Carole clearly didn't like Jane. And Carole liked everyone.

Jane's gaze scanned all of us before settling on the detective. "I can't stay here with poor Euan dead in the garden." She spun around and pushed the police officer aside on her way out. "If he died here... Oh, it's all too horrific."

Carole hurried after her, back out onto the snowy drive. Detective Rodgers was right behind them. "Find out who did this," Jane shouted over her shoulder as she pulled out a tissue. Tears were streaking down her cheeks.

"We'll come and make sure you're all right," Carole said soothingly, but the kindness of her words didn't match her manner. She had the same polite, wary expression she wore at the dentist.

I studied her, wondering why her behavior was so out of character. At the very least she was being too quiet, too reserved, and I knew that there must be a story to tell.

10

Carole
Thursday, February 8, 3 p.m.

Carole had warned Bella that meeting Euan McGovern was a terrible idea. But Bella wasn't one for taking advice.

At first, when she'd given Bella all her Scottish contacts, including a number for young India McGovern, she'd warned her to stay away from India's father, Euan—but Bella had other ideas. Carole was deeply annoyed at herself for suggesting that Bella go to the castle in disguise. She would now have to fill Freya in about what a nasty piece of work the laird had been. But not while they were in the company of the police.

There had always been something distinctly unnerving about Jane too. So even though Carole had wanted answers about why those Scottish antiques were listed in Arthur's third journal, and even though she was keen to follow up every possible lead, she'd been in no hurry to contact Euan or his girlfriend for advice. They were both antique dealers and collectors, but even that hadn't been enough to entice her to reach out.

Because she'd known that if she did, she might not be able to hold her tongue.

Now, however, she was slightly ashamed that she hadn't suggested to Freya that they should contact Euan and Jane. Instead, she had told Bella about them.

Carole had justified her actions because a month or so ago she'd had a small disagreement with Freya over the need for evidence before making any sort of move. It had been Phil's suggestion to build their case first before making a trip to Scotland, and Freya had backed him up. This new stance had irritated Carole. Their usual approach of "diving headfirst" into a case had always delivered results so far. Freya herself had always said that gut feelings were there to get you going, and then you could find the proof you needed. But as soon as Phil suggested they bide their time, Freya had seemed to forget her previous position.

Carole had tried to argue that antiques experts were often said to have "the eye"—which meant an instinct for telling in a split second whether an item was genuine and valuable. However, Freya had insisted that "the eye" came only from expert knowledge honed over decades. They needed to do their research into the Boston paintings case first. Experts used instinct first and then investigated an item thoroughly.

Carole knew that Freya's new preference for staying safely at Crockleford Antiques and following leads from afar was a way of protecting herself. It was difficult for her niece not to cocoon herself away from the world after the loss of her parents, her first love, and her marriage. She didn't trust easily. But to take up Arthur's mantle as an antique hunter, she would have to go out into the wide world just as he had done—talking to people, making connections.

Which brought Carole's mind back to the first time she'd met the laird of Fawside and his significantly younger girlfriend at a hotel bar in the Highlands. From that first meeting, she had known they were rotten to the core. She'd had a deep-in-her-bones feeling about it. But she'd had no proof—until now. Until Bella had gone missing.

Now Jane was the only one who might have some answers. So Carole pulled her shoulders back, plastered on a smile, and prepared to play a role. Bella's life might depend on how well she could play it. Because Carole would not put it past either Euan or Jane to have thrown Bella into a dungeon just for the fun of it.

Jane was running toward a Range Rover parked in a far corner of the drive, and Carole hurried to catch up with her.

"Jane, please wait—" Carole's foot slipped on the ice, and Freya gasped behind her. "Let us help."

Jane spun around, her face creased with pain. "Is he *really* dead?" she cried. "Who saw him . . . like that?" Jane took out her car keys and brought the Range Rover flashing to life. She opened the passenger door and lifted the dachshunds inside.

Carole gave a brief nod. "I'm sorry. Freya and I came here looking for a friend of ours who was meant to meet with Euan yesterday. We're the ones who found him." She paused for a moment as Jane sobbed into her tissue. "Look, why don't we help you get some things together? And then you can give the detective details of where you'll be staying—all right?"

Carole might not have liked Jane, but she couldn't help feeling sorry for her. This all brought back memories of the previous year when she'd discovered Arthur, her best friend, dead in his shop.

Freya looked lost. She was clearly wondering what Carole was up to, but now wasn't the time to explain. First, Carole needed to get Jane on her side and talking. As she studied Jane, she noticed that her handkerchief was dry. Was she witnessing crocodile tears?

"Are you sure you're all right to drive? Can't we give you a lift somewhere?" Carole asked.

"I'm—fine, thank you. I'm just . . . it's a shock." Jane looked up at the snow-tipped castle and shuddered. "I have to get away from here."

She looked utterly bereft. Carole found it hard to reconcile her memory of the cruel-hearted woman she'd met over a year ago with the one who stood before her. Jane might have been awful to Euan's daughter, India, but it was true she'd seemed dedicated to Euan and the life they had built together.

"I'm sure you're devastated." She was ashamed of herself for not saying she was sorry about Euan's death, but . . . well, she wasn't.

"What am I going to do without him?" Jane blew her nose.

Carole pulled her into a hug and rubbed her back. "Let's get your things. Where are you going to stay?"

"I'll just need a few minutes first," said Detective Rodgers. "It won't take long." Carole and Jane spun around to see him standing a short distance away, watching them.

Carole nodded reassuringly at Jane. "We'll wait here for you." Freya gave her another quizzical look, which Carole ignored.

"Euan owns the village pub . . . *owned* it. I'm going to see if they have room. God, this is all so terrible. And to think that if the storm hadn't come in, I would have been here when the robbery happened."

"They took the silver collection," said Dolores, appearing beside the detective. "Probably one of those dodgy men you're always with."

Jane's mouth opened and her cheeks reddened. "I do not . . . I never did. Don't you go believing anything that witch says."

Dolores blinked, her expression stony, but said nothing. It was clear there was no love lost between the two women.

Rodgers stepped between them and raised his hands. "Ms. Campbell, if I could just have a few moments of your time. I understand you'd rather not stay here, so I can have an officer take you to the station—"

"What?" Jane glared at him. "I'm not being *taken to the station* like a criminal. Are you arresting me?"

"No, Ms. Campbell. But you did say you couldn't stay here, so I was providing an alternative." Rodgers's tone suggested he had come up against this situation a number of times before. "Shall we talk in the kitchen instead?"

Jane cocked her head as if wondering whether this was an offer or a demand, then began walking back toward the castle with her lips pursed. It was clear that she didn't feel she had a choice.

Carole nudged Freya as they watched the detective herd Jane inside. "I want to know what's said, don't you?"

Freya motioned to the female officer standing by the back door. "We won't get to eavesdrop through there." She scanned the castle, her eyes narrowed. "If we slip back the other way and go around the back, I think we'll come to the kitchen windows."

Carole's face lit up, and she hurried off before Freya could stop her. She followed a path that swept to the far side of the castle. It didn't take her long to discover the large kitchen windows and pull Freya in beside her as she pressed her back to the wall and bent her head to peer inside.

Jane was sitting at the kitchen table, Detective Rodgers opposite her. With the sound of the waves breaking forty feet below and the wind whipping around their ears, it was hard to make out every word. Luckily, Jane had one of those irritating nasal voices that carry through the air, like nails down a chalkboard.

"I wasn't with anyone last night . . ." There was a pause as Rodgers asked a question, his voice a low rumble. "Okay . . . look, I might have had some male friends. But so did Euan. What we had was an open relationship, and just because his beloved housekeeper didn't agree doesn't make it wrong!"

More murmuring from Rodgers.

"Of course he can confirm it."

Carole looked over at Freya, worrying that her hearing was well and truly going. "Who's she talking about? Did you get all of that?"

Freya shook her head. "She has another man living locally, and the detective got her to give him the address. She has an alibi for the time of the murder. And she told the detective to talk to Euan's daughter."

Jane had straightened up. Her lips pursed with malice as she said to the detective, "You mean India? Her mother died years ago, and Euan took her under his wing and gave her the best of everything. She went to a very exclusive boarding school until she wanted to come back to study. She's had everything she ever wanted, and she's so very ungrateful. And so violent that we had to . . . send her to her room a number of times."

"Lock her up there, she means," Carole whispered to Freya, who widened her eyes in shock.

"That girl hated us both, for no reason. He should have left her in New Zealand, but he was named in the will as her guardian, so here we all are . . . Or *were*." Jane's dramatic sobs were clearly audible through the windowpane.

"I want to feel for her, I really do. But . . . I don't buy all her grief. I don't know why, but I don't. She's a drama queen," Carole muttered. "Let's get back out front and faff about until she comes out. She's my number one suspect in all of this, and I can't wait to see her locked up."

Before Freya could suggest that they try not to jump to conclusions without any real evidence, Carole swept through the snow and back toward the drive.

It didn't take long for Jane to emerge and join them.

"I hear it was a bad storm. Where were you stranded?" asked Carole, hoping Jane might reveal who she had been with the previous night.

"I'd been in Edinburgh and was meant to come home, but . . ." Jane's gaze tracked back to the white forensics tent surrounded by melting snow.

"Why don't we follow you to the pub, and we can all have a nice stiff drink?"

"Oh!" Jane was already shaking her head. "That would be so kind of you. It's lovely to see a friendly face, but . . . It's been such a shock, coming home and seeing all this. I don't think it's sunk in yet."

"Even more reason for us to make sure you're safe," Carole insisted.

Freya gave her another quizzical frown but didn't say anything, and Carole was grateful. She could fill her niece in on her disastrous past encounter with Euan and Jane while they drove into the village.

11

Carole

Eighteen months earlier, on the Glorious Twelfth—a date in August marking the start of the grouse-shooting season—Carole and Arthur had been staying at a hotel in the Highlands which had been booked exclusively for a weekend of hunting. From the very beginning it had seemed like a strange event for Arthur to be invited to, as he had no interest in shooting birds or animals of any kind. He only had eyes for hunting antiques.

Everyone seemed to be there for the birds, but Arthur had done his normal thing of hurrying off to "meet a friend," which was a code for doing some business. Carole had decided to have a glass of wine at the bar.

A young woman with a sharp blond bob and a *Breakfast at Tiffany's* black dress sat at the end of the bar, trying to ignore the barman, who couldn't keep his eyes off her. Carole was well versed in these situations and knew the young lady needed a helping hand.

"That is a stunning dress." She gave the young woman her warmest smile and it was met with a look of relief. "I'm Carole. May I join you? Because if we ladies don't stick together, we get stuck with unwanted male attention."

"I'm India . . . and thank you." The young woman motioned to the stool next to her. "I think my father hopes I'll find a rich husband at one of these things."

Carole sat down. "How very archaic of him." This type of mentoring needed a drink, so Carole waved at the barman, who was more than happy to dash over to India's side. "Would you be a love and get us two glasses of Prosecco and two glasses of water?" She squeezed India's arm. "Always drink water when you drink alcohol... I'm Carole Lockwood, by the way. Are you here with the shooting party?"

"I..." India's voice shuttered and her gaze drifted to the barman. "I hate the shooting, but my father and his girlfriend said I should come." The glasses were placed in front of them.

"Ah yes, to find a husband." Carole gave India a knowing look. "And are you looking for a husband?"

"I'm just eighteen. I'd like to wait, but..." India tilted her flute to her lips. She had the poise and grace of a ballerina and her sad, watery eyes made Carole think of Princess Odette in *Swan Lake*. Trapped by a curse, with no way out.

"What would you rather do instead?"

"I like music—piano, the violin, and I'm learning the harp. I travel to Edinburgh for my lessons. It's the only time..." She trailed off and took a sip of wine. "I'd love to get a music fellowship, and perhaps one day find a chair in a symphony." Her voice was almost a whisper, as if speaking the words aloud could make the hotel walls come crashing down around them.

"Then I'm sure you will."

But India shook her head and sighed. What had made the young woman so doubtful and anxious?

"I'm glad someone has faith in my dreams. Most of the time I'm told I'm not good enough, that no one would want to listen to me play... Jane screeches that at me if I ever practice at home." She pressed her lips together as if she regretted revealing so much. "Sorry, I'm fine. Just tired. I think I'll go to bed."

Someone—perhaps this Jane woman—had damaged her confidence and weakened her determination to follow her dreams. Dreams, Carole knew, needed full-bodied drive to even get close to becoming reality.

India's stomach rumbled and Carole touched her thin wrist. She couldn't bear hearing such unkind, untrue words from such an accomplished young woman. She needed to provide an antidote. "No. No, no. I just can't listen to such tosh. I'm having dinner with my friend Arthur. Come and join us. He's the sort of person who can help you see that anything is possible. Would you like to meet him?"

"I'm . . . no, thank you. I need to watch my weight."

"You certainly don't." Carole squeezed her shoulder and murmured, "Darling, I'm not leaving you alone at a bar with a crowd of drunken middle-aged men and no umbrella to beat them away."

"I've dealt with worse." India scanned the bar as if looking for someone. Several men raised their heads, like a pack of wolves catching the scent of fresh meat. She bristled at their movements. "Actually, I think I would like that. Thank you."

They had left the bar and were heading down the corridor toward the long dining room when a man's voice yelled from behind them, "Where do you think you're going?"

India shuddered to a stop and Carole turned. A man in his mid-fifties was catching up to them. He wore full field clothing and was broad-shouldered under his thorn-proof jacket, with knitted shooting stockings under knee-length breeches. His salt-and-pepper hair was cut so short that it bristled. He ignored Carole, too busy glaring at India. "I said, *wait* for us in the library. It's a simple order."

Carole knew that a charm offensive was the only way forward. "I'm

Carole Lockwood," she said. "And you are?" Her tone was warm, but there was a warning edge to it—one that implied he was on the edge of being rude, and she was not the sort of person who would tolerate such behavior.

"Euan McGovern. And this is Jane Campbell." A woman in her early forties with bleached-blond hair and a green shirtdress hurried up behind him. "You"—he stabbed a finger at Carole, which made her bristle—"seem to be walking off with my daughter."

"She isn't, Daddy . . . she just . . ." India was silenced with a pointed look. "Sorry," she whimpered.

Carole forced herself to smile sweetly, trying to ignore the way Euan towered over her. She had decades of experience dealing with this type of man. "I've just met your lovely daughter, and I insisted that she join my friend Arthur and me for dinner. She looks hungry."

"But didn't she tell you she was meant to wait in the library? I was too busy for lunch. Are you telling me you found her in the bar?" Euan flipped his stare to India.

"I was just getting some tea."

"Young ladies do not sit in bars on their own. You know the rules."

A question was on the very tip of Carole's tongue, demanding to be set free. Had India been sitting dutifully all afternoon waiting for a father who never showed up, and not even able to have lunch? She wasn't sure how to handle the situation, but she was definitely going to have dinner with the young woman and get to the bottom of what was going on.

"Hello?" Arthur called from somewhere down the corridor, and Carole relaxed. Backup had arrived in the form of an immaculate gentleman in his early eighties wearing a three-piece herringbone tweed suit in shades of tan, brown, and blue, with a bright orange cravat. Arthur liked to carry a cane on these occasions, although he did not need one.

"Do you know Arthur Crockleford?" Carole beamed as Arthur reached her side. He gave her a slight tilt of his head to ask if everything was all right. Carole and Arthur had known each other a very long time. They went all the way back to Arthur's days as an archaeologist.

Euan took an involuntary step back, which confirmed to Carole that he did indeed know her old friend—and she sensed that he and Arthur were not on good terms. She fought the urge to dig a little deeper into the nature of their relationship. For now, she would use the evening to show India what female empowerment looked like, in the hope that the next time a man told her to wait for him without a care for her own welfare, she would do no such thing.

"India is joining us for dinner." There was no question in her tone.

"Mr. Crockleford isn't the sort of man I want my daughter associating with. I know the work he does." McGovern glared at Arthur, but neither man backed down.

"Whatever does that mean?" Carole gripped the strap of her bag. Arthur was the most honorable man she knew.

"It's all right, Carole." Arthur's mild tone settled her quickened pulse. He could handle this vile specimen of a man.

Standing shoulder to shoulder with Carole, Arthur looked Euan up and down. "We have a reservation for dinner." He held out his arm for India to take. "Carole and I would be delighted to have your company, young lady. Do you like opera? We were talking earlier about the Verona opera season, where you can watch *Carmen* in a Roman amphitheater. It's a truly exquisite experience. But of course, if you wish to talk about antiques or art, or advice on how to purchase something at auction . . ." He gave Euan a calm smile, but the challenge in his tone was clear. ". . . We could also do that."

Carole didn't know exactly what was going on between the two men, but she wanted to get moving. She liked antiques and had a real fondness for Egyptian revival jewelry, which had reached its peak after the discovery of Tutankhamun's tomb in 1922, but there were more pressing things she needed to discuss with India.

"She has no interest in art, Arthur," Euan said through clenched teeth. The temperature of the hallway seemed to have risen by a few degrees.

"Not even your private collection?" said Arthur.

Carole was well acquainted with his every tone, and this one was a warning. She just didn't know what he was warning Euan about.

"No," the man barked, clenching his fists before regaining control and stretching out his fingers, placing his arms stiffly by his sides. His clenched jaw was his only tell. He forced a smile. "Enjoy your dinner." He gave India an unreadable look, but she flinched as their eyes met, which made Carole reach for her hand and weave their fingers together.

A woman flinching was a learned response, and it told Carole that she had to help this girl in whatever way she could.

12

Freya
Thursday, February 8, 5 p.m.

As we followed Jane's red Range Rover toward St Abbs, Carole filled me in on what she knew about her—and the recently deceased Euan McGovern. Hearing the story of her first meeting with the couple, I understood why she'd disliked them so much. A man openly bullying his daughter while his partner enabled the behavior was not a scenario Carole, or any woman, would easily be able to stomach. My aunt's response toward me had always been the opposite of everything she'd seen in them. She had gladly stopped her blooming acting career in its tracks to take me in when my father and mother—her brother and sister-in-law—died in a fire. I was a twelve-year-old who wouldn't talk to anyone but her and had terrible nightmares, but Carole was always calm and kind. She gave me all the love I needed without ever trying to take the place of my parents.

We drove through the pretty coastal town of St Abbs and headed toward the sea, where the Old Ship pub looked as if it had been standing watch over the harbor for generations.

Jane had parked out front, and we found a space slightly farther down the road. I gave Carole a look and nodded toward Jane. "What's the plan?"

"I think she knows a lot more than she's letting on. She and Euan were thick as thieves when I saw them together. The gossip mill is rife in the antiques world and I never heard anything about an open relationship. It's an easy thing to say when the other side is already dead, isn't it? Let's stick close to her until we find out what she knows. Bella was at that castle for a reason—she doesn't go to all the trouble of disguising herself without good cause. I think that Bella had found some kind of a link to the Boston paintings . . . And then there's the silver."

"The Scottish silver that was stolen from the castle last night could easily have been the pieces listed in Arthur's journal. And I suppose it really could be a robbery gone wrong," I said, and Carole tutted. ". . . Yeah. I don't think so either. We don't believe in coincidences, do we?"

"We don't, and Bella is a clever cookie. She was onto something before it went all wrong. Let's ask Jane about the silver. Do you have pictures on your phone of the Scottish silver pages from Arthur's journal? Perhaps we can show her some of them, see how she reacts." Carole linked her arm through mine as we walked toward the pub's entrance.

"I do. And as you've met Jane before, I'll let you do most of the talking," I said, lowering my voice as the old pub door opened. We stepped into a low-beamed room with a bar along the back wall.

The warm, cozy room had been well worn in by the fishermen who'd frequented the place for generations, denting the floorboards with their welly boots while their pipe smoke, long since extinguished, stained the low ceiling.

Jane was leaning over a long wooden bar, talking to the barman, when we entered. As the door banged shut behind us, their heads snapped around in our direction. Jane schooled her face to neutral, but the barman's glare didn't abate.

"Are you both looking for rooms too?" Jane asked.

"Oh . . . no." Carole's face went from wide-eyed surprise to a conspiratorial smile. "We're staying at the hotel down the road for tonight, but if you have a room for tomorrow night?"

It wasn't the original plan, but perhaps the village was the place to be if we wanted to find out what had happened to Euan and where Bella might be.

"I'll let Oliver talk to you about that." Jane smiled at the barman, who was in his late twenties with a beard and tattoos. "I'll take the four-poster at the front if it's free."

He grunted again and moved to the computer at the far corner of the bar. "Would you two ladies like a drink?" he called. His voice was deep, with a distinct English accent—he wasn't local.

"Some tea would be very welcome." Carole took three strides to stand next to Jane at the bar. "Come and join us while Oliver deals with your room. You must be in such shock." Without waiting for a reply, she placed a hand on Jane's back and almost pushed her toward a small round table by one of the leaded windows looking out to the sea. The pub was dark in the old-fashioned way: dark beams overhead, dark brown furniture with maroon cushions, the smell of stale beer seeping out of the tiled flagstone floor.

Happily, it was a room that modern interior design had never touched—it was a building that had been doing the same job for a lifetime of seafarers, a reminder that despite the ever-changing tide, some things stood firm. On entering, it told a weary soul that they had weathered the storms and were home now, and it was time for a drink. It was a place for respite before the next day's trials had to be faced.

Oliver brought over a pot of tea, and Carole played mother and poured everyone a cup. "Oliver, dear, you wouldn't happen to have any biscuits, would you? I'm thinking we'll need them," she said, patting Jane's arm. I didn't miss the way Jane flinched at her touch.

I picked up my cup and blew on the steaming tea. "I'm so very sorry for your loss." I waited for the words to sink in. "I can't imagine what it would be like to find that someone you love has been . . ." This was a lie, because I had been in exactly that position.

I didn't know how to ask Jane everything that I wanted to know, so I caught Carole's eye and pleaded silently for her help. Jane sank back in her chair and pulled out a tissue to blow her nose.

"I was meant to be at the house last night. Do you realize that?" We both nodded. "If I had been, they probably would have killed me as well. I just don't understand why they couldn't have taken the silver without harming Euan. What will I do without him?" For the first time, I recognized genuine worry creasing her brow.

However, it was much the same as she'd said back at the castle. I had a feeling these were the same lines everyone was going to hear.

"What exactly was taken?" I asked. "Can you remember the silver that was on display? Would your insurance company have a record of it?" A collection that large would certainly have been insured, unless it was stolen or bought on the black market.

"Euan and I are . . . were . . . dealers. He dealt in Scottish antiques, mainly Scottish silver and paintings, but I didn't pay much attention to it. It wasn't my thing. I'm into Mauchline and Wemyss Wares more than the silver and paintings, but I dabble a bit. It's how we met. That detective said there was a woman at the house last night, caught on CCTV. Maybe she's the one who stole the silver and killed my poor, dear Euan." Her eyes closed as if she were fighting back tears, and she rubbed her nose again.

After giving her a minute to compose herself and meet our gaze, I showed Jane the photos on my phone, not telling her where they came from. To each photo she replied, "Maybe," or "I don't know, looks like it." But it was the way her frown grew deeper and deeper with each image that made me think she really did recognize some of the silver.

"Did the detective show you a picture of the woman?" I asked.

"Oh, he didn't have to—I could see her on my phone. It's linked to the camera. I've no idea who she is. At first she seemed familiar, but when I looked closer, I didn't recognize her."

"Who did she remind you of?" I was intrigued. I wondered if Bella had dressed as someone Euan or Jane might know.

But Jane shrugged. "No one. The picture's a bit grainy. I kept telling Euan to get a new security system but he said the quotes he got in were astronomical." She looked at us. "Was she the friend you were looking for?"

Carole's gaze met mine—we needed to tread carefully. "She might be the friend we are looking for," Carole said carefully. "You're sure you haven't met her before?"

"Nope, but the police have started looking for her. I overheard the detective saying to a policeman that it looked like Euan was killed by a nasty bash over the head, and then I noticed them taking away one of his prized candlesticks."

"Killed in the library with a candlestick. Sounds like a game of Cluedo, doesn't it?"

I nudged Carole, trying to remind her not to make light of the situation. She straightened up suddenly, as if she had just come up with one of her cunning plans, and I stifled a groan as she patted Jane's hand. "Do you know that Freya here is an antique hunter? While the police are looking into poor Euan's death, she may be able to track down the silver that was stolen."

Jane dabbed her already-dry eyes. "That won't be necessary. I'm sure the police are quite capable of dealing with it."

"We wouldn't ask for a fee, because if it was insured, we could negotiate with the insurance company to get paid if we are successful. It's the way most antique hunters work. Perhaps if we find the silver, we can find who did this to Euan."

Jane paused, and I thought she was about to agree, but then she shook her head. "I'm sure the police will find the silver and the killer. I can't even begin to think about it. It's all too much."

I had a niggling feeling that she was trying to shut down the conversation regarding the silver and its insurance. When I worked with Arthur, we hadn't come across many people who didn't want help recovering items stolen from them. Even if Jane had no sentimental attachment to the pieces in Euan's collection, if there was a chance that tracing them could help to find his killer, why wouldn't she want the help we were offering at no cost?

I decided to approach the subject from another angle. "How long have you been collecting and dealing?"

"Mauchline Ware and Wemyss Ware? Over seven years. I export to America to sell. The Americans love Scottish antiques. I . . . before Euan . . . I was with someone who loved Scottish antiques, and he made me appreciate them too. He taught me *everything*. Then I met Euan, and he liked the money he could make from the things, but not the items themselves. That *Outlander* TV show has done great things for the Scottish antiques trade, in my opinion."

Exporting to America—the words echoed in my mind. The Boston paintings we were looking into for the FBI had been shipped from Edinburgh to the US. Jane had just become my first suspect in the Boston case. But had she also murdered her boyfriend? And did she know more about Bella than she was letting on?

I reminded myself to spin the questions out slowly; I didn't want to show my hand too early. "And Euan kept the stock in the castle?" I asked.

Jane nodded. "If that woman on the door camera murdered him and stole the silver . . . I wouldn't be surprised if her fingerprints were all over the candlestick that killed him."

"It does sound very convincing," Carole cut in, but her tone was that of someone who wasn't convinced in the slightest. "I do so wish we could help you. A friend in need, and all... We have a lot of resources at our fingertips."

Jane frowned and took a sip of tea. It was clear she didn't want us involved, and I didn't want to annoy her so much that she shut us out altogether.

"Did Oliver ever bring those biscuits?" I asked, trying to move the conversation onto safer ground.

"He said he would," Carole replied, helping me change the subject.

"I'll look out for him. What were you hoping for, some shortbread?" I scanned the pub—Oliver was in the very far corner, talking into his mobile. He saw me looking, said something to the caller, and pulled the phone from his ear with a fake smile in my direction. Jane was glaring at him, as if she knew exactly who he was talking to and disapproved.

"Do you know Oliver well?" I asked.

"What? No, he's just the landlord. Euan deals... *dealt* with all that," she said.

My phone pinged and I pulled it out. I read the message and disguised a smile by draining my teacup.

"I'm afraid a friend of ours has just arrived at our hotel... um... for dinner, and we must go and get ready. I had quite forgotten about it." I stood up, giving Carole a meaningful look. We needed to leave. "I'll go and get the car and meet you out front, if you wouldn't mind getting the bill?"

I had an idea. And we needed to get back to the hotel as soon as possible.

13

Thursday, February 8, 6 p.m.

Snow started cascading down again as we drove to the hotel. The windscreen wipers struggled against the onslaught and the gray clouds above us smothered the horizon. I had to keep reminding myself to take my foot off the pedal; the weather conditions were too unsafe for speed.

After following the long, winding drive, we were greeted by two police cars parked in front of the building. The moment I stepped out of the car, boots crunched on the gravel behind me and I spun round.

Phil.

"You're here fast," I said, though in truth it didn't surprise me. I studied him as he approached us. He was wearing jeans and a Henley with a plaid shirt over the top and looked like some kind of cowboy American tourist. There was a new lightness to his step, and it made me hope that solving his late FBI partner's case in Jordan last October had had a healing effect on him.

His dark eyes met mine and he raised a questioning eyebrow. "I messaged," he said, as if getting to us as quickly as possible from across the Atlantic weren't a big deal. Carole beamed at me. I shook my head at her to try and stop her voicing any opinions.

"Where've you both been?" he asked.

I didn't get a chance to answer as Carole had flung her arms around him, and he grunted as the air was pushed out of his lungs. After a few beats his shoulders relaxed into one of Carole's wonderful bear hugs and a warm smile brightened his face. "Or should I ask, what trouble have you been getting into?" he said. She pulled back to look him over as if he were a long-lost family member who might be injured, not an FBI agent with whom we had just signed a consultancy contract.

When you love a person as much as I love Carole, it would be easy to feel twinges of jealousy when she directs the full blaze of her attention on someone else, but I have always preferred to focus on the joy she brings to everyone around her. Sprites like Carole should never be contained, no matter how much we want their attention for ourselves. Extroverts find their energy in crowds, whereas I have always preferred to make smaller, more intimate connections.

Phil extracted himself from Carole, but her hug had softened his stance. "So, have you found her?"

He didn't need to specify that he meant Bella. When we didn't answer, he continued, "The local police are here searching her hotel room, but it seems she hasn't been back since yesterday. Although I'm told someone entered her bedroom this morning claiming to be her." Folding his arms, Phil pinned us with a stern look. "Want to tell me about that?"

"How about some champagne?" asked Carole, making for the front door, apparently in a hurry to get out of the snow.

When Phil didn't move, she called back, "Coffee, then? You Americans love the stuff, don't you?"

"Come on." I placed my hand on his biceps. "We can all talk over dinner."

He didn't budge. "You're going to have to explain why you told a member of housekeeping staff you were Bella and entered her room." His breath brushed my cheek. "I'm sure it's a good story."

I tilted my chin to look up at him, hoping he couldn't sense the attraction buzzing through my veins. "We need to find her, Phil, because when we went to her last known location we found a dead laird there instead."

Phil stepped back and shook his head. "You're telling me she *killed* someone?"

"What? No, of course not. I'm saying I think she's in real trouble."

Snow was floating around us and a few flakes landed on my cheek, but I didn't feel the icy sting. I crossed my arms around myself and glared at him in the hope of making him understand the seriousness of the situation.

"You're cold." He gave my arm a squeeze. "Let's get inside and you can fill me in on what you've already found out." He took a few steps before saying, "But I'm not crossing any lines for Bella. I'm here for you."

"Fine," I replied, ignoring the last sentence. We both knew full well that Carole and I were not shy about crossing lines if needed.

∼

After we had explained to a young policeman that we were friends of Bella's, and that we had entered her hotel room earlier out of concern for her well-being after she'd gone missing, it became clear that the police thought she was on the run after killing Euan McGovern. Carole told them that Bella had hired a rental car and they promised to try and trace it but giving them that information only made them assume Bella had fled the scene. Phil promised to go into the station and provide all the information he had on Bella and what he believed she had been doing at the castle that night.

I tutted at him when he mentioned that she could have stolen the Scottish silver, based on her past "career choices," and I updated him on what we had learned from Jane.

"Bella didn't do this!" I said, as we left the policeman waiting for the hotel's CCTV footage to be handed over.

"But you don't know that, do you?" He glared at me. "Stop trying to protect her. She wouldn't do the same for you!"

"I'm not . . ." But I was. "And I'm sure she would." But I wasn't.

Phil shook his head but had the good grace to leave the conversation at that.

We entered the tartan-carpeted dining room and sat down for dinner, but my stomach was too clenched with anxiety to eat. I needed a minute to get my thoughts straight—I needed to work out a plan to find Bella. I left them to order and went up to my room to put our coats away. My worry had increased tenfold, for she was not only a missing friend, but she was also now wanted for questioning about a murder and believed by the police to have fled the scene.

When I returned to the dining room, Carole was gripping Phil's forearm. He looked quite uncomfortable. He was not, it seemed, used to the amount of physical contact that came naturally to Carole.

"We need to find her before the police do," she was saying urgently. "You must help."

"Absolutely, Phil, your resources are far greater than ours." I picked up my napkin, realizing that I'd probably missed my chance to order food.

"Where could she be?" Carole's gaze swept the room and mine followed, in the vain hope that Bella was somewhere in the hotel. "Do we think she's on the run? Is she hurt? Or maybe she's been . . . kidnapped and thrown into a dungeon."

I groaned. "There's no dungeon."

"We're all talking about Bella, right?" Phil shook his head in disbelief. "The international art and antiques thief? The woman who can morph into anyone she chooses, of any age? Sneak in and out of any situation? The—"

"We get the point. You don't like her," I cut him off. We needed clues, not a character evaluation. "But she's one of us, and we're all she has."

I was not naive; I knew Bella would very likely be capable of murder if provoked. But perhaps that could be said of any of us. We didn't know what had gone on the previous night in that castle with the bullying laird. On the Red Sea, I had felt the need to calm Bella's somewhat violent desire for revenge when it came to her ex-boyfriend, the antiques trafficker Chris Prince. But what motive could she have had for killing the laird of Fawside Castle while she was hunting the paintings in Arthur's journals?

Unless it was self-defense. Though a blow to the back of the head wasn't really consistent with that theory.

Phil sighed, and I smiled at Carole. He was going to help us.

"I don't trust her." He leaned toward me so that he wouldn't be overheard. "I'm an FBI agent, and she's a criminal. Whether I *like* her has nothing to do with it. She needs arresting! And you two"—his index finger flicked between us—"shouldn't be working with her. When the case was allocated to your agency, there was no mention of Bella being involved until she showed up on our video calls. And I let her be part of your team, I gave her a chance, and now look where we're all at. She once locked you into a vault, remember? If that doesn't tell you she's bad news, I don't know what will. She's a walking red flag." He focused his attention on Carole. "And you . . ." Carole beamed at him while he frowned at her. "Have been aiding in deception, I'm quite sure of it."

"I did no such thing. What an accusation, darling. I merely gave her some lippy and a bit of good old encouragement." Carole flicked her hair over her shoulder in defiance. "And you don't get to decide who's on the team. We do."

"We agreed on two lines of inquiry. First, finding out where the Boston paintings came from, and the other was assisting the insurance company in retrieving the stolen Scottish silver. But it seems to me that you have now made a third line ... of finding Bella."

"Excellent. Now that's all agreed," said Carole, pouring everyone some water. "Do we get special FBI badges and firearms training? I think I would make a great female James Bond if you gave me a hidden gun." She tapped her handbag, which was hanging on the back of her chair. "I think one would fit in here."

"What? Good God, no!" Phil raked his hand through his hair and sighed. "I'd forgotten what this was like with you two ... I don't even know how you think that's possible. First of all, no one in their right mind would ever give either of you a gun."

"Rude!" I chuckled. "I've actually had firearms training, decades ago, with Arthur." Although I wouldn't trust myself to remember any of it, but Phil didn't need to know that.

"That's settled, then. I get the first lessons." Carole winked at me; she enjoyed winding Phil up. I couldn't help the laugh that bubbled out of me.

Phil cleared his throat. "Shall we get back to reality?"

"Have you found out anything more about the other paintings in the journal?" I asked.

"The three paintings identified in Boston as forgeries were of the highest quality, and this has made everyone nervous. It raises the question, how many of the paintings in private collections were bought as genuine but are fake? And where are the original paintings?" replied Phil.

"Do you now think that *all* the paintings in Arthur's journal have been forged? Or just those three?" I asked.

"There's no way of knowing unless we find the others and have an expert authenticate them. The Boston paintings were sent from Edinburgh, although they could, I suppose, have originated somewhere else. Someone did a very good job of covering their tracks."

A plate of steak and chips was placed in front of me. When I looked up to question the waiter, Phil said, "I thought you'd be hungry, so I ordered for you. I hope that's okay? I figured everyone likes steak?"

It had been a very long time since anyone other than my aunt had cared about whether I ate or not. "Thank you," I said, deliberately avoiding Carole's look of glee as I picked up my knife and fork. ". . . We told Bella about the Boston paintings, but do we now think that she suspected that the paintings in the journal were in the castle? Or did she think that the three Boston paintings were connected to the castle and Euan McGovern? Seems to me that she was quite a few steps ahead of all of us. Perhaps if we locate her, we'll find the answers to what is going on with the paintings too."

"Even if she has answers, can we trust what she says?" said Phil.

"We have one other line of inquiry. Bella went to see Alexandra Pattern, who works at an auction house in Edinburgh." A thought occurred to me. "Perhaps Bella was impersonating an Edinburgh auctioneer when she visited the castle, and that was how she intended to get inside. It would be a good cover story for Bella." I gave Carole a knowing look, but still didn't let on that it was her idea that Bella went to the castle in disguise.

Phil opened his phone and started typing. "I shall have Sloane arrange a meeting with the auction house tomorrow morning at nine. Let's meet with this Alexandra Pattern and see what Bella was doing at the auction house."

Carole shifted in her chair and took a large sip of her wine.

I looked at her. "Is there something you need to tell us?"

"Carole?" said Phil as he rested his elbows on the table and stared at her. She squirmed under his attention. "Tell us."

"Now, I don't want to get Bella in trouble . . ."

"She's already under suspicion of murder. I don't think any information you have could make it worse, do you?" he said.

I waited for Carole to accept that he would sit like this in the dining room all night if necessary.

She pointed her knife at him. "Sometimes you're a fun-sucker, do you know that?"

"Well, that just depends on what type of *fun* we're talking about." He smirked, and I snapped my attention to my food, not wanting him to see me blush. "I'm good with *legal* fun, Carole."

Carole beamed at him. "I think I'm finally rubbing off on you." She glanced over at me. "Look how red Freya has gone."

"Can we get back to what you've been keeping from us?" I mumbled.

"Bella said she was going into Edinburgh. And I've always thought that she needed more friends, so I arranged for her to meet India—Euan's daughter—and have a coffee. They're both in their twenties, and . . . and then we found out that Euan is dead, and I didn't want people to think the wrong thing."

"And?" There was something else Carole wasn't saying.

"Now, don't jump to the wrong conclusion." Phil gave her an "out with it" look. "I could be wrong, but I think it was India who told Bella about the auction house and a woman who works there, Alexandra Pattern. But neither of them has anything to do with what happened at the castle."

"And this is the daughter that you believe hates her father?"

Carole started shaking her head. "No. No. No. I can see what you're thinking, that maybe Bella and India came up with some sort of plan to kill off the laird. But they're both very lovely young ladies, and they would certainly never do a thing like that." The slight crack in her voice betrayed a trace of doubt beneath her words. She waved at the waiter, lifting up her empty glass.

"I think we need to pay India *and* the auction house a visit," I said, placing my napkin on the table.

"Not at this time of night," said Carole, motioning to the window.

She was right; there was nothing we could do this evening, with everything closed and everyone on their way to bed. But necessity called for invention, and we did know someone who could help.

"All right, then we should call Sky," I said, "and ask her to dig up as much information as possible on Alexandra Pattern and India McGovern."

We might not be much of a team yet, but Phil showing up had made me realize that we had a lot of valuable skills between us. Together, surely we could uncover why Arthur had listed those paintings and antiques in his journal—and find Bella.

14

Sky
Thursday, February 8, 7 p.m.

Sky was not going to be left out of all the fun this time around. Months ago, when Freya and Carole had jumped on a specialist antiques cruise from Greece to Jordan, she'd been happy to stay behind—at that point, she'd only been working as an assistant at the shop for a few weeks. But it was different now.

Being left on her own hadn't gone well. Her ex, Aaron, had paid a visit, and it had taken the might of the whole Suffolk village to make him leave and stay away. Telling Freya and Carole that all of that was behind her was one thing; making her own brain believe it was another. She didn't like to admit that shudders still ran down her spine with every creak the old shop made.

Owen, the local mechanic she was dating, had offered to stay over while her employers were away. That was lovely of him, but it wasn't just being left in the shop on her own that bothered her. She wanted to join in with the thrill of the hunt.

Her mobile rang. "Freya—have you found Bella?" she asked, freezing as her pulse picked up.

After Bella had come back from Jordan, she'd stayed with Sky in the flat above the antiques shop for a weekend, and it had made all the difference to Sky's ability to remain living there. Ever since Aaron had broken into the shop and held her hostage, being on her own there made her jumpy—Bella sorted that for her. She put extra locks on all the doors and placed cameras everywhere that Sky could access from her phone, and she did it all without a word. She saw right away what Sky needed to feel safe, and she didn't hesitate.

By the second evening, as they sat and talked over pizza, Sky recognized Bella's deep understanding and mistrust of dangerous men. They'd both dated them. Seen the traits in the flesh, day in and day out. And they had both spent time on the wrong side of the law. Their family set-ups were almost the same: raised by single parents, they'd fended for themselves from an early age, making them both appear strong and independent. But really neither of them had been given any other choice—it was the way they'd survived. Bella had pulled Sky into a hug when she left, and an unspoken pact had been made—they would help each other out if needed.

Though Sky had no idea where Bella was, they had messaged quite a lot, so when Bella had asked Sky to help her find someone, she had happily agreed. Bella didn't want anyone to know, and Sky was fine with that—it meant Bella trusted her, and she would never break a friend's trust. But for a long time, it had seemed as if Bella was hunting a ghost. Eventually she got a break and found her target: an elderly man who had been sent to prison six years earlier for dangerous driving resulting in the death of a passenger.

While Freya filled her in on Bella, the missing silver, and the murder, Sky pinched the bridge of her nose. "This really isn't good, is it?"

"It's not. We need to find her as quickly as possible and understand what happened last night at the castle. The only way I can think of to do that is retrace Bella's footsteps. Can you look into Alexandra Pattern and India McGovern? And see if there's any connection between the Griffin & Thompson auction house, Fawside Castle, and the three forged paintings found in Boston?"

After she had hung up, Sky sat at Arthur's old partners desk in the shop and opened her laptop. With a few strokes of her fingers over the keys she was feeling lighter, and her mind had been filled with the love of the hunt. Freya loved hunting stolen art and antiques—and now a missing Bella—and Sky loved the hunt for information. Especially the type of online information people didn't want her to find.

She was about to go over the Boston case when she remembered she'd never told Freya about the man Bella had asked her to search for. Bella was a friend, and she didn't want anyone to know her business; Sky respected that. Bella had told her to keep the whole prison business secret. But now Bella was missing, and while Sky didn't want to betray her confidence, her safety was more important.

She began to search for a connection between the man Bella was looking for and the two people Freya had just asked her to research.

It didn't take long to find a small link between two of them, and guilt twisted her stomach—even though there was no way she could have known.

"Sorry, Bella," Sky said to herself, after she'd hung up the phone and sent a text to Freya detailing all the information on the elderly man she had given Bella. "But Freya needs to know everything, even if you made me swear to not say."

The night was setting in as Sky dialed another new friend—Agatha from the Teapot Tearooms.

"Hi, Agatha. I was wondering if you could look after the shop for a couple of days? Freya and Carole need me in Scotland."

"Oh, my dear, you absolutely must go. Don't you worry, the Neighborhood Watch will be put on red alert the moment I inform the Parish Council, and I'll sit in wait at the shop. The Teapot is overstaffed at this time of year anyway, but I just don't have the heart to drop anyone's hours."

"I'm not quite sure this is a red alert situation, but I'd love your help." Sky smiled at the phone. Her love for the village and the people who lived there continued to grow.

"You pop in as you're passing and I'll give you some food for the road. Can't have you living on processed motorway food, can we?"

The only thing left for Sky to do was pack and tell Owen she was going to Scotland. She had a friend to find, and she wasn't going sit this case out.

15

Freya
Friday, February 9, 9 a.m.

The next morning, we hurried to Griffin & Thompson's auction house at 29 Hanwell Place, Edinburgh. It was a grand Victorian building with four towering columns supporting a pitched gable over three royal-blue double doors. Snow had settled on the roof and around the building, making the scene look like something out of *A Christmas Carol*, even though Christmas was long gone.

"How impressive," remarked Carole as she pushed open the front door. "It looks like it was made to house art and antiques, doesn't it?"

"I've heard it called one of the most beautiful salerooms in the UK. And wait until you see the inside."

We crossed the threshold, and even Phil, who normally wore a mask of indifference, stopped in his tracks to gaze at the sweeping two-tiered auction gallery. It could have been a theater, with its maroon walls and classical balcony overlooking the main auction floor.

In one of the display cabinets was a large collection of Mauchline Ware. "Those look like the pieces in Arthur's journal," said Carole. "What are they again?"

I was fond of Scottish Souvenir Wood and had researched it quite a bit after seeing the large collection catalogued in Arthur's journal.

"They're mostly souvenirs for nineteenth-century tourists. I think they started by making snuff boxes from locally sourced wood and when the demand grew, they branched out into other items." I pointed to a collection of four wooden rings in the cabinet. "They weren't easy to make. The finishing process could take months. I'm pretty sure most souvenirs nowadays aren't made with such effort."

Carole stood looking into the cabinet. "Makes me want to take one home and put it on a shelf, like they would've done."

There was a part of me that wanted that too. "Detective Rodgers told me they'd found a desk diary in Euan's office. The name Emma Page was jotted in for five p.m. the night before last—just around the time when Bella rang the doorbell. Rodgers wanted to know if I knew an Emma Page, and I told him I didn't . . . it's not a good look telling a police detective that your friend has lied about her name. I've had a text from Sky to say that she found emails from Bella to an Alexandra Pattern, who works here. It seems Bella was planning to come here to see her about the Mauchline Ware and some of the other items in the journal." I turned back toward the main reception area and said to the porter, "We have an appointment with Alexandra Pattern—I rang earlier."

As we waited, I pondered, "It's no surprise that Bella likes using aliases, but why would she have decided to go undercover to the castle? Why all the subterfuge?"

Phil nodded. "It's a good question. Bella didn't want anyone at the castle to know who she really was or what she looked like. There must have been a reason for that."

It didn't take long for Alexandra to appear, but even in that short amount of time Carole had managed to circle at least twenty items in the catalogue for an upcoming auction that she "absolutely must buy." The moment I saw Alexandra's hairstyle, I knew Bella had gone to the castle disguised as her. It was a strange turn of events. Why would Bella have gone to the castle looking like this Edinburgh auctioneer and using a different name? Had that turned out to be a dangerous mistake?

"Can I help you?" Alexandra Pattern was in her late fifties or early sixties with a French bob and striking lipstick—exactly as Bella had on the CCTV footage. She was dressed for the cold in fingerless cashmere gloves, a black polo-neck jumper, and thick tweed trousers.

I stepped forward and held out my hand. "I'm Freya Lockwood, from the Lockwood Antique Hunter's Agency. You may have known my predecessor, Arthur Crockleford?"

"Of course, I knew Arthur. Who didn't? But then, the antiques world is quite small at the end of the day. How can I help you?"

Phil and Carole introduced themselves as I pulled up a picture of Bella from October's cruise. "I think you may also know a friend of ours. I believe she came here to meet you recently. Did she ask you about Mauchline Ware or any paintings? Did she show you any pictures? She's gone missing, and we're trying to retrace her steps."

Alexandra studied the picture on my phone. "I did have a visitor recently . . . maybe a couple of weeks back. The hair is different, but the face looks the same, I think. When did she go missing?" She tugged at her neckline as if the jumper was now too hot, then rested her hand on her stomach. "I don't remember her showing me any photos, but then, it does get very busy here."

"Over twenty-four hours ago, and I'm ever so worried," said Carole. "Anything you can tell us may be helpful."

"There's nothing I can tell you. I'm sorry." But as I flicked through the pictures, her gaze lingered on one of the three Boston paintings, and when she saw me notice she shrugged. "I think she was asking about the auction next week or maybe the charity event." She tugged at her collar again, and a bead of sweat glistened on her top lip.

She was lying. There was no way Bella had arranged a meeting with her just to talk about an upcoming auction or a party.

I decided to try a different tack. "Bella *was* looking into these paintings, and she believed they had a connection to Griffin & Thompson." I held up the photo of the three paintings again.

Alexandra's jaw clenched, and the tension in the room became as thick as soup. "She may have mentioned some paintings. I really can't remember."

She was underestimating how well I knew the antiques world and the people who worked within it. In my experience, they had wonderful powers of recall about any items that crossed their path.

Phil tapped my phone. "What can you tell us about these paintings?" he asked, clearly sensing she was holding back. Alexandra took a step back as he pulled out his badge. "I'm with the Art Crime Team of the FBI. We're looking into the paintings, and we know they were sent from Edinburgh to Boston to be sold."

Alexandra tugged nervously at her jumper sleeves. "And what does that have to do with me?"

I tried to make my smile warm. "Perhaps nothing, but Bella was interested in the paintings and so are we. Can you help? Even the smallest detail could be significant."

Maybe Alexandra realized we had no intention of leaving without the information we needed, or maybe she just wanted to get us away from the main floor of the auction house. She gestured toward a door. "Follow me."

She led us back into a small office overflowing with catalogues and papers. "I have never seen those paintings before, but . . ." She stopped, put her reading glasses on, and took my phone from my hand studying the photographs of the Boston paintings. "These look like the work of Sir Henry Raeburn, or they are exceptional reproductions. Are they prints?"

"These paintings are being held by the FBI. We believe that they are fakes which were sent to Boston to be sold as originals."

"Well, I have nothing to do with anything like that, but the lady you were asking about was talking about his works, along with other Scottish antiques. Maybe she is involved in some way?"

Bella was looking into all the items in the journal.

"But I will tell you what I told her: we haven't had anything like this through the auction house." Alexandra handed the phone back and pressed her hand to her stomach again. "I'm sorry—I'm not feeling well. Is there anything else?"

Phil and I exchanged a knowing glance. Alexandra was trying to get rid of us, but Carole hadn't seemed to notice.

"How do I know that name, Rayburn? Isn't it a make of wood-burning stove?" Carole asked. I just shook my head.

"The spelling is different." I gave her arm a squeeze to let her know that I had already put the pieces together.

"Tell me," she whispered.

"Later," I replied. I wasn't sure if I could trust Alexandra. I'd remembered now that a number of the other paintings recorded in Arthur's third journal were also by Sir Henry Raeburn—but they were not the same ones we had just shown Alexandra in the photographs.

As we stepped out of the office, a noticeboard in the corridor caught Carole's attention. "Oh, that auction house is sponsoring a charity dance the evening after tomorrow?" she said brightly, turning back toward Alexandra.

"What?" Alexandra was mopping her brow with a tissue.

"A dance—I do love a good Scottish ceilidh. How do we get tickets? Can we get them here?"

"Tickets were on sale through the website, but it might be sold out. Now, if that will be all?"

Carole took out her phone. "I'll get onto that right away. Will we see you there?"

"Um... maybe." Alexandra smiled, but it was more like a grimace. "Please close the door behind you."

Conversation over. I had a feeling that I was being steamrolled but it was clear Alexandra was done talking, for now at least. What secrets was Alexandra Pattern keeping, and had Bella found out the truth?

16

Friday, February 9, noon

We were meeting India McGovern at a café in Leith called Two Shots. I was almost sorry for Carole when, to her dismay, I told her we would drive there and didn't need to take the tram.

When we arrived, my aunt was delighted to see images of two crossed rifles on a sign above the café door—she took it as a sign from the universe that she should practice with firearms. I had to stop her phoning Phil and demanding a shooting lesson as soon as we returned.

"You should just let me persuade him. I'm very good at getting him to do things for us." That wasn't strictly true, but there was no point in arguing.

I was hungry, and brunch sounded wonderful. "I don't need to look at the menu to know we'll be having smashed avocado with a poached egg and chili sprinkled on top," I said, taking in the spiced coffee scent and relaxing.

Carole had suggested we meet India in St Abbs, but she was staying with a friend in Leith and had suggested the café instead. "India was only told about her father's death yesterday. Are you sure she's up to meeting with us?" I said to Carole as I looked around, wondering if the young woman might have changed her mind.

"It's why I insisted that Phil go to the police station to meet with Detective Rodgers and we came here by ourselves. I didn't want to overwhelm her with strangers. But to be honest she sounded quiet on the phone, which concerns me."

The café was full of people with noise-canceling headphones and laptops sitting on stools at a long bar that stretched along a bare brick wall. Above them were neon signs saying things like *Hot Lips* and *Not All Those Who Wander Are Lost*. It was too dark and too bright all at once.

"Hello," said a voice behind us. Carole turned and flung herself at the speaker, a small, pretty woman with a blond fringe, wearing a long puffer jacket. She enveloped her in a hug.

"India, darling, how are you? Thank you for coming. But we could've, *should* have, come to you."

India's shoulders were hunched and she looked pale, but I didn't know if that was a sign of grief or just her normal complexion.

"Do you need anything? Can we help in any way?" asked Carole, searching her face anxiously. Before India could reply, she added, "This is my niece, Freya. We now run the Lockwood Antique Hunter's Agency together."

India linked her arm through Carole's as if my aunt could keep her from fracturing apart. Her puffy red eyes told me she was anything but all right. She looked me up and down but still didn't speak.

"I'll get some coffee," I said, pointing to a free table in the far corner. "Why don't you both sit down?" It seemed as if they needed space to get reacquainted.

Carole steered India to the table, and I could see India starting to talk.

A few minutes later, with three mugs on a tray, I headed back over to them and placed a cappuccino in front of India. "It must have been a massive shock?"

"It was." India scanned the café, looking anywhere but at us until she focused on Carole. "You know that I had a complicated history with my father. For years he was just a face on a video call once a week. But when my mum got sick, she started making us chat more... made him promise to take me in when she knew she wasn't going to make it..." Tears ebbed down India's cheeks. "He said no over and over again, and then he changed his mind. He never wanted me to come here, but Mum found a way to make him take me in, and I wish that she hadn't. It's bad to feel like I'm free now he's dead, isn't it?"

"What do you mean, that your mother 'found a way'?" I asked.

India shrugged. "She was very persuasive." But she didn't sound very convincing. It occurred to me that her mother might have known something about Euan that she'd used to bribe him into caring for their daughter.

India picked up her cup, but her hand was shaking so much that coffee spilled over the rim. Carole took it from her while I mopped up with a napkin. "It's all right to have complicated feelings about his death," said Carole gently. "We're not here to judge. I just wanted to see you and check how you were doing."

India took a deep breath. "Can we change the subject? How's your new business going?"

"It's good. We have a contract with the FBI, can you believe it? Freya is *very* happy about it." The way she said "very" made me blush.

"We've successfully solved a couple of cases on our own, and this third one is our first as consultants for the FBI." I heard the pride in my voice; we had come so far in such a short time.

"Wow, the FBI, that sounds... important." India rubbed her nose with a tissue Carole had handed her.

Carole beamed at me. "Freya is quite the detective."

India's expression brightened with hope. "Are you here to find out who killed my father?"

"Oh no. I'm sorry if we gave you that impression. We're on a case, but our focus right now is looking for Bella. Carole tells me that she gave Bella your number. Did the two of you meet up or talk? Have you heard from her recently?"

India shrugged. "We met quite a few times and we really hit it off, but I haven't heard from her in about a week. I just needed to see Carole in person." She put a hand on Carole's arm. "You and Arthur were always so very kind to me after . . . well . . . it's not good to speak ill of the dead, is it?"

"You don't need to say anything at all if you don't want to in that regard," Carole soothed.

"You're worried about Bella, aren't you? That's the same look you had when you found me at the bar that evening."

Carole sighed. "I'm very worried. We haven't heard from her in days. She went to the castle to meet with your father and hasn't been seen since. The police want to question her . . . after they found . . . him."

"Why was she meeting my father?" India asked.

"That's what we're trying to find out," I replied. "Have you spoken to the police?"

"They contacted me, but I didn't know what to say. I wasn't there when it happened. I live at the castle because I don't have the money to move out yet, but I try to spend as little time there as possible. When I heard there was a storm, it was a good excuse to stay away—but then maybe if I had been home, he wouldn't have been killed . . ." She pulled the sleeves of her jumper down, twisting them around her hands. "I never wanted him dead. I wanted him to just . . . see me. *Like* me, even, or something like that."

I was touched by the depths of her despair and wanted to offer her some comfort if I could. "We can never know what's around the corner. It won't help running through the what-ifs in life; it never does. Trust me." My free hand closed in a fist around the burn scar on my palm, trying to shut down the memories. Trying to block out the guilt of surviving that fateful fire that my parents hadn't made it out of.

India noticed the movement, and I reopened my palm to show her the burn. Carole looked away—she hated to see the mark that night had left on me, but the grief would have been etched into me regardless of what my hand looked like. "When I was twelve, we had a house fire. My mother had caught my cold and she was using an electric heater in their bedroom. Sometime in the night, it caught fire. I tried to get to them, but . . ." My gaze lifted from my palm to meet India's eyes. "I know all about what-ifs."

"You've lost both your parents, like me?" India asked.

"I have, but—" I smiled at Carole. "Then this wonderful woman came to the rescue, along with Arthur Crockleford; they gave me time and space to heal. I found my passion for antiques in Arthur's shop, and when I was older I traveled with him."

"Just like Bella?" India said. "She told me that you were the only two people she trusted."

If that was true, Bella had a funny way of showing it. "You do know her quite well, then?"

"I know her well enough to know Bella wouldn't do anything wrong." India sighed. "I know she thinks she's morally gray, like in all those dark romantasy books we both love. But she's not. She's just lost and doesn't know where she fits into the world. The police are wrong to be looking for her in connection with my father's death." Her shoulders straightened. "You're a detective agency—maybe you can find out who killed my father? Prove that Bella is innocent? I'll pay you whatever you want and help in whatever way I can."

Before I could explain that we were not that sort of agency, Carole reached over to take India's hand. "Of course we can. But we wouldn't dream of taking your money."

I took a deep, steadying breath. Yet again, Carole was offering to work for nothing, but I wanted to help India get the answers she needed if possible. "You could hire us to look into the Scottish silver that was stolen—and if we find out anything about your father's death while we're at it, well . . . But are you sure you'd really want to know, if it turned out Bella was involved?"

"She's not. She's a good person."

A good criminal, I wanted to say, but didn't.

"You seem very sure of that," I probed.

"If you want to look at someone who *isn't* good and could definitely have murdered my father, then you should be looking at Jane. She's a bitch. And my father was getting tired of her—all they ever did was argue. He accused her of having an affair last week."

"There was no open relationship, then?" asked Carole.

India scoffed. "My father was possessive and domineering. Do you really think he would allow anyone that kind of freedom? Who told you that there was?"

Carole shook her head, and our eyes locked. Jane had lied to the police.

17

India
Friday, February 9, 1:30 p.m.

A tear slid down India's cheek as she walked out of the café. Talking to Carole and Freya had brought things to the surface, and it was hard to quiet her mind once it started spinning its painful cycle. Her chest twisted with a confusing type of grief she hadn't experienced when her mother died. It was almost unbelievable that the father she'd hated so venomously was dead and gone. Forever.

Now there were all these *feelings* that no longer had any direction. She'd half believed that once all the verbal abuse stopped, she would feel free, but his voice was still in her head. She was still trapped under the weight of his poisonous disappointment. Every time she'd borne the brunt of his rage she had wished him dead, but now her ingrained need to make him proud had no chance of ever succeeding. It was all so very complicated.

Her hatred of Jane was still alive too. Jane had been in India's life for nearly five years; she was one of the first people Euan had introduced her to when she'd arrived from Napier, New Zealand. India had been so innocent back then, desperate for a new family to fill the hole left by her mother's death from cancer. She'd been willing to ignore all kinds of warning signs. But she had quickly learned that any friend of Euan's was bad news—and anyone he was sleeping with was probably rotten to the core. It only took a week for India and Jane to settle into a deep loathing of each other, and for Euan to find his grieving daughter a place at boarding school. As a full boarder, she only came back to the castle a few times each year, and if she could arrange to stay with friends instead, she always did.

They had found a rhythm that everyone was happy with until India had said she wanted to leave boarding school when she turned sixteen. She had decided to go and do her Highers in a school in Edinburgh and, as the castle was close enough by train, she would live there with her father. She tried to avoid Euan and Jane as much as possible, which wasn't hard as they mainly spent their evenings in the library doing business that India was never told about. It was during one of these hushed evenings that India had answered the front door to find Alexandra Pattern, an auctioneer from Griffin & Thompson, standing before her.

Alexandra was warm and friendly at first, chatting to India about her music and studies—until India asked if she was selling some antiques for Euan. Alexandra just glared at her, and from that day on she never rang the doorbell again; instead, she came around the back and went straight into the library. But her strange reaction to the innocent question stayed with India, and it may have been the reason she started sitting in the dining room reading her romantasy books—which just so happened to be next to the library. Through the thin dividing wall between the rooms, she learned quite a lot.

Alexandra's visits settled into a routine that coincided with a lot of boxes coming and going from the castle. While at work, she may have been an honest and reliable employee, but it was what she did out of hours that intrigued India. The only person India knew who might be able to shed light on what was happening was Arthur Crockleford, so she arranged to meet him for coffee one winter morning. Without using Alexandra's name, India discussed the situation with Arthur in general terms. He suggested that she try to find out what was in the boxes and take photos of the contents—and he handed over an old-fashioned Polaroid camera she could use.

India loved the idea of uncovering the secrets of the castle, and maybe learning something that would help her convince her father to give her some money so that she could move out. She wouldn't call it blackmail.

When Carole arranged for her to meet Bella, they talked about Arthur, but India didn't mention all the photographs she had sent to him before he died. She told Bella vaguely what she thought her father was up to—buying and selling stolen art and antiques—and that he wasn't doing it alone. Had she mentioned Alexandra Pattern to Bella? She couldn't remember.

Bella didn't seem in the least bit concerned with whatever Euan or Alexandra was doing—she was only interested in tracking down some paintings. She showed pictures of them to India and told her she believed some of them were hidden in Fawside.

When Carole had called her after Euan's death, India hadn't intended to answer—she'd suspected that Carole would be looking for Bella, and she didn't want to give anything away. If Bella wanted to be found, she would be. But India had needed the warmth and comfort that she knew Carole would offer.

India climbed into her old Jeep but didn't start the engine. Perhaps she had told Carole and Freya too much about her relationship with her father. Maybe she should have tried to cover up her true feelings and play the distraught daughter everyone so clearly wanted to see. She'd managed that on the phone with the police, but as soon as she saw Carole she'd known that she couldn't lie to her—she had already told her too much when they'd first met. Carole had a way of getting everyone to open up, spilling all their secrets to her, despite their best intentions.

Or perhaps India should have told Carole and Freya about working with Arthur. But they were working with the FBI—she didn't want the police in her business.

India picked up her phone to call her boyfriend, Oliver, who was a barman at the Old Ship pub. The moment the ringing tone started, she relaxed back into the car seat. Oliver always had a solution, was always looking out for her. He was her safe haven.

"Hello, love, are you coming over?" She could hear the smile on Oli's lips and allowed herself a small sigh as she turned on the engine.

"Are you busy?" She didn't care if he was; she would just wait at the end of the bar or upstairs in his flat for him to finish his shift.

"The lunchtime rush is calming down. Come around—I want to see you."

After they hung up, India checked her makeup in the mirror, rubbing away the tear-streaked eyeliner and mascara that had run down her cheeks.

"Just hold your nerve, Indie. That's all you have to do," she told her reflection. There was a real chance now that she could get her very own happy-ever-after, in a fairy-tale castle with her prince.

All she had to do was keep out of the way until the police called off the hunt for Euan's murderer, and they would be home and dry.

18

Freya
Friday, February 9, 4 p.m.

Carole, Phil, and I had settled in the hotel's sitting room for a traditional afternoon tea when Sky launched herself into the one free armchair and plucked a scone from the cake stand.

"Sky!" I was pleased to see her, but her arrival was unexpected.

"Thank God there's food. I'm starving..." She paused as if she were about to explain why she was in Scotland and not looking after the shop. "How do they eat scones in Scotland? Clotted cream first and then the jam on top?" She glanced at Carole's scone, which was cut in half with jam on the bottom and a plump dollop of cream on top.

"Jam first... trust your elders." Carole winked at me as I lifted mine to my lips. It had clotted cream first and jam on top. "Darling, I'm thrilled you're here. I love us all together." She leaned across and clasped Sky's hand. "Have you left Owen in charge of the shop?"

"Owen's a mechanic!" I said, my voice a little too high. "And we've an antiques fair to attend next weekend. Someone should be making an inventory and packing stock." My pulse picked up.

"Don't panic, I would never... he's like a bull in a china shop." Sky chuckled, seeing the look on my face. "Freya, you know I'd never do that, and I've sorted most of the things for the fair. Agatha's looking after the shop while we all hunt together." She took a large bite of scone. "It's a great plan, right?" She lathered more jam on top of the clotted cream and took another huge bite.

I shook my head. Agatha wouldn't have been my first choice. "... I guess it is."

"Look, I know I should've asked first, but I didn't want you to say no. I wanted to help. I love Bella . . . I'm worried."

Phil groaned. "Of course you love her. You're a hacker and she's a spy. It's a match made in heaven."

"Want to talk about our meet-cute? Or should we talk about you and Freya?" Sky bit back. Phil clenched his jaw, and Sky narrowed her brown eyes at him while I inwardly cringed. "Thought so. I'm reformed, and so is Bella. I'm here because I'm worried about her *and* I've found a clue." She straightened her back the way she always did when she was about to tell us an important discovery.

"I suppose your employer, this one"—he pointed to Carole—"has you hacking into something for that?"

"I haven't done so this morning, darling, but the day isn't over." Carole raised her teacup to him.

"Hacking is like a gateway drug. Then it's on to all sorts of cybercrime for these computer genius people," Phil said, placing a tiny cucumber sandwich in his mouth.

"All I heard was 'genius,'" replied Sky, picking up the last cheese sandwich and devouring it whole.

"Sky is *very* innocent now." Carole winked at Sky, letting us all know that she certainly could still do some hacking if the Lockwood Agency—or more precisely, Carole—wanted it done.

Sky waggled her knife at Phil. "You've a problem with Bella and me because we weren't born into your white male privilege and had to climb our way out of our situations. Do you know what it takes to survive a childhood like ours?" She didn't wait for Phil to answer; instead, she moved to sit down on the floor, as close to the coffee table and cakes as possible, and picked up a custard tart. "Can we get more of these? And I'm not sure yet where I'll be staying..."

"Phil?" I raised an eyebrow that hopefully said "play nice." I wanted to hear about the clue Sky had found, and first he needed to apologize.

He sighed. "I'm sorry. The moral vacuum that you and Bella reside in when it comes to your work puts me in a difficult position. It's not in my nature to turn a blind eye, and as you're working as my consultants..." He ran a hand over his day-old stubble. "It makes me... uncomfortable."

"Can we all agree to put this to one side while we try to solve everything? What did you find out?" I asked Sky.

Sky chewed and swallowed. "Sure, as long as I don't get any more comments like that." She looked over at Phil, and he nodded. "There's a guy in prison in Edinburgh who Bella's been looking for. I found him for her. And it turns out that Alexandra Pattern also went to visit the same prisoner six months ago."

"Around the same time the three paintings were shipped to Boston?" asked Phil.

"Four days before they were shipped. It might be a coincidence?"

"So, Bella gets you to find this man in prison, she visits Alexandra Pattern at the auction house, and then she books an appointment to see Euan?" I asked and Sky nodded. "When did she ask you about this prisoner? Why didn't you tell me earlier?"

"And who exactly is he?" Phil asked.

"There were details of Edinburgh prison visiting hours in Bella's notebook," said Carole.

"Bella told me it was a personal case. She never mentioned it in the context of the agency, so I had no reason to think it was to do with agency work." Sky shrugged. "I wanted to help her out by finding Cedric, but I didn't really look into him much, because I was busy with our case." As we all stared expectantly at her, she continued, "The prisoner's name is Cedric James. And I'm here because I think we need to go and talk to him, just like Bella did. Maybe he'll tell us why both she and Alexandra visited him. I thought Bella's search for Cedric and the hunt for the art and antiques in Arthur's journal were two entirely different things. But I don't now."

"Was everyone here in contact with Bella apart from me?" I tried to keep the hurt from my voice. Arthur might have left me a legacy, but sometimes it didn't really feel like I was running the show.

"It's not like that," Carole reassured me, topping up my cup with hot tea. "I think she wanted to prove to you that she was valuable, and she believed that this one over here . . ." She jabbed a finger at Phil. "Didn't want her anywhere near the case after their little spat."

There was a moment of silence as everyone drank tea and munched on tiny cakes or scones.

"I think we need to trace Bella's exact steps in sequence. Who did she turn to first for help?" My gaze flickered between Sky and Carole. "And did either of you know the other one was helping Bella?"

They both shook their heads.

"We're going to have to come up with a better way of communicating, don't you think?"

"I'll set up a group chat, and we can all share what we know in there. Would that work?" offered Sky.

"Oh, a group chat, that fills me with joy. We can all share . . . everything." Carole clapped her hands together, and I put a hand up.

"Ground rules. This is just for work. No dirty jokes, no spicy memes. Is that clear?" I asked Carole.

"And you call *him* the fun-sucker." She pointed at Phil.

Sky spat out her tea. "What are we talking about? What's a suck—"

"Nothing." Carole was alight with mischief.

"Back to the timeline. Carole, you first."

"Bella told me she was in Scotland doing some research into the items in Arthur's third journal. She asked me who I had met there with Arthur in the past, because she knew we had traveled to Scotland quite a few times together. So I mentioned a young woman I'd met with Arthur whom I'd stayed in touch with—India. And I said that her father, Euan McGovern, was in the antiques business. I told her to stay away from Euan as he was bad news, but that India might know some of the same people and might be able to help."

"It sounds like that was after I had already done the digging into Cedric James for her." Sky licked her fingers free from crumbs and we all waited, but she didn't continue.

"And?" I encouraged.

"He's not going to like this." She nodded at Phil.

"But I'm on the edge of my seat, darling, so out with it," Carole urged.

"First Bella asked me to look for a Lester White or Frank Sargent born in St Thomas' Hospital, London, around 1942 to 1944. I found both and gave her the details, but these men had very little in terms of a digital footprint. No bank accounts, credit cards, etc. The strangest thing was that each man had an arrest on record—Lester three years before Frank—and then they had disappeared. It reminded me of what my ex, Aaron, used to do when setting up fake companies. So, I started to search the death records. Both Lester White and Frank Sargent had died in childhood. It's a very common way to create an alias. I only found Cedric James because Frank Sargent and Cedric were both registered on an apartment lease, and council tax, in London fifteen years ago. Then I found out that Cedric James was in prison for causing death by dangerous driving. I thought Bella would write to him, not actually visit. And I never thought any of it was related to agency work. This was well before Phil told us about the Boston paintings being found," said Sky.

"And where did that lead you?" Carole encouraged.

"Before I drove up here, I did some more digging. Cedric James was charged with dangerous driving, but he was also an artist. A very talented one."

Phil leaned forward.

Carole gasped and I froze.

Had Bella lied to Sky? Maybe her "personal" hunt for those men had been professional after all. It was a leap, but had Bella been searching for the forger all along?

19

Saturday, February 10, 10:30 a.m.

I had never been inside a prison before, but as soon as the first gate locked behind me, I knew I never wanted to enter one again. The clank of metal reminded me of the Copthorn Manor vault door slamming behind me and Bella locking it. My pulse picked up, and I wondered if I really was grateful that Phil and his FBI connections had been able to get us an appointment to meet Cedric James at such short notice.

Phil must have sensed my hesitation. He touched my back lightly, looking down at me. "This won't take long, but I can go in on my own if you want. He's not a violent criminal. I don't think there is much threat in here with him, but . . . Freya?" His tone was low and warm. "I'm here. Nothing will happen to you." He motioned to the security machines. They looked like the ones you see at an airport. "Come on, and stay close."

When he moved his hand from my back to my elbow and nudged me forward, it seemed to quell some of my indecision. He was tall and broad; his shirt was tight, as if he spent all his free time at the gym or perhaps in some FBI self-defense training program. But it was more than his imposing physique that made me feel safe with him. He had, from the moment I met him, been looking out for Carole and me.

Making myself take another breath, I relaxed. It was time to find out why Bella had visited Cedric in prison—and why she hadn't told us she had a lead on an artist whose expertise was consistent with the Boston forgeries.

"It's just down here," the prison guard said. "Wait. He'll be brought in. Don't get many FBI coming here. Must be important?"

Phil nodded but didn't reply.

Officially, we were at the prison to talk to Cedric James about the painting he was charged with faking. Thanks to Sky's research and the FBI's information network, we had found that years ago Cedric had been convicted of fraud, and one of the paintings that was used as evidence was a forged Raeburn that had been offered to the National Portrait Gallery in London. Their thorough assessment uncovered the forgery, and a plan was set in motion to apprehend Cedric. However, before this could be accomplished, Cedric had been involved in a break-in at a manor house on the outskirts of Glasgow. The car chase that ensued had ended in a crash where a man was killed.

"The information sent over by my partner, Sloane, indicates that Cedric had the talent to forge the Boston paintings. If he didn't paint them himself, I'm quite sure he knows who could have done it. The forgery world is small, and there are very few with the aptitude to copy those masterpieces." Phil sighed. "It's probably too much to hope that he might own up."

We walked down a long, sterile corridor that smelled like a hospital and through another steel door. As it locked behind us, I stilled my panic by looking up at Phil—he was in his element. I had only known him as an undercover agent, but now he had a presence about him that was confident and self-assured. I recognized that I was seeing who he truly was for the first time.

"Freya, are you okay?" Phil had stopped before another set of doors and turned to face me.

"Yes, sorry, I was just . . . thinking. But here . . ." I pulled out a photo and handed it over to him. "I had Sky print out a photo of Bella."

A last set of doors opened into a large room with a number of tables and chairs. It was clinical and cold. Phil motioned to a table in the far corner. "We'll sit over there." Before I could reach for the chair, he had pulled mine out for me, which made me hesitate because it wasn't something I was used to.

"He'll be here soon," he said softly, with his hands resting on the top of the chair. "Freya?"

He was waiting for me to sit. I tried not to smile at the thought of Carole's glee if she saw Phil being the perfect gentleman.

"Thank you," I said, sitting down on the blue plastic chair. Phil sat down next to me and placed the folder on the table in front of us.

Moments later a thin, elderly man who had to be in his eighties walked slowly through the door a guard had opened for him. He had thinning gray hair that curled at the ends and round spectacles balanced on his Roman nose. The guard smiled and pointed to us. Cedric said something, and they both chuckled. He looked as if he needed a nursing home, not a cell.

"Cedric James?" asked Phil, rising to his feet. "I'm Phil Jacobs from the FBI, and this is Freya Lockwood from the Lockwood Antique Hunter's Agency. She consults for us." I expected Phil to offer his hand to shake, but he didn't. Instead, he sat down and opened the file.

Cedric was wearing a polo shirt with flecks of color over it and jeans that hung loosely from his slim frame. He saw me looking. "The governor lets me paint. It's the one true pleasure of this awful place. I must base it on my imagination, though." He winked at me, and I couldn't help the smile that began to form on my lips.

"That must make a change for you," I said, warming to him despite myself.

"Aye, for now," he said, and I wondered if he would be right back to reproducing the Old Masters when he got out of prison.

Phil cleared his throat. "You went to the Royal College of Art, which is impressive. You must be very talented."

Cedric wove his fingers together, resting them on the table. "Enough of your flattery. Get to the point."

"Very well. There have been some paintings removed from sale in the US because they are believed to be forgeries. I've got an analyst comparing your known techniques with the painting we recovered. What do you think we might find?"

I thought Cedric would bristle at the accusation, but instead he relaxed back in his chair, one hand rubbing the back of his neck. "Come, come. I've no idea which painting you might be referring to, and you're not expecting me to incriminate myself, are you? Aye... I didn't think I needed my solicitor, but perhaps you should come back when she's here?" It was clear that Cedric James didn't miss a trick. His body might be succumbing to the passage of time but his mind was still sharp, and he was quite able to insist on receiving his legal rights.

I decided another approach was needed, so I pulled Bella's photo from Phil's file and slid it over the metal table to Cedric. "I believe this woman came to visit you recently."

His gaze flicked to the photograph and he shuffled in his seat before pushing it back to me. "Nope, no idea who that is."

"I don't really have to get Phil here to ask the governor to show us the CCTV, do I?" I pointed to the cameras all around the room. "She might not look exactly the same on-screen—she's brilliant at disguises—but if you look closely..."

"Why do you want to know?" He was now totally ignoring Phil and focused on me. "Who's she to you? Because I don't help this lot"—he stabbed a finger in Phil's direction—"put people behind bars."

"That's not it. Bella is my friend. She helps us sometimes, and she was looking into some Scottish paintings for us. We know she came to visit you. And not long afterward, she went missing. I'd like to know what you talked about." My fingertips touched the edge of the photograph and my gaze fixed on Bella's face. "I'm worried about her and I'm hoping she said something to you that could help us find her."

"And the police . . ."

I silenced Phil with a look and was surprised when he didn't say anything further. Was he going to mention that Bella was wanted for questioning in connection with the murder? I hoped not, because we needed to keep Cedric on our side.

"We haven't heard anything from her in days now. Her room at the hotel still has all her stuff in it. She never went back there after visiting a castle, and the laird of the castle, Euan McGovern, has been murdered."

Cedric's jaw clenched and he folded his arms, studying me and then Phil. "Euan's dead? That's . . . interesting," he said.

"Did you know him?"

Cedric shrugged a reply—not a confirmation but not a denial either—and looked pointedly at Phil. "What do you want with that girl?"

"I'm concerned for her safety." Phil sighed as if he was reluctant to let the truth slip out.

"I'm locked up in here—what has it got to do with me?"

He had a point but he was avoiding answering the question, so I asked again. "What did Bella come here to talk to you about? Was it about any paintings that you might have painted?"

Cedric unfolded his arms and placed his elbows on the table, leaning toward me. "She never asked me about my painting. She wasn't here for that."

Therefore it was personal, not professional.

"You've used the aliases Lester White and Frank Sargent in the past," Phil stated, and Cedric shrugged another reply. We were getting nowhere fast.

"Please. Bella may be in grave danger. We need to know why she was here," I pressed.

"Fine, but only because you're barking up the wrong tree. That crazy girl showed up and announced that she wanted me to take a DNA test or something like that. I refused, and then she wanted to know about my sons. Apparently, her mother told her about me when she was a child and then asked some man . . . what was his name? Arthur something . . . to help find me. When that didn't work, she got some new computer girl in."

"Arthur Crockleford?" I asked. The connections just kept on coming, but I still didn't understand how everyone was connected.

"That's him. That old boy was an antique dealer back in the day but worked with all the unsavory types. Everyone knew him, everyone liked him, but I never had any dealings with him one way or the other. He ran with folks I wanted nothing to do with. He was as wrong as them."

"You knew Arthur?" I dug into the scar on my palm as I fought the urge not to correct Cedric. Arthur wasn't "wrong." He'd had one foot in the underworld of antiques dealing to help the FBI as an informant.

"Well, apparently Arthur Crockleford found out about me but didn't get around to telling Bella that I was in here," he continued. "I'm out soon, did you know that? Maybe Arthur wanted to wait until then to tell her, or that's what I think. But she didn't seem convinced."

"Why a DNA test?" asked Phil.

Cedric winced under the glare of Phil's attention, but I was quietly impressed with his ability to dominate the conversation when needed. "As soon as she asked me to do some weird DNA test and harped on about my boys, I told her to leave. But she just kept going on and on. I lost my temper a bit. I warned her not to go looking for my kin. They were both bad, bad news, which I blame their mother for. She is malicious and conniving, and they grew up the same."

"Who is their mother?" I asked, but Cedric gritted his teeth.

"Do you know Alexandra Pattern?" Phil asked, changing the subject and trying to keep Cedric talking.

"I s'pose you've checked the visitor log? She was an old friend who comes to chat sometimes, nothing more." He glared at Phil. "You leave her out of all your questioning."

Was he worried about her?

"Did you know Euan McGovern?" Phil asked.

Cedric cocked his head and chuckled. "The laird of Fawside Castle? I've never met him, but I've heard his name before. Everyone has. He's not well liked."

"So you don't care that he was murdered a few days back?" Phil continued.

The air fizzed with tension as Phil and Cedric stared at each other. Then Cedric squared his shoulders and rose to his feet. "We're done here."

Just as he was turning away, a thought struck me. "Why Raeburn?"

"What?" Cedric stopped and looked down at me.

"I'm just curious." How could I word this so that he wasn't incriminating himself? "Why do you . . . admire him so much?"

A flash of understanding danced across Cedric's face. He smiled, the first genuine emotion I'd seen in him since we arrived. "When I was a young man, I visited a Raeburn exhibition at the Glasgow Museum and one of the paintings there—*John Stuart Hepburn Forbes*, it was titled . . . well, it moved me. It was a little boy with a dog, and I'd always wanted a dog. I started learning about Raeburn. In his time, he was a painter so celebrated that you weren't really anyone until you'd sat for him and that portrait hung in your entrance hall." He turned to leave but hesitated. "My father loved Raeburn's work too, but he never supported my desire to paint. He insisted I join the family business. Instead I packed up and went to art school in London. He never forgave me. Disinherited me for most of my adult life, until . . ." He stopped, and his eyes glazed over.

The room's silence echoed around us. "Until?"

He shook his head. "My family is cursed with early death, and I was welcomed back not because I was wanted. I came back to Scotland because I was the last resort... do you know what that's like?"

I shook my head. "I'm sorry. And how did you end up in here?"

Cedric shrugged. "Painting was the only thing I was ever good at. But making a living from it is hard going. I found my own way to make the money I needed."

By forging Masters and selling them.

I needed to tread carefully. "Your father never discovered what you did?"

"My father would've loved to have a Raeburn hanging on his wall, but he could never have afforded one." But Cedric could have had many on his wall, because he could paint them himself. I understood the edge of pride in his voice, although his eyes were shadowed with regret.

I changed tack. "Do your sons visit you?"

He didn't answer directly, but looked down at me. "I know what you're thinking. I could have been so much more than all this." He waved at the room. I hadn't been thinking that, but it was clearly what he believed of himself. "I wasn't brave enough. It takes a certain type of soul to be able to authentically create. To have an understanding of light and darkness... not in paint, but in the heart. To paint a person, you need to show someone's story truthfully, but more than that, you also need to be comfortable showing your own. When the two combine, what you produce is truly original. I wasn't... capable. My father bashed the confidence out of me. But at least I passed it down to..." He snapped his mouth shut and walked toward the waiting guard.

Phil and I looked at one another. "... His sons," I said.

"And that means one or both of them paint," replied Phil. "We need to get Sky to look into who Cedric's sons are. Maybe that was why Bella was here asking for a DNA sample?"

When I didn't answer, he touched my arm, and I realized I was still staring at the door Cedric had walked though moments before.

"We should go."

I nodded and followed him out.

~

Phil and I got into my car and sat waiting for the windscreen to de-mist.

"That was strange. Bella was there to get proof of who Cedric was, or who he was related to. But why?" I gazed out at the snow-covered road.

"Can we talk about something else for a moment?" Phil said, turning to me.

I ignored him. "Cedric's DNA will be on file. I'll ask Sky to look into it some more." I slipped the car into gear.

"Freya?" His voice was quiet. "I . . ." He paused and shook his head as if he were lost for words. "You were great back there. Coaxing out of him about his sons."

My pulse picked up. I got the feeling that wasn't what he had planned to say, but the praise still bloomed in my chest. Phil reached over the console and briefly touched my arm. "I haven't seen you since Jordan. You look . . . well. I'm glad we could make this . . . the consultancy . . . work . . . that I get to be here."

I took in a long breath, not ready for where Phil seemed to be going with this conversation. I had a feeling he wanted to talk about *us*. "Because of you, I get to really focus on the agency. You giving us this case to look into . . ." I looked down at his hand, which was still on my arm. He tracked my movement and removed his hand. "Building the agency is everything right now." I was pushing him away by saying that, but I didn't see any other choice. I couldn't risk ruining the tentative relationship our agency had with the FBI. "The Cedric lead wasn't what I expected," I went on, trying to ignore the tension in the car and steer us back onto the safer ground of work.

"Yes, the case . . ." He opened the file in his lap and took a deep breath. "Cedric's skill level confirms he could have painted a few, or all, of the paintings in Arthur's journal. He told us he didn't know Euan, but he knew that we had found out Alexandra had visited him. I don't buy that Alexandra was there just as a friend. Could she be the one who sold paintings for him while he was inside?"

"Are all the paintings in the journal forgeries, or just the Boston three? And did you notice that the one painting Cedric mentioned—the painting of the boy and the dog—was one of the Boston paintings? Why would he say that?"

"So many questions," said Phil, staring out the window.

I thought back to Bella and her relationship with Arthur; the way Cedric had said that Bella had told him she'd asked Arthur for help, and then asked Sky. "This reminds me of Jordan, when we helped you solve your old FBI partner's case. Arthur wasn't just trying to lead us to valuable antiques with his journals—he was trying to set things right. Maybe he hoped to do the same for Bella by leaving her clues to follow," I said.

"Yes, I've thought about that too."

Silence sat heavily in the air around us as it started to rain.

20

Carole
Saturday, February 10, noon

Carole had only been inside the Old Ship for an hour or two, but she already felt at home. Freya had dropped her off at the pub before setting off for the prison. Carole was there to support India through a meeting with Jane—India didn't want to face her father's girlfriend alone.

The log fire was roaring and her cup of tea was steaming hot, but the chill between Jane and India made Carole shudder. It seemed as if nothing had changed since the first time Carole had met them. If anything, their loathing for each other seemed to have deepened.

"You need to pack up all your shit and leave the castle for good once the police have finished," said India through gritted teeth. "You're not family. You never were. It's my home, not yours."

Jane relaxed back in her chair and smoothed her highlighted hair with one hand. If she was ruffled by the venom in India's voice, she didn't show it. She was a master at schooling her features and now they were portraying a sorrowful victim. "It is my home, and of course, we need to work together to sort everything out. We need to talk to Euan's solicitor, don't you think?" Her eyes widened in innocence that Carole knew she didn't possess. "Who knows what everyone inherits? And

I'm devastated by the loss of the love of my life. It will take years to get over."

India scoffed. "Whatever you were to each other, it wasn't lovers. You didn't even share a bedroom. You hated him perhaps even enough to kill him."

"You little—" Jane stopped herself. "As I've told the police, I was in Edinburgh all evening. I have the perfect alibi. Were you here with Oliver, or somewhere else?" Jane asked as India turned to Oliver, who was pretending to polish glasses at the bar while listening intently.

"Were you with that not-so-secret boyfriend all night?" Jane nodded at Oliver; she didn't wait for an answer, as she clearly already knew it. "Did you think that if you killed your father then you would inherit the castle and save your boyfriend from losing his job? Is that it?" India glared, and Jane smiled. "Euan knew all about the two of you. He was going to sell the pub to someone else, anyone else, just to get rid of him." She picked up her teaspoon and it clinked against the china as she stirred more sugar into her tea. "Why did you kill my poor darling man? So that you can now live out your musical dream without begging us for money, and Oliver's livelihood remains intact? Both of you have it all set now, don't you?"

Jane was still maintaining the same sweet, perfectly even tone. To anyone watching the conversation from elsewhere in the pub, it would have looked as if she was consoling India. Carole had to admire what a talented actress she was. She leaned forward to say something, but before she could, Jane continued, "Have you seen Euan's will? Just because he told you that everything was yours when he died doesn't mean it was the truth. Euan had a very loose regard for the truth. He made an appointment with his solicitor not long ago."

India picked up her cup, but it rattled against the saucer. Oliver came to stand behind her with a hand on her shoulder.

"What's going on?" His voice was quiet and rough. His plaid shirt was rolled up to his elbows and his strong arms were covered in tattoo sleeves. Carole studied them and noticed a few... well... not-so-pretty ones. She knew exactly what they meant: prison. Oliver's accent wasn't Scottish; it was from down south somewhere—if she had to guess, she would have said Kent. Having been an actress in her younger days, she was well versed in accents.

So, Oliver was from the south, had once been in prison, and was dating the laird's daughter. Carole was utterly thrilled that he had transformed his life and settled down. She beamed up at Oliver to let him know as much.

"I'm glad you're here, Oliver," she said, reaching out and tugging on his shirt. "Why don't you come and sit down with us? I'm quite sure you would be welcome, given the circumstances." She gave Jane a look, one that she hoped meant "stay in line."

"I might just do that. How about you fill me in on why Indie looks upset?"

Carole was happy to oblige. "Jane was just informing her that she thinks she knows what was in Euan's will. Oh, and she accused you both of murder. Is that about right?" she asked Jane.

The other woman shrugged. "My point is that once I am allowed back into my home—and I'm told that it will probably be tomorrow—I'm not going anywhere until we all know where we stand."

"So you're going to try and live at Fawside when you so clearly hate Indie?" Oliver asked. "Why don't you just pack up your stuff and move on, Jane? Your golden goose is dead. And as anyone in the village would tell you, good riddance."

"They would not. Everyone loved Euan."

Oliver huffed. "No, they didn't. Euan was a boor. He showed up here six years ago after his brother died and took over the castle. He never did have a proper job, so where did all the money needed to run that place come from?"

Carole nodded. It was a very good question. Euan had accused Arthur of swimming in the underbelly of the antiques world, but there was every possibility that it was actually Euan who'd been doing just that.

Jane glared at Oliver. "I would be very careful if I were you. I overheard a lot of very interesting things while living at the castle." Without another word, she picked up her handbag and breezed out of the room.

Carole reached for her phone and sent Sky a text to ask her to have a dig around and find out what she could about Jane. By the time she had put her phone away, India's face was cradled in Oliver's strong hands. Carole surreptitiously picked up her phone again and sent a second text to Sky telling her to investigate Oliver's background too.

Carole was very fond of India and was glad that she had found a man who so clearly adored her, but she couldn't ignore Jane's words either. India had given Carole the impression that she didn't believe Bella had murdered Euan. Perhaps it was because she knew all along who had killed her despicable father.

India soon excused herself and went to wipe away her tears in the bathroom, and Oliver retreated back behind the large mahogany bar, which still looked far too small for him. Carole sipped her tea and waited for Freya and Phil to finish at the prison and come and pick her up.

Her phone pinged. It was a message from Sky.

Sky: *Oliver Stanton, 31 years old. Grew up in Maidstone, Kent, and was in prison for GBH when he was twenty-one but it seems he got a reduced sentence as he went after the man who sexually assaulted his sister. They should have given him a medal really. Isn't it interesting that his grandmother, Dolores, is the housekeeper at the castle? Also, I can't find much on Jane. Is that her real name?*

Carole: *Freya is currently visiting Cedric James in prison. Can we cross-reference and see if they were ever held in the same prison at the same time?*

Sky: *I'm on it.*

Carole watched Oliver and realized something rather important—Oliver was a protector of women, and Euan was an abuser. Had something happened on the night of the storm to cause Oliver to snap once and for all, killing Euan? Had he been protecting the woman he loved while at the same time keeping the pub?

Freya pushed the old pub door open, quickly scanned the room, and then hurried toward Carole. It seemed they had both uncovered some leads in the time they had been apart.

21

Freya
Saturday, February 10, 4 p.m.

After we picked Carole up at the pub, our drive back to the hotel became a debriefing session, with Phil unable to get a word in. We decided that the next person we needed to talk to was Dolores Fraser—Oliver's grandmother, and the housekeeper we'd met after discovering Euan's body. A housekeeper who worked on weekends. I found Dolores's earlier explanation a little suspicious, but we hadn't had time to talk to her much as she'd been quite shaken.

With Sky's help, she was easy to track down. If anyone knew what had really been going on in that castle before Euan's murder, it had to be Dolores—"Housekeepers see everything, don't they?" Carole said.

Dolores lived in a small bungalow at the outer limits of the castle grounds. Although built in the 1930s with a pebble-dash exterior, it was in immaculate condition. The path to the door had been cleared of snow, swept, and gritted. There was a warm, inviting glow from the windows.

It was still early afternoon, but dusk was already setting in. It was the deepest, darkest part of winter and constant weather warnings blared from the radio. Carole's expression told me she was still worried about

India even though she had left her in Oliver's strong, capable, tattooed hands.

Phil pressed the doorbell.

"I'm not sure we should all have arrived unannounced," Carole said, coming to stand shoulder to shoulder with Phil. "All three of us might intimidate a woman on her own."

In Phil's outstretched hand was his FBI card. We all knew it had no real sway in Scotland, but it was always a good bet that people watched a lot of American telly and would think differently.

The front door creaked open with the safety chain still in place and Dolores smiled at us through the crack. "You again?" She breathed out a shaky breath. "How can I help you?"

Before Phil became too official, Carole shimmied in front of him and stuck her hand through the small space. "We wanted to check if you were all right."

Dolores frowned as if she couldn't decide whether she wanted to see us again.

"How are you holding up? It was a shock for all of us, finding your employer like that," I said. I was about to introduce Phil when Carole pushed forward.

"This is Phil." She beamed at Dolores. "He's . . . an American tourist with an impressive . . . business card."

Phil scowled at Carole, but she ignored him, and their typical routine made me inwardly chuckle. Carole had good instincts for people. If she thought Dolores would be more accommodating and forthcoming without knowing Phil was with the FBI, then I trusted her.

"Still haven't found your friend?" Dolores asked. "Well, I haven't seen her. The detective has been asking a lot of questions about her and Euan's business, but I don't know anything. I'm sorry, but I need to go and sit down again." She made to shut the door.

Carole placed her hand out to stop her. "We don't want to disturb you, but might we trouble you and come in for a moment? I think we desperately need your help."

"My help?"

I gave her a pleading smile. Perhaps she gathered that we weren't going anywhere or perhaps she felt sorry for us; either way, she unlatched the door. "Well, I am never one to turn down someone in need. How about a hot toddy? It's so cold out, I think we could all do with one."

Carole breezed into the bungalow as if they had been friends for years. "I do hope that we're not intruding, but I'm most concerned about Euan's death."

Dolores was halfway down the hallway. I had just closed the front door behind us and was toeing off my snow-covered boots when she froze and turned round. "What do you mean, concerned?"

"I'm going to be very honest with you. I'm not a fan of Jane, and . . ."

Dolores's face brightened. "You see through all the smiles and the crocodile tears, then? She's a nasty piece of work, that one. We all think so. Come and sit down." She pointed to her left. "I have always kept my peace on the matter, as Euan was a good employer to me, but that Jane . . . she was bad news. And the poor child. Imagine losing your mother and then ending up in that house, with a man who never wanted children and a woman who outright hated them. I think the bottom of it is that Jane didn't want to share Euan. She wanted to play lady of the castle all by herself."

Dolores's sitting room looked like it hadn't been updated for fifty years but had been cleaned daily. The gas fire was blazing and she had floral curtains, a floral sofa and chairs in a completely different pattern, and swirling brown carpet. She disappeared for a few moments and came back with a tray of drinks. I gripped my very strong hot toddy and said, "Did you arrive before or after India came to live with Euan?"

"Just after. Around five years ago, I think, or maybe six. I'd heard in the village that everyone who worked here before me was let go. I think Euan wanted his privacy and believed that Jane would look after the place," she said. "I'm betting that woman never lifted a finger. So when India arrived, he hired me to make sure everything was in order. Get some good home-cooked food into her, as she was far too wee. I'm a bit of a mother hen. It's one of my talents."

"And how did everyone get on? Jane was in the pub earlier making some... accusations," coaxed Carole.

Dolores's cheeks reddened. "Is she still staying at the Old Ship? That woman is a Jezebel. I bet she's not even paying. What did she say? No. Don't answer that. Let me guess. She has found out about Oliver and India, and she thinks that they killed Euan so that the pub wouldn't be sold, because India would inherit everything." She spat. "What other lies did she rattle off?"

"He was definitely going to sell?" I asked, noticing that Dolores hadn't yet admitted Oliver was related to her. "That would have been bad for Oliver and India. They do seem very much in love."

Dolores's gaze fluttered to a silver photo frame on her mantelpiece. It contained a picture of two boys, around eight and ten years old. "At least I have one of my wonderful grandsons living nearby. Oliver is everything to me." It was a relief to hear her say that. "I wasn't sure about him going out with India at first, because I presumed that Euan would be livid. He was always trying to set the poor child up with every rich old man in the Borders, but as soon as she saw my Oliver at the village Christmas carol evening when she was playing the piano, it was love at first sight."

"Euan wasn't happy when he found out?" asked Phil, his untouched mug in his hand. He never drank while he was on the job, and after only a few sips of the hot toddy I had decided he should drive back to the hotel.

"Oh, he didn't know. We all kept it very hush-hush. She used to tell him she was staying over in Edinburgh for a recital or a lesson, staying with friends. Then she would go and see Oliver at the pub."

"Perhaps someone else told him?" Because Carole seemed quite sure that if Jane knew about Oliver and India being in a relationship, then Euan must have as well.

"I don't think so. Euan didn't go into the village unless he had to, and after all the issues when he first got here, it's not like anyone was going to tell him anything. No one talked to him."

"And what were these issues?" asked Phil, leaning forward and putting his mug on the coffee table.

Dolores waved her hand as if it was all rubbish.

"He didn't get on with anyone around here?" Phil prodded.

"From what I hear, the family has never been well liked in the village." She leaned forward a little. "I think they might have English ancestors, and . . . well. Rob Roy, and all that. But I think it's just that they keep to themselves, and that starts people speculating."

"About what?" I asked, intrigued as to what the villagers thought.

"Always said that they were a bit dodgy." She shook her head. "But before you ask, I have never seen anything like that in all my years here. Euan was an antiques dealer, and he made good money, but that woman of his . . ."

I had a feeling the village was onto something, but Dolores seemed very protective over her late employer. I decided to leave it there and ask Oliver the next time I saw him.

Dolores leaned toward Carole. "India has to get that hag out of the castle, and she isn't going to go easy. You mark my words. She had all those bookcases built to showcase her antiques and wooden boxes, and all that equipment to film herself for the things on the phone."

"I'm sorry, darling, what things on the phone?" Carole had finished her drink, and I was surprised she could still follow the conversation with that amount of alcohol inside her.

"You know... the social thingy."

"Social media?" said Phil.

"Yes, that's it, it's the social media thingy where Jane sells all her bits and bobs and sends them to America."

Phil cocked his head. "What do you know about her business in America?" he asked.

"Oh, aye, America is where she sends everything. Sometimes I even dropped the bigger packages in Edinburgh for her when I was going into the city. She makes good money and has no bills to pay."

"And did you ever send anything the shape of a picture frame or painting size?" he asked.

Dolores's brow furrowed. "Oh no, I don't think Jane knows anything about paintings. That was the previous laird, Mr. Euan's brother. The one who died. He was the one who loved paintings. But after he went, they all got put in the attic." She yawned and stood.

"And what was the name of the previous laird?" I asked, reaching for my phone to send Sky a message.

"Oh, it was..." She frowned. "Something beginning with C... Charles or Christopher... Christopher, I think. But it was before my time."

"Thank you so much for your time, Mrs. Fraser." I pulled out a business card and handed it to her. "If you think of anything else, please let us know."

"But you didn't tell me what you needed me to help with." Her cheeks had paled a little and she was looking anxiously at me, obviously wondering if she had spoken out of turn.

"We'd love it if you would help India when she moves back into the castle. Make sure Jane doesn't get her claws into her and convince India she needs to stick around," Carole said.

"Don't you worry. I had already resolved to do exactly that quite some time ago." Dolores held out her hand to Carole and they shook on it.

My aunt motioned for us to go and winked at me as we made our way to the car—because tonight we had an attic to break into.

22

Saturday, February 10, 11:30 p.m.

Carole, Sky, and I set off for Fawside Castle in the dead of night, while the snow was falling fast and the wind had picked up. The farther we went from the hotel, the less convinced I became that we were doing the right thing—I couldn't stand the idea of Carole or Sky getting hurt if we hit a bit of black ice. However, they were both determined to search the castle and we had discussed the priorities—take another look in the study and photograph the silver that was left by the thieves. Next, Jane's collection, and most importantly, try to find a way into the attic where the paintings belonging to the previous laird, Christopher McGovern, had been moved.

I had decided to keep Phil out of it, because what we were planning was trespassing, and the moment I'd mentioned this to Sky and Carole they had seemed to relax. We were on a Lockwood Antique Hunter's Agency mission. It might be a little bit . . . illegal, but we were in it together.

Phil had informed us over dinner that police forensics had finished with the garden and castle. We could only hope that the castle had been locked up and the local police force were too stretched to guard the castle throughout the night.

Carole was dressed head to toe in black—although this did not, in any way, mean that she was wearing appropriate attire for breaking and entering. Black leather trousers, a ruffled sparkling black shirt, knee-high boots, and a velvet bomber jacket with red rhinestone lips on the back. It had more rock concert vibes than dead-of-the-night stealth investigation, but I wasn't going to be the one to tell her. When I locked eyes with Sky as Carole pulled on her red bobble hat, we couldn't suppress our smiles.

Carole noticed me frowning at her pulling down the passenger-seat mirror and applying bright red lipstick. "Don't be judgey, darling, it doesn't suit you."

I coughed out a laugh and turned down an even smaller lane than the one we were just on. "We're going to break into a castle and you're putting on lippy like we're going to a party. This isn't one of those Jilly Cooper novels you love. There isn't anyone in there to impress."

"And what if the police show up and I'm not looking fabulous? What then? I know we think that they won't be here tonight but we can't be sure." I sighed, which she took as having won the point. "Don't you worry. I've got us these from the local shop." She dug around in her handbag and pulled out two fluorescent balaclavas. "Here." She threw one at me as I slowed to pull up next to a snow-covered hedge and let an oncoming car pass us. "Now I'll be able to see where you are, and no one will be able to identify us in a lineup." I opened my mouth, but no words came to me. "I know, you're thrilled that I think of everything."

"I was actually wondering if wearing these will mean that we'll be seen from space. And if St Abbs is anything like Little Meddington, everyone in the village will now be discussing why you bought them."

We carried on down the long drive to the open parking area, then parked under a tree in the far corner from the castle. There was no police car or police officer in sight.

"This is taking time we don't have. Put that on and let's get going," said Carole, taking off her bobble hat and then rolling the end of the balaclava up and placing it on her head like a hat—therefore totally defeating its purpose, although she didn't seem to notice.

"Sky?" Carole noticed Sky was studying her balaclava technique. "I have one for you too."

"Um, no, I'm good." Sky tapped away on her laptop, then scrubbed her arm across the steamed window. "You see the alarm box up there? The old one?"

We all looked up at the towering castle outside the car window, but it was shrouded in pitch-black night. There was no sign of life. It was as if the snow clouds had reached down from the heavens and covered the turrets, tops of the trees, and swept over the surrounding farmland until we were enclosed in an eerie vacuum. My mind couldn't help but picture the hand we had discovered beneath the snow the last time we were here.

Sky was too busy tapping on her computer to worry about the ominous scene before us, but Carole shuddered.

"I'm quite sure that CCTV camera is off," said Sky. "Don't you think it's strange, after there's been a theft and a murder, that they don't have everything switched on? That police tape isn't going to do much, is it?"

It was true that the yellow tape crossed over the front door wouldn't stop anyone from entering.

"I think it's very strange, but we shouldn't look a gift horse in the mouth," said Carole, climbing out of the car and taking a few steps toward the door, wobbling on the ice.

Sky hurried over to help her but instead skidded into her with an *oomph*. They both squealed in delight and then made out they were ice-skating toward the castle.

Watching them gleefully, and loudly, slip-sliding to the front door, I did concede that Sky and Carole were probably not cut out for the hushed nature of breaking and entering. I was just glad that at least as far as we could tell, nobody was home.

Having discovered the front door was locked, we hurried around to the back, where Sky insisted on practicing her lock-picking skills. However, after standing in the freezing snow for three whole minutes, Carole vetoed the idea and insisted that I should take over.

"Next time we break in somewhere we'll make sure it's during summertime, and I promise that you'll be the woman for the job," Carole soothed Sky.

"We're not making a habit of this," I whispered, and Carole winked at me. This was exactly the sort of habit she wanted to keep up.

I had debated telling Phil what we were up to after our dinner together, but after discussing it with Carole we'd decided against it. Phil had a black-and-white view when it came to the law. Breaking into a castle was very much on the wrong side of it, but we had to follow up any clue that could lead us to Bella. I also knew that this would be our only opportunity to look around the castle, because tomorrow India and Jane would be moving back in.

I took hold of the lock-picking tools and was about to start when some instinct made me reach out and turn the handle. The door clicked open.

We all paused. "This isn't right, is it? It shouldn't be unlocked. The alarm shouldn't be off. Do you think someone is inside?" I groaned softly. "I regret not telling Phil where we were going now."

Sky took a few steps back. "Okay, so, seeing this place up close makes it look . . . haunted. Are we all sure this is a good idea? Like, a ton of poltergeists could start throwing ancient daggers at us the moment we step inside." She pulled her coat around herself. "Have you seen that TV show about ghost hunters?"

I linked my arm through hers. "You don't have to go inside. It's fine if you want to wait in the car and keep an eye out for the police."

Her mouth popped open in a wide O. "There is no way you are leaving me alone. Not ever."

"Right, *Ghostbusters* it is," said Carole, clapping her hands together as she stepped into the boot room.

I shook my head and switched on my torch as Sky did something on her phone—when I gave her a questioning look, she said, "Location tracker. You've got one on your phone too. I don't want any more of my friends going missing."

"We will stick together and it'll all be fine. Find that attic, keep an eye out for the Scottish silver, paintings, and anything else of interest." Sky and Carole both nodded in reply. "Dolores said Christopher McGovern's paintings had been stored in the attic, but we need a thorough sweep of the whole castle."

I had only taken a few steps inside, Carole and Sky in front of me, when a light came on behind us, casting our long shadows down the boot room.

"What's that?" whispered Sky, spinning around and stepping closer to Carole.

Hurrying to the back door, I stuck my head out. The glare of headlights lit the snowfall, but it was hard to make out the type of car coming toward the castle.

"Is it the *police*?" whispered Carole from over my shoulder. "We should hide." We retreated farther into the boot room and waited on the threshold of the servants' hallway, her hand gripping Sky's arm.

"But we aren't trespassing if we aren't inside," I hissed. "Shouldn't we go out, shut the door, and see who it is?"

Sky's gaze flickered between the hallway and the back door. Slowly, she shook her head. "There's no going back now. And this is a warmer place to hide. We should all stay together."

In the dim light of Sky's torch I could see the hallway, and she took a few steps down. "Where are you going?" I whisper-shouted.

"Don't get hysterical; the police won't like it," Carole said. "When they come for us, you both follow my lead . . . Sky, put some lippy on, darling. It will help."

"I'm not putting lipstick on for the police. Are you out of your mind?" Sky hissed. "I'm a Black woman in a house that's not mine in the middle of the night. So, how about *you* distract them with your lippy, and I find a place to hide until they leave with you in handcuffs?" Sky didn't wait for Carole to answer. Instead she sped down the hall and through a door at the end, her anxiety at the police catching her greater than her fear of ghosts.

I shook my head at Carole, and she gave me a sheepish look. "Right . . . as you seem so confident about handling the police, you go meet them. But you'd better come up with an excuse quickly . . ." I caught her eye and saw regret in her expression. "I'll go after Sky."

"Tell her I'm sorry . . . I didn't mean . . . I just like lippy." Carole puffed her hair out and faced the back door. "I'll go and charm the officers. I only meant that we might even get away with murder if we look like butter wouldn't melt. And Sky *is* utterly stunning . . ."

I held up my hand to stop her going any further. "We'll discuss it later. Let's get out of here first."

My boots echoed on the flagstone floor as I hurried after Sky. As I reached a dark door with stags' heads carved into it, I turned back to check on Carole. She was facing the oncoming snow, which swept into the boot room and settled on the floor around her feet. A moment later, a tall, dark figure came to stand in front of her—and my instincts took over, fear making me hurtle back toward her. The new arrival shone a large torch directly into Carole's face, and she flinched as I came to a halt behind her. The glaring light blinded us.

Carole held up her hands and squinted. "Don't shoot! I'm an unarmed pensioner with a wonderful sense of fashion."

"It's debatable, if that's what you wear to break the law," Phil said, stepping up to Carole. "So, where's Sky?" He sounded bored, and it made me quite pleased we'd left him out of our break-in plan, but I also couldn't stop the smile that lifted my lips.

"What are you doing here?" I pushed his gloved hand down and his torch lit the floor.

He pointed at Carole. "Making sure this one doesn't get you all arrested."

"Well, darling, if we're breaking the law, then so are you," she said.

"You really think that the moment Dolores said the paintings were in the attic, I didn't know you'd come straight here after dinner?" said Phil. "I followed."

"You should have said so. You nearly gave me a heart attack, and that was after my heart was already painfully sad about having said all the wrong things to Sky." Carole was babbling and had placed a hand over her chest.

I closed the back door and turned to Phil. "Now you're here, are you going to come and search the place with us?"

"I intended . . . well, to stop you doing something reckless."

"Oh, you're decades too late for that. Onward and upward, I say." With that, Carole's shoulders lifted. She was clearly happy that Phil was now with us and spun around on her ABBA-style boots. "You two take the downstairs, and I'll find Sky and profusely apologize, and we'll go upstairs," she called back as she hurried down the hallway.

I followed after her. "Come on," I called back. "We don't have all night with this trespassing thing."

Phil mumbled something I couldn't hear, but within a few strides I sensed his warmth at my back. "How did you get in here?" he said as I pushed open a paneled door to our left and found myself standing in a drawing room with tapestries on the walls.

"That's the strange thing. The door was unlocked, and the alarm was already off."

Phil swept his torch round the room. "There's nothing here that is in the journals. We should move on to the next room." As we stepped back out into the hallway, he said, "Police forensics searched the castle from top to bottom after they removed Euan's body. I've asked Detective Rodgers about an attic, and he says they didn't find one but will be back to look around on Monday when India is here. I showed him the paintings we believe to be forgeries but apparently they've seen nothing like that here. The only thing they can confirm is the Scottish silver was stolen, and it wasn't catalogued for the insurance. It seems Euan's insurance company knew nothing about his collections." Phil opened the door at the end of the hallway, the one Sky had gone through earlier, and we found ourselves in a large medieval entrance hall with the main door in front of us.

Large wooden coats of arms hung on the walls, faded and flecked with age. Four polished full-size suits of armor, complete with swords or spears, were arranged at either side of the large front door. On one wall there were three stags' heads, which seemed to loom over us and made me shudder as I tried to rid my mind of what Sky had said earlier.

"What was Bella doing here?" Phil's torch beam was searching methodically over every item.

"I'm still not sure. I believed that she was looking into the origin of the Boston paintings and perhaps also looking for the other paintings in Arthur's journals . . . but after talking to Cedric, I wonder if it was more than that? After we found Euan's body we went into the kitchen, study, and drawing room at the far end, but I wasn't really focusing on the paintings or the furniture then. I have this feeling that I missed something. Was Euan's murder really a robbery gone wrong? It doesn't make sense." I was thinking out loud as I scanned the paintings along the back wall, none of which were familiar from Arthur's journal.

"They have really gone all out on the whole Gothic castle theme," said Phil.

I hummed, averting my gaze from a stuffed stag's head with dusty fur and glassy eyes that bore into me, and noticed a stone archway in the far corner with three steps leading down to another small, dark wooden door. "Do you think there's a dungeon down there?" A part of me wanted to head straight for it, but another was too scared to enter a castle dungeon in the middle of a winter's night.

"Worried?" Phil asked, holding up his gun an inch higher and shining his torchlight around the door frame.

"Of course not," I said, putting a mask of indifference on my face. "We're meant to be looking for the attic, not a cellar." Phil's gun was held next to his torch, and I wondered what he was looking for. "Do you think bullets will work on ghosts?" I nodded toward the gun.

He tutted. "I can't see a light switch for the stairs, and I don't want to turn on the hall lights . . . it's too obvious." And then he said something under his breath about there already having been one death in the castle grounds that week, and walking around in the dark. He sighed and changed the subject. "Yesterday I had Sky look for the blueprints of the castle. Apparently there was once a staircase leading to a door at the left-hand side of the castle, near the cliff. Could be a way in and out, which would be hidden from the cameras." Phil seemed to sense my hesitation, as he said, "Come on, Hunter. I'll protect you." He strode toward the stairs and stopped at the top to turn back to me. "Against criminal ghosts, if necessary."

"Not necessary," I replied, but I was glad he was going first. Even for a medieval castle, this place was cold and unsettling. There was nothing welcoming or homely about any of the rooms I had been in. The antiques were of the finest quality, but there was a museum-like atmosphere to the decor. Considering the castle wasn't open to the public, it took someone with a lot of money and a strong need for privacy to keep up a fortress of a home like this.

Phil pushed at the door, and it creaked open. Beyond it was a narrow spiral stone staircase with a rope handrail on the right. With each step I took, the air became mustier. The odor of earth and rot filled my nose.

"It's too damp down here to store anything you don't want to get moldy. Upstairs, all the art and antiques are in pristine condition . . ." I was mainly talking to myself as we descended, but Phil hummed in agreement.

There came a *drip, drip* below us, and I shuddered.

"Cold?" asked Phil, turning to look up at me. I wondered how he had noticed with his back to me.

"I'm fine." I wouldn't allow my vivid imagination to get the better of me, and I really wanted my curiosity satisfied. We needed to search every inch of the castle while we had the opportunity—and then run like hell.

I stepped into a cavernous space with a concrete floor and stone walls, which were black with mold.

A rattling, clanking sound echoed out of the darkness, like chains against metal.

"What was that?" I jumped and stepped closer to Phil. "This place really is a dungeon."

I expected Phil to laugh or find some witty comeback. Instead, he swept the beam of his torch around once more, pausing at each and every corner.

Drip. Drip.

My heart thundered in my chest.

Torch and gun placed together between his hands, Phil stepped into the center of the large cellar just as my own torch illuminated a row of metal bars at the far end.

"What's that? It looks like a cage."

I held my breath and forced my legs to move toward it.

23

Sunday, February 11, 12:30 a.m.

The cellar's damp, musty air seeped into my bones and I wrapped my arms around myself as Phil's torch followed mine to illuminate a wall of wrought-iron bars. In the center was a gate bound with chains, a large padlock resting in the middle. My skin crawled as I reached out to touch the cold, clammy metal.

"Is that a cage?" I whispered again. It was probably irrational, but I couldn't help my imagination spiraling. My first thought was that perhaps Bella hadn't gone missing; maybe she had been taken. Maybe she was *caged*, and that's why the police hadn't found her when they searched the castle. The awful image of Bella trapped behind those bars for all this time made me grip the padlock and give it a tug. My other hand went into my pocket for my small lock-picking kit.

"We need to get in there." I didn't wait for Phil to answer.

I put my torch between my teeth until Phil took it and held it for me, angling both beams onto the padlock. Icy fear seeped through the metal and into my bones as I placed the first pick inside, then the next. Beyond the bars was a wine cellar with huge barrels against the back wall and dusty bottles in wine racks on the right-hand wall, rising up to about waist height.

Drip. Drip.

I took in a deep breath to steady my fingers, but it was only when Phil placed a hand on my elbow that I relaxed. "Freya, Bella's not here." His torch lit the area beyond the gate. "It's just a normal wine cellar... No one is down here."

"What are those?" There were footprints in the dust heading in both directions to the very back of the cellar.

The padlock clicked open and I slipped it, unfastened, into my pocket—I had learned my lesson at Copthorn Manor, never to leave a lock behind. The gate groaned open as Phil followed me inside.

"From the blueprints, there must be another staircase or something that leads to an outside door." We walked farther down, and something glinted in the torchlight that wasn't the same color as the wine bottles. "There's something between those bottles..." It didn't take long to find the motion-activated camera. "I need Sky to find out what it's been recording."

Phil nodded. "The police must have missed this. There must be a strong reason for someone to be recording down here."

"Would Euan go to all this trouble to catch a wine thief? I don't know much about valuable wine." I picked up a few bottles and studied them. "But none of this is that old. Maybe he suspected someone was using this passageway to steal something more valuable?"

"Let's get out of here and find Sky. Breaking into a castle in the dark like Bella did is exactly what started all this mess in the first place. It's..."

"*Reckless.* I know." Annoyance twisted in my chest. "Did you ever think that I'm not trying to be reckless on purpose? I'm just trying to get the job done in the best way that I know how, and I am trying to protect the people I care about. I'm trying to build something with the Lockwood Agency without putting everyone in danger. But I need people like Bella to do that. And you..." I pointed an angry finger at him. "You're pushing her away with all your digs and mistrust... she won't even attend the team meetings anymore..." I was rambling, giving in to my frustration.

I turned to leave, not wanting to say any more, but the wine cellar was so narrow with the racks on either side that my back bumped into a wine bottle behind me as I tried to get away.

Phil stepped up to me. "Freya, stop..."

He was so close that his breath feathered on my cheek and his hand landed on my wrist—his fingers circling around in a firm hold that was at the same time soft and warm. "That's not it. At first, when Arthur asked me to look out for you, I was annoyed, but then I saw you at Copthorn Manor... and then again, on the cruise..." He took a deep breath. "Listen, it is *you*, not your aunt, that I wanted as an FBI consultant. I may not always agree with your methods, but you do get results. I just don't want your plans for the agency... your fledgling career hindered by people who never seem to listen to you."

I stopped myself saying anything else by biting my cheek, but I tilted my chin to look up at him. For the first time that night, I didn't want to get out of the cellar and back to Carole and Sky. His thumb brushed back and forth over the underside of my wrist, and I held my breath.

"I..." My mind went blank for a moment. *What are we doing?* "I have to find Bella; she needs us. This is my team. I need you to trust that I know what we have to do to get the job done... I'm not asking for your approval. If the FBI doesn't like it, then I suppose we can go our separate ways."

Phil's forehead furrowed, but I continued before he could speak. "The journals Arthur left me are not just a log of past crimes, but of potential ones. I would solve them all a lot faster with the best team available."

"I don't..."

"Let me finish. Be part of the team, Phil. All I'm asking is that you give Bella the benefit of the doubt. Because Arthur certainly did, and if she could earn his trust, then she has mine too. As does Sky."

He sighed, brushing a fingertip down my palm as he let me go. "I will . . . try." He ran a hand through his hair. "For your sake. But I don't trust easily, and until I see that Bella is no threat to you or your aunt, I will be watching her." There was such conviction in his voice that I nodded, and I leaned toward him.

"Okay . . . but I'm holding you to that." A small smile tugged at my lips, and his eyes flashed to it.

"Freya . . . I . . ."

A muffled scream shattered the moment.

It hadn't come from the cellar. I slid sideways out of the wine room and headed toward the door. "Was that Sky?"

We jogged to the bottom of the stairs. Just as I was about to climb, Phil gripped my wrist again.

"As you don't have a gun, I think it's best I go first, don't you?"

"This time, but Carole's right. We want lessons after we close this case."

He groaned, but a small chuckle escaped his lips. "You're both a pain, you know that?"

I wasn't going to argue, but I wasn't quite joking either. We seemed to have a habit of getting ourselves into these situations at the Lockwood Agency. I let Phil pass me with his gun held high and hurled myself up the stairs after him, my heart pounding.

Back in the hall, an eerie silence met us—I scanned the room, wondering which way to turn. As I opened my mouth to call out, Phil gripped my arm to stop me. But I did it anyway. "Sky? Carole?" I pulled out my phone to call them, but there was no signal.

"No more shouting," said Phil, standing directly behind me. "We aren't meant to be here." He paused and listened. "I think the scream must have come from upstairs."

The stairs at the back of the hall were shrouded in darkness but that didn't stop us from running up them. They led up to a balcony that overlooked the hall below and then led on to a long corridor, which turned a corner toward the other side of the castle.

"Should we split up and start looking through the rooms?" I asked Phil. He was still keeping far closer to me than necessary.

"No more splitting up." He opened the door in front of us; it led into a sparsely furnished bedroom. He opened his phone and pulled up the castle blueprints. "All these seem to be guest rooms?"

I nodded and opened the next door. Door after door was opened down the corridor; most rooms were evidently not in use. At one end was what looked like India's room, and at the other a room that could have been Euan's. Still no sign of Sky or Carole.

"Where are they?" I whispered, my stomach tense. "I'm going to shout out for them again."

"Let's check the next floor first."

The third floor was the same as the first and second—there was no one around. I took to being bold and turning lights quickly on and off in each room to speed up the search, to much grumbling from Phil. After checking what felt like the hundredth room, I leaned against the wall in the hallway and tapped my head against it in frustration. I couldn't take the not knowing anymore.

"Sky? Carole?" I called again. "Are you here?"

Phil, returning from the last room at the end of the corridor, shook his head. "That was—"

"If you say 'reckless,' I'm leaving you for the ghosts to deal with. I'm clear that's what you think, but that is my aunt and my friend that we can't find. And we've no idea which one of them screamed."

There was a creak of floorboards over our heads. I gripped Phil's arm.

"Freya?" called Carole from above us.

"Are you all right?" I shouted back.

"We've found another floor!"

Sure enough, behind a tapestry was a door we had missed in the darkness. Phil pulled back the dusty fabric. "Almost looks like someone was deliberately trying to hide this entrance, doesn't it?" I whispered as we climbed the stairs. "Carole?" I called again.

We rounded a turn in the staircase and saw light streaming out from under an old, boarded door at the top. My heart shuddered as Phil reached for the handle.

"Darling? Is that you?" There was worry in Carole's voice. Phil must have heard it too, because he lifted his gun.

"Are you okay?" I asked, my pulse picking up.

"Well . . . just wait . . ." she replied through the door.

I gripped Phil's arm. "Something's wrong."

He reached for the door. "Stay back until I tell you it's clear."

"Sure," I replied, knowing that I'd do no such thing. The slight smile on his lips told me that he knew it too.

The door crashed open and Phil said, "FBI!" Then he stopped dead and lowered his gun. ". . . I shouldn't be surprised, should I?"

My legs wobbled with adrenaline as I raced up the remaining two steps and crossed the threshold.

24

Dolores
Sunday, February 11, 12:30 a.m.

The police had been called, but Dolores wasn't going to wait for them to arrive. They never should have left the castle unattended. Someone was creeping around in there—she had seen lights flicking on and off in the bedroom windows when nobody should have been home. Whoever was in there, she was going to confront them.

Dolores knew that what Euan and Jane were up to wasn't aboveboard. She wasn't a fool. But she also needed to keep her job, because keeping her home depended on it. It didn't sit well with her that these people, who already had so much more than she did, also had something so important that they could hold over her head. So, while she was cleaning, she was also keeping watch.

That was how she found the long-forgotten entrance to the wine cellar and the boxes of ceramics hidden behind the empty wine bottles. It was how she knew about the paintings in the attic and the letters that had sat on Euan's desk. Letters that she *might* have read and then she *might* have taken before he burned them. When Euan asked if she had seen them she played the elderly, forgetful cleaner, and he never asked again. Although she did mention that she had possibly seen them in

Jane's room—this caused quite an argument between Jane and Euan, and Dolores slipped out early that day.

Now she pulled on her warmest coat, mittens, hat, scarf, and snow boots and set out to collect the large torch and baseball bat Oliver had put in the car for her. Dolores didn't like Jane, and the feeling was mutual—Euan and Jane might have been lovers once, but now they only just about tolerated each other. Dolores had been married once, for six years, over fifty years ago. She knew very well that Euan and Jane could have lived happily as friends and business associates. That sort of relationship would never have worked for Dolores—she'd hated her ex-husband.

Baseball bat in hand, she wondered if she had enough power in her arm to make a swing or if her arthritic fingers would be able to grip the handle tightly enough. Well, she would give it a go. Maybe she should have called Oliver, but it was late, and he might not have arrived before the police. She took a few tentative steps on the footpath, hoping that the grit he had put down was still keeping the paving stones safe to walk on, and made her way toward the castle—she could do that walk blindfolded. If Jane was sneaking about stealing things, then Dolores would keep her there until the police arrived.

25

India
Sunday, February 11, 12:30 a.m.

Oliver's flat above the pub was furnished with a collection of dated things that looked as if they came from his grandmother's house—although his place was far, far messier than hers.

India sat on the window seat in his bedroom and watched the sea lapping against the snow-topped harbor walls. The moon made the scene look magical, but she was too old to believe in anything other than cold, hard facts. She had grown up in Napier, on the east coast of New Zealand's North Island. Sea-breeze-swept hair, sand-covered toes, and salted lips had been the constant joy of her childhood years. Her mother had owned an old, beaten-up sea kayak which they'd taken out on the water every sunny Sunday. The lapping water calmed all the money worries and bullies away. The sea and her music were all India had thought she would ever need—until her mother died, and their flat above the souvenir shop was taken back by the landlord.

Those days after her mother's death, when she'd sat alone in the flat before her father had sent her a plane ticket, had been so quiet it was frightening. The drive to never experience that again had taken root, and silence was now a shadow on her very soul. She practiced her instruments more after her mother died than she ever had before.

India had submitted to her father's rules and rages for that very reason: even when he was cruel, he was still *there*, all the family she had left. Boarding school had been the perfect solution for both of them. She was rarely alone while at school; it enabled her to play the music that she loved. But when she came back to live full-time in the castle while studying in Edinburgh, nothing was easy.

There were very few people who truly understood what it was like to be that lost, but when India had met Bella, she had recognized in her a mutual need to belong and never have to be alone again. It had made her want to help Bella find the paintings she was looking for. Bella had shown her pictures of Scottish silver that looked very similar to the ones in her father's study, and India had decided that Bella needed a closer look.

Now it was India who needed to search the castle under cover of darkness. She was desperate to see what was in her father's will, and there had to be a copy somewhere in his study. If she was going to start a new life with Oliver, they would need her father's money. Was Jane right? Had she really been disinherited? The thought chilled her to her bones. She would do whatever it took to keep what was rightfully hers.

"Indie, come to bed," a sleepy voice grumbled from the bedroom, but she couldn't rest.

"I need to go back to the castle. Jane is up to something... I went to check, and she's not in her room." She strode into the bedroom. "Can I take your 4x4 again? It's better in this weather."

Oliver groaned. "You'll not go over there on your own. I'll drive you. And, yeah, it might be good to have a look about before Jane gets in there tomorrow. What are we looking for exactly?"

He flipped back the covers and padded over to her. He was tall and broad, enveloping her slim frame, and he made her feel safe and protected like no one ever had before. His scent wrapped her like a warm hug and his fingers gently tilted up her chin. "You really want to go right now? In the middle of the night?"

India gave him one determined nod. "I can't sleep. We need to find the will. And if we know Jane isn't going to be there, we can look for all those boxes Arthur told me to photograph. I was never interested in them before, but I think I need to take another look . . . the contents must be valuable."

"Just get someone to come around and value it, like that woman from the auction house you said was always hanging around. Do you need to go there now?"

"Yes, before Jane takes them for herself." That wasn't the only reason, but there were things that Oliver didn't need to know. "I like them." Or rather, she would like to hide them from Jane. "There's a little piglet in one of those boxes, and I'm really fond of him." After a moment, she gave him a little bit of information to keep him happy. "The Wemyss Ware cats always remind me of my mum. She had two of them in our New Zealand flat that sat on a chest of drawers in her bedroom. They were given to her on her wedding day by a great-aunt. She used to polish them every week with such care, you would think those cats were the Crown Jewels. They had roses painted all over them, and they seemed to smile back as you looked at them."

"But it's not just that, is it?" He frowned at her even as she folded into his chest and wound her hands around his waist, hoping it would be enough to distract him from his train of thought.

"I won't be able to sleep until I check everything is in order at the castle and Jane hasn't already removed Dad's antiques." She was talking about the paintings in the attic, but she couldn't tell Oliver that.

"Do you think she would?"

"Don't you?" What she didn't tell him was that *she* would be the one doing the taking.

She gave Oliver a brief peck and pulled on her boots, then retreated to the kitchen while he dressed and made coffee to go. She hoped he wouldn't push too far. There was so much he didn't know and she wished she could tell him, but Bella was very insistent that men were never to be trusted, no matter how infatuated you were. No matter what they would do for you in the name of love.

26

Freya
Sunday, February 11, 1 a.m.

The glare of the bare light bulb hanging from the attic ceiling made me shield my eyes with my hand.

"I think you owe us an explanation," growled Phil, stepping forward.

"You'd think you'd be a little less grumpy, growing up with all that American sunshine!"

Phil huffed, and I breathed out a relieved laugh. "Bella?"

She was standing with Sky and Carole on either side of her. Phil stayed just in front of me as if trying to protect me from her, but I placed a hand on his arm and swept around him. "You can put that away. We're on the same team," I said as I hurried to Bella's side, but he didn't holster his gun.

"How did you find each other?"

"Oh . . . Well, darling, I bumped into Bella when she popped out from behind that tapestry. It gave me quite a fright. Sky thought she was a ghost. And then I may have become a bit overexcited."

"That was the scream?" I asked. I glanced back at Phil, who was glaring at Bella. "We've discussed this."

Phil sighed and muttered, "I'm glad to see you're all right, Bella."

"Oh, he's still got that charm you love so much, hasn't he, Freya?" Bella smirked.

My gaze swept over Sky and Carole, checking for injuries. "You all okay?"

They nodded sheepishly.

"We were going to come and find you, but Bella wasn't keen..." Sky nodded at Phil. "When I told her he was here."

I studied Bella and she shrugged. "Are *you* okay? What happened? Why haven't you been in touch?" I said, stepping in and pulling her into an unwanted hug. She smelled of dust and earth. "Where have you been?"

"I lost my phone, and I didn't think... No one worries about me." She pulled out of my grasp. "I was looking into who might have shipped the three paintings to Boston." She brushed a cobweb from her sleeve, and I had the impression that there was a lot she wasn't telling me.

"Of course we were *terribly* worried, darling. It's why we are here," Carole said, touching her arm. Bella merely shrugged her off and stepped farther away from both of us.

"When we couldn't get hold of you, we jumped in the car. That's what friends do when they care." I tilted my head to catch her eye, trying to infuse my words, but she looked away and scanned the room. "You need to tell us everything. We've had to trace your movements—visiting Alexandra Pattern and Cedric James?"

Bella glared at Sky. "You told them?" She stabbed a finger in Phil's direction. "You told *him*?"

"You were *missing*!" Sky raised her hands in despair, but her voice cracked with guilt. "What was I supposed to do?"

"I said it was..." Bella bit her lip. "Never mind." She motioned around the attic. "This is what I've... we've... been looking for." She was changing the subject, but I couldn't push her while it was clear she didn't trust us.

Phil scanned the pitched, cobweb-covered room and said, "What, exactly?"

Carole flung her hand around, indicating the dustcovers shrouding unknown objects at the far end and twenty or so removal boxes. "Everything."

Phil strode past Bella. She grimaced behind his back as he bent down and started pulling dustcovers aside.

Bella took my arm and steered me aside. "Why did you call lover boy? We don't need him here. I've almost solved this case of yours. Lots of the items in Arthur's journal are in here."

I studied her face and shook my head in disbelief. "And that's all you've been hunting for?" I kept my voice low. "If that's true, then what has Cedric James got to do with this? Why were you visiting a prisoner, the same one Alexandra Pattern visited, and asking him for a DNA test? What's really going on?"

"It's a long story, okay?" Her glare fixed on Phil's back. "You have found the items in the journal. Case closed."

"Bella." I couldn't keep the exasperation out of my voice. "We were employed by the FBI to find out who shipped the three paintings to America and where they'd come from. We don't have those answers yet because we have been hunting for you. We also haven't found the Scottish silver that was in the journal. So no, the case is not closed."

"Right, so if I get to the bottom of the Boston thing, then he'll go home? Or is he really just here for you?" Bella said.

I shook my head, not knowing how to get her to open up to us.

Sky had come to stand beside Bella. "You have a bigger problem than Phil being here. The Scottish police want to question you about Euan McGovern's murder. If they have your phone . . . ?"

Bella waved a hand toward her face. "They can't get in without the code or my face. And there's nothing on there anyway."

"I'm sure it's all a massive misunderstanding," said Carole, joining our huddle. Sky had folded her arms and was watching Phil closely, as if she were Bella's bodyguard.

I had never truly believed that Bella killed Euan, but I needed to hear it for myself, and I knew Phil certainly did too.

"Why did you decide to come here to see Euan? Did you believe the paintings were here or were you coming here to meet him for another reason? And what happened after you got to the castle three nights ago?" I asked her. "We need the whole story, Bella."

"All right." She sighed. "I went to see Alexandra Pattern. A contact in the US had told me that she was dealing in paintings—sending them to American auction houses to be sold. I had no idea if this was a money-laundering, black-market thing or a legit dealer selling art abroad, so I paid her a visit and showed her some photos of the paintings. She denied ever seeing them but I thought she was lying. So I searched her office when she was busy with another customer and found a desk diary from last year. In the back there was a Christmas party mentioned at Fawside Castle. Arthur had been in Scotland with Carole, and so I called her, and she said the only people she knew were Euan, Jane, and India. Carole gave me India's number and I met up with her. India and I talked about Arthur, and I got the feeling that they'd had quite a lot of contact..."

Carole frowned. "Arthur never told me that." I put a hand on her arm, knowing that it pained Carole to find out Arthur had kept secrets from her.

"I'm sorry," said Bella. "He was probably just looking out for her. Indie and I planned to look around the castle while Euan was away on holiday in May, but I didn't want to wait that long. I had already swiped Alexandra's business card, so I copied it and made an appointment under the name Emma Page.

"I didn't know that Alexandra had visited Cedric, and I don't know why she did. I showed up here and thought nobody was at home, so I decided to look around. I was still downstairs when someone smacked me over the head and I hit the ground. I might have passed out, because I've no idea how long I was there for. I didn't see my attacker—I heard scraping noises and, well, I wasn't going to wait around to find out who did it to me. Anyway, my wig and hat were probably the things that kept the blow from killing me. So I jumped in the car, dropped it around the corner from the rental place knowing they would find it eventually, and fled to a discreet little holiday rental that I knew about in Edinburgh. I had a concussion, and I waited a few days before I decided to come back here while it was empty and really have a look around."

"Why didn't you go back to the hotel?" asked Phil. "Why leave all your stuff there?"

"Because my wig had dropped off and someone had just tried to kill me, Phil." Bella hugged herself before saying, "I didn't feel safe going back in case someone followed me. Cities are far easier to get lost in."

"You didn't see Euan's body while you were here? Or anyone else in the castle that night? No other cars?" I asked.

"Nope. I thought it must have been Euan that attacked me. Or maybe Jane, as they were meant to be the only ones at home that night. I didn't know Euan was dead until I saw it on the news." Bella wasn't looking at me now—she was glaring at Phil. "I didn't kill anyone."

She had shifted a little closer to the door as if getting ready to run again.

"Bella." I reached out to stop her. "Back up a bit. What has Cedric James got to do with all of this?"

She froze. "Nothing."

Carole tutted. "Out with it, darling."

"Fine. He was an art forger, so I wanted to know if he had painted the Boston forgeries." She shrugged. "Nothing more."

That wasn't what Cedric had told us. If there was something illegal going on, Bella wasn't going to tell me in front of Phil. "Show us what you found up here."

Bella strode down the center of the pitched attic, dodging cobwebs and low-hanging light bulbs, to stand next to Phil in front of the cloth-covered boxes. She pulled back one of the sheets as dust particles clogged the air. "This is what you need to see."

27

Sunday, February 11, 1:15 a.m.

I crouched down and flipped through paintings of stormy seas, Victorian buildings, portraits, and landscapes with livestock and lots of dogs. The forger really liked painting dogs.

"These look exactly like the ones in Arthur's journal... But why are they here? None of the paintings were registered on the Art Loss Register or reported stolen as far as we know. Are these originals or forgeries? We would need to get that expert in Glasgow to verify them."

Phil opened a removals box. "And this is a large collection of Mauchline Ware, very much like the one shown in the journal." He looked straight at Bella, as did I. "Got any answers for us?" His tone was less biting than it normally was, and it didn't go unnoticed.

"Turns out I'm good at this hunting thing, doesn't it?" She tipped her chin up. When Phil ignored her dig, she sighed and said to me, "I don't think any of the paintings listed in Arthur's journal were stolen. I think they're a catalogue of fakes that have been painted and sold on the black market for years, maybe decades. More recently they've been popping up in legitimate auction houses. Like the case in Boston with the three Raeburn paintings... that portrait in particular." She pointed to an unframed painting of an old-fashioned woman in a bonnet that I recognized as one in Arthur's journal. "I assume that someone, maybe Euan, thought it was good enough to fool the experts."

Phil picked up the painting and flipped it over. A slip of paper was pasted to the back and he read out, "'Sir Henry Raeburn, *Portrait of Mrs. Johnstone*. Valued around $160,000 to $180,000.' Someone has gone through all of these and 'valued' them."

"Yes. Earlier this evening, I sent photos of some of these paintings to the Glaswegian curator and Raeburn expert who was brought in to look at the Boston paintings. He confirmed that the original *Portrait of Mrs. Johnstone* and all the other eighteen here are held in private collections, and those paintings are original. Nine of the original paintings, duplicated here in this attic, he has appraised in person. He would like the opportunity to test the paints on these but I'm quite sure all of them are excellent forgeries," Bella said. I saw Phil give an approving tilt of his head, as if he were seeing something in her for the first time.

"So all the paintings in Arthur's journal are forged? We were never looking for stolen paintings. He was pointing us toward a forger or forgery ring," I said.

"We have no records of any other auction houses reporting forgeries shipped through Scotland. One or two may have gone undetected, but not many," Phil said. "It looks as if this is an organized operation that's been going on for a while, given the number of items here. But I think they've recently changed the way they're working. That made them sloppy, and we got lucky. It's clever to sell them on the black market, where provenance and valuation can be hard to verify. Perhaps that's where Arthur came into contact with them, realized what was going on, and started to catalogue the fakes that he saw."

"Or he got someone else to," Bella said, so quietly it was almost to herself.

"Arthur was undercover and reluctantly involved in all aspects of the black market. If he valued the paintings as real while working for the FBI, then he couldn't out the forgery operation while he was alive. He left this for us to uncover after his death, just like in the Copthorn Manor case. He didn't report it at the time; he didn't tell Phil when he was his informant—but he did keep a record for a later date, when he could bring it all down," I said as I studied the paintings.

"And if all of these were stashed up here by Christopher McGovern, then he must have been involved?" asked Sky.

"It's a good guess. Perhaps his younger brother, Euan, took over after his death," I replied. "And he brought in Alexandra to sell them."

"It was a very talented artist that painted these. And we have recently met with a very talented artist in prison," said Phil. He lifted up a painting of a boy with a black-and-white-spotted dog, and I understood what I was seeing—it was an exact replica of one of the paintings recovered in Boston and the one Cedric had mentioned.

"How many are there?" I asked. "We need to show them to an expert. Cedric could have painted them, and maybe they were sold behind his back while he was in prison. Perhaps that could have made him angry enough to kill, but he didn't have the opportunity, did he? Who else do we suspect? We have to assume this is connected to Euan's murder, don't we?"

"We have a likely chain of events... Cedric painted these years ago. Euan was selling them. Perhaps Alexandra was sending them abroad. And Arthur knew every part of the operation, and he didn't tell me," said Phil with a sigh.

"But he has now," I said. "He was waiting for someone to slip up, like they did when they sent the three paintings to Boston. Once that happened, we would have as much information as he could give us to take the whole operation down."

Sky was frowning at the portrait over my shoulder. "I mean, that boy looks so downright miserable, and it's such a dark painting. Who wants that in their house?" she said. "And who is this Raeburn person?"

As there were several Raeburns in the journal, I was well versed in the painter, but it was Bella who replied. She stepped nearer to Phil, who was examining the painting of a woman in a bonnet.

"Sir Henry Raeburn was a Scottish portrait painter, born in Edinburgh in 1756. He was basically self-taught, married to a rich woman, and spent time in Italy, like they all did back in the day. God, I love Italian men, don't you?" Sky chuckled, and Bella continued, "Then after he returned, he rarely left Scotland, but his paintings went back and forth across the Atlantic during his lifetime." She reached for an envelope that was attached to the bottom of the painting. "He became hugely popular in America in the eighteenth and early nineteenth centuries. His works sold for a ton of money at auctions over there. I suppose that's why Euan wanted them shipped to America to be sold." She opened the envelope and pulled out what looked like a magazine clipping. "This is interesting..."

She handed me a torn-out page from an old auction catalogue. Reading it, I felt as if a lock was clicking open in my mind. "Now, that *is* clever..." I huffed out a laugh at what I was seeing.

Carole came closer for a look. "What is it?"

I read, "'*Half-Length Portrait of a Lady in Lace Bonnet* is a previously unrecorded portrait by Sir Henry Raeburn. From an early date in the artist's career, its recent rediscovery at a regional US auction house represents a significant addition to the artist's known body of work.'"

I refolded the page and placed it back in the envelope. "They're using auction catalogues as provenance, then sending the paintings over to America to be sold."

Phil shook his head. "I've got to hand it to them, it's a good idea. No one in the black market is going to check."

"Well, this is all very exciting. Have we solved the case?" said Carole. She bent to pick up a small Mauchline Ware figure of a boy. His mouth could be opened and closed by means of a lever on the back. "And what is this—is this also a fake?"

"I don't think so. It's a treen nutcracker," I said, joining her in looking through the box of Mauchline Ware. "But there is one exactly like it in Arthur's journal."

"Do you think India knew all this was here?" Sky asked, and then without waiting for an answer said to Bella, "If she told you she could get you into the castle while her father was away, then maybe she wanted to show you all this?"

"Or she had no idea and was just trying to help Bella?" said Carole. Always the protector, just like Arthur.

"*Or* she knew they were here and wanted to be with Bella when she entered the castle to make sure Bella didn't see anything she wasn't meant to—and India had already planned her father's death before Bella gained access," said Phil. "We cannot rule anyone out."

I tried not to smile as I realized, by the way Phil had phrased his last sentence, that he had ruled Bella out as the murderer.

"India told you that on the night of the snowstorm, she was staying with Oliver at the pub?" I asked Bella to clarify.

"She did," Bella confirmed. "It's hard for me to believe that Indie killed her father, but I do think she knew all about all this." She nodded toward the paintings.

"The pub isn't far from here, and we all know she hated her father. Oliver had a motive to kill him. Could they have done it together?" I asked. "Until we find the real murderer, Bella will still be a suspect, so we need to find who did this and clear her name." Everyone nodded in agreement, and Bella's cheeks reddened ever so slightly.

"This is nonsense. India is as delicate as a ballerina. She didn't kill or plot to kill anyone. I won't believe it," said Carole. "And Bella didn't either. So who else is left?"

"We need to find out whether India is a consummate liar or an innocent bystander," I said. "Then we have Jane. Cedric could have hired someone to do it, I suppose. Dolores could have walked here that night, but given how frail she is and her reaction to the body, it's a stretch. Oliver has motive and means . . . Maybe there's someone we haven't met yet who worked for the forgery ring and had reason to kill Euan?"

I scanned the faces around me, waiting for someone to come up with an idea.

Bella shrugged. "You've forgotten Alexandra Pattern. She was in on it all."

"So many suspects with flimsy motives," said Sky. "But this might help." While we had all been standing around discussing India, Sky had continued to search through the boxes. She held up an open Victorian writing box, and inside I could just make out some papers.

Bella got to her first and took the box, pulling out a folded sheet of paper. "Got you . . ."

We gathered around. The handwritten note read: *I have proof that you are not the real laird. I think that we can come to an arrangement.*

"Someone was blackmailing Euan?" said Phil. He picked up a few more pages and glanced through them. "They all say the same thing. The poison-pen writer knows Euan McGovern isn't who he says he is, and they want paying off."

"Blackmail is a good motive for murder, isn't it, darling? But if it was Euan who was being blackmailed, it's more likely he would have killed the blackmailer, not the other way around. India would know the true identity of her father, but I can't imagine her writing that." Carole was peering over Phil's shoulder. "If she believed Euan wasn't her real father, I very much doubt she would have stuck around. Or maybe she did know that he wasn't the real laird and kept quiet?"

"It raises an interesting question, though, doesn't it?" I took one of the letters from Phil and read it: *Time is running out. Meet me at the castle, 3 p.m. tomorrow.* "Blackmail only works if the information the blackmailer holds is correct and damaging. What if the writer is correct, and Euan was an impostor?"

Phil put the letters back into the box and took out his phone and said, "I'll get Sloane to look into the McGovern family history and dig up photos. And look into Cedric James's background again and see if she can find a connection between the two men."

Bella was still holding the box, staring down into it. "I need to know where the real Euan McGovern is," she said, so quietly that I wasn't sure we were meant to hear her. "I need to find him." Her cheeks had paled and her hand trembled briefly as I gave her back the page I still held. She closed the lid and sighed. "I thought . . ." She shook her head and stepped closer to Carole.

"We will get to the bottom of this. All of us," Carole said, giving Phil a pointed look.

"Of course," he replied. He took the box of letters from Bella and gave her a nod of thanks—it was such a small moment, but also a huge step forward. Bella was asking for help in the only way she knew.

"Why do you need to find the real Euan?" asked Carole. "There seems to be more to this than just these paintings."

"It's not important," said Bella, turning away toward the door.

The rest of us exchanged glances. "We should get out of here," I said after a moment. "I don't think we're going to find anything else, and the police could arrive any minute."

We were filing down the attic stairs toward the main staircase when I heard car tires sloshing through the snow. I stopped, listening.

Phil placed his hand on his gun but didn't draw it this time. "Everyone behind me."

As we emerged into the main corridor I took Sky's arm, pulling her back. "Before anyone sees us, I need to show you a motion-sensor camera we found in the cellar. I want to know if you can get into it and find out what it has recorded."

"Do you think we'll see something that could help the case?" Sky said.

"I'm hoping so, as we seem to be at a dead end."

Carole caught my eye. I didn't need to say a word; she understood that I needed her to occupy whoever was arriving at the castle, and we would be right behind her. She gave me a little salute.

"Then quickly..." said Sky, tugging at my jacket.

We hurried quietly down toward the cellar.

28

Bella
Sunday, February 11, 1:30 a.m.

A knot had tied in Bella's throat when she'd read the blackmail letters in the attic, and it hadn't released since. She gulped down the oncoming emotions—they never helped anything. She needed cold, hard facts. That was the only way she would find her father.

She took in a deep breath and focused her mind on the main question. If Euan McGovern was not Euan McGovern, then who had been murdered? And had Arthur known that there was an impostor at Fawside Castle? Was that why he hadn't sent her to Fawside last year?

She had known that Phil was studying her as she stood over the box filled with Mauchline Ware. He had never trusted her, but that night there had been a shift in him. His tone of voice was a little softer; his eyes no longer narrowed when she spoke; his arms didn't cross over his chest when he saw her. Bella suspected that was Freya's doing—she was the only one Phil listened to, even if she didn't see it yet. Carole had always provided the warmth in the Lockwood Agency, but knowing that Freya had defended her in some way was a foreign but not unwelcome sensation. Bella had always had to fight her own battles, and she had been fine with that, but now there were others standing by her side.

They had walked through the castle together in a silent line. Phil was now opening the back door to check they were still alone. When he didn't see anything, he waved everyone forward. He was closing the door behind them, the silence outdoors broken only by their boots crunching gently on freshly laid snow, when the sound of someone else's footsteps came from the direction of the front of the castle.

They all stopped. The horror of being caught froze Bella's bones in place.

Dolores stepped into view, and Bella breathed deeply again; the old woman didn't seem the type to carry a weapon. Then she noticed the baseball bat in Dolores's hand. None of them wanted to hurt a little old lady, but no one should carry a weapon to a fight they couldn't win, for the weapon would only get turned around. As Bella stepped forward, her mind racing for an excuse, she saw two uniformed police officers and a man in a suit striding down the path behind Dolores. Right behind them were India and Oliver—India's jaw was hard with rage. Gone was the porcelain-ballerina delicacy Bella had come to admire; the India standing before her looked as if she was about to grab the bat and start swinging.

The man in the suit placed a hand on Dolores's shoulder to stop her approaching them. "Bella Demire—or is it James?" he called out. "I hear that you think a prisoner may be your grandfather. Cedric James?" Bella bit her lip, and the detective continued, "I'm Detective Rodgers. You're wanted for questioning in connection with the death of Euan McGovern. If you would come with us."

How had he made that connection? Bella herself had only recently learned about it, when Sky had found Cedric.

"*James?* Does he mean *our* Cedric James?" Carole whispered, turning to face Bella, who shrugged in reply. "And I don't know if I ever knew your surname, darling." Her eyes flicked to Phil, questioning.

"I have it on record as Bella Demire," he replied. "But I'm quite sure that's an alias."

"It's not James," said Bella, trying to sound convincing, but her stomach was churning with the truth. She grabbed on to Carole, suddenly desperate to explain before the police could haul her away. "I was looking for my father, but there was no lead with the name I had. So I asked Sky to dig into the information I had on my grandfather."

Carole gave a small nod as she put the pieces together. "You thought Cedric was your grandfather—that's why you asked for his DNA? You think one of his sons is your father?"

"I don't know . . ."

Detective Rodgers motioned the uniformed officers toward Bella. Her pulse picked up and her hold on Carole strengthened.

"One of Cedric's sons died. I've no idea if I'm on the right track, but I asked Arthur to help me, and he said he'd written it down . . ." In the *journals*. But Bella clamped her mouth shut as one of the officers touched her elbow.

Phil shook his head and drove his hands into his pockets. "Detective Rodgers, as I've explained to you already, I am part of a joint task force. These are some of my colleagues."

The detective cleared his throat. "That may be so, but this is my crime scene you're all trampling over. I think it would be a good idea if you all joined us at the station."

"It's very late, darling, and the back door was unlocked when we arrived. Perhaps one of your officers forgot to lock up?" Carole asked before continuing. "Couldn't we just come in tomorrow morning? I'm far better at interrogation after a beauty sleep."

Bella averted her eyes. She didn't want to admit that she had been the one to break in.

Rodgers looked as if he was trying not to laugh. "So it's only breaking and entering that you're capable of in the middle of the night?"

"Not *only* that, darling." She winked at him.

Phil spluttered, and even Bella couldn't help but smile. The detective was going to be in for a long night if he intended on questioning Carole.

Phil stepped forward, wearing his expressionless FBI face. "We will of course cooperate and come to the station with you. I'm sure everyone here will be happy to be interviewed as soon as our lawyer arrives." He turned back to the team. "Wait for the lawyer. Right?" He made eye contact with Carole, and she nodded as his gaze shifted to Bella. "Right?" he asked her again with a small frown, as if she might be the one to start talking first. It was as if he didn't know Carole at all—she would be bending their ear for hours with nothing but funny stories and not-so-subtle innuendo.

"Let's get this over with." Bella was mentally preparing herself to spend the night in a cell. She knew that as soon as the duty sergeant took her fingerprints, everything was going to go to hell. Before the police escorted her away, she said to Phil and Carole, "If you get out before me, tell Freya to go talk to Alexandra Pattern again. She knows more than she's letting on. When I showed her the pictures of the Boston paintings, she wasn't surprised they had been confiscated . . . she seemed amused. Perhaps *she* was blackmailing Euan."

~

Bella's rage simmered as the policeman placed his hand on her head to guide her into the car. "I'm capable of getting into a car," she hissed, but he said nothing in reply.

It was going to take all her willpower to keep calm.

There was no type of authority Bella could get on with, from a school crossing guard telling her when she could cross the road to the policeman she now sat behind in his car.

After being betrayed by her ex-boyfriend Chris Prince last year,

Bella had raised the drawbridge against everyone. She liked the Lockwood women, but she wasn't a team player. She was a lone wolf. That's why she hadn't called anyone after she was injured that night at the castle. The first day had been scary, with the blinding headache and the swirling nausea, but she had managed to get through it, and it had solidified her resolve.

Through the car window, she watched the car's lights reflect off the blanket of snow covering the hedgerows and then morph into city streets, and her mind went back to India. She had thought they were friendly. But did India know what was hidden in the castle attic? Did she know that her father was being blackmailed? India was quiet, but she wasn't stupid—she knew a lot more than she had let on. "We need to talk," Bella had called to her as she was taken away. India had shuddered in a way that told Bella she was hiding something.

Bella was determined to get away from the Edinburgh police as soon as possible and then pry answers out of India and Alexandra Pattern. Alexandra and Euan must have had a close relationship. Maybe they were lovers? It seemed likely to Bella, but if that was the case, she couldn't understand why India hadn't mentioned it. Goose bumps prickled over her arms at the realization that by showing up to the castle disguised as Alexandra Pattern, she could have ended up like Euan.

As the car pulled up outside a police station, Bella realized she had no idea where she was. But she knew she'd be fine; it wasn't the first time she had been arrested. The memory of Carole's warm bear hug from an hour ago came back to her; the pride in her voice when Bella showed her that she had found some of the items in the journal. The look on Sky's face when she had told her about the Scottish artist Sir Henry Raeburn. Her chest clenched as she decided these responses were fleeting and false. Bella came from a world where it was dangerous to trust other people.

An hour later, Bella was sat in a cold interview room. It was empty—

apart from a desk and chairs—and seemed larger than normal. Detective Rodgers and a young officer with a brown folder sat opposite her. Bella's lawyer, a young Sikh called Parvinder Singh Johal—dressed in a navy suit with a pagri wrapped around his long hair—sat next to her. He had been summoned at short notice thanks to Phil's connections.

The detective proceeded to run through all the typical questions. Who was in the room? What time was it? Same old, same old.

"Well, now, you're wanted for a few things, young lady. Wanted for questioning for a theft at Copthorn Manor in England last year—we'll be informing the relevant force about your detention. You were also placed in the vicinity of another robbery in 2022. And then there's our force's concern: Euan McGovern's murder."

Bella shrugged. "I think it's best that we get this over with now. No. Comment," she said, leaning back in her chair and folding her arms. "You can keep me here for twenty-four hours, and then I'm off. We both know you don't have anything on me."

Parvinder gave her a stern look.

"How did you know Euan McGovern?"

"No comment."

"Are you related to Euan McGovern?"

"No comment."

"We have three other surnames on record for you: Demire, Jones, and White. Your most recent record states Demire. Which one is the real one?"

None of them. "No comment."

"What is your current address?"

Bella glared at him. "No comment."

The last time she'd had a place to call her own had been while she was sharing a flat with Chris Prince in Edinburgh . . . a flat that Arthur had recommended to her. It had also been Arthur who reluctantly introduced Bella to Chris at a party in the Highlands, although he'd warned her to stay away from him. Arthur couldn't have known that after his murder she would end up falling for the man, whom he clearly didn't like. Chris had stayed over regularly at Bella's flat and eventually moved in without asking if he could. He'd said something like, "It's convenient for work, being here." She hadn't questioned this at the time. She'd believed he was genuinely happy they were living together.

But what if there was more to all that history? Bella knew now that everything Arthur did had always been methodical and well planned. Had he wanted her in that particular Edinburgh flat for a reason? And Chris was an art and antiques trafficker and a black-market dealer, so what did "convenient" really mean for him? He and Arthur had been involved in the black market together. She closed her eyes; it was all so glaringly obvious when she thought about it. What if the art trafficker who had moved the paintings to Boston was far closer to home than she'd thought? What if she had lived with him?

Bella opened her eyes and gripped her hands together. She needed to get away from here, talk to Alexandra Pattern again, and find out if she knew Chris Prince. The art and antiques world was far too small for her liking, and the black market was even smaller.

"Let's try something else," Detective Rodgers continued. "Your fingerprints were found on a cabinet from which a collection of Scottish silver was stolen. Did you steal the silver?"

"No comment." In her mind, Bella was running through all the items Arthur had listed in the journal. Those strange words, "Man Alive"—what did that mean? Arthur had mentioned that he was helping her find her father; he'd written down everything he could find about him and his "interest in Scottish art and antiques." What was Arthur trying to tell her?

"You are wanted for questioning in connection with a number of burglaries." Rodgers was unrelenting; Bella forced herself to focus on him again. "Why were you at Fawside Castle on the night of the seventh of February?"

"No comment." She clenched her teeth. She didn't have time for this; she needed to *think*.

"Was your friend Carole Lockwood also involved in the robbery at Fawside Castle and the murder of Euan McGovern? We found her breaking and entering with you. What were you both doing there? Where were Freya Lockwood and her assistant while all of this was going on?" The self-satisfied smile on the detective's face made Bella's annoyance bubble to the surface. She opened her mouth to reply.

"Don't you dare." Her lawyer glared at Bella again.

She bit the inside of her cheek before muttering, "No comment."

Rodgers sat opposite her with his head tilted, trying to work her out. Bella made her face relax into a blank canvas while internally swearing to get to the bottom of it all. She wasn't having her decade-long quest to find her good-for-nothing father—the only family she had left in the world—get her friends into trouble.

Friend... friends... She sighed, realizing that she hadn't thought of anyone in those terms since Arthur Crockleford's murder.

What games were you playing, Arthur?

Bella cursed herself for getting too close to the Lockwoods. They had somehow seeped their way into her cold, damaged life and she couldn't quite work out how to push them out. She knew she needed to try harder, but it was difficult to deny the relief that had swept through her when she'd set eyes on Carole, Sky, and Freya back at the castle. It had been a long time since anyone had cared enough about her to drive across the country just to make sure she was all right.

She blocked out the constant questions, trying once again to make sense of everything she had learned so far. The phrase "Man Alive" echoed over and over in her mind.

"In Edinburgh we have on record that you lived at number five..."

"What?" Bella's attention snapped back to Rodgers. She leaned forward. Her flat number was number four, not five, but he didn't need to be corrected.

"I said..." huffed the detective.

"Actually, never mind. No comment." Because Bella didn't need to hear anything else. She had just worked out what "Man Alive" really meant, and she needed to tell Freya and Carole immediately.

29

Freya
Sunday, February 11, 6 p.m.

It had been a sleepless night and a worrying day. Sky and I had spent quite some time in the cellar looking at the camera before deciding that we had to leave it in place, and she would try to hack into it from the car. When we left the cellar, we heard voices. It didn't take long to work out that Phil, Carole, and Bella were being taken to the police station in Edinburgh for questioning. I tried to run after them but Sky held me back, saying we'd be better off helping from the outside.

Carole and Phil were back at the hotel by 7 a.m., but Bella was kept in custody. The thought of her locked up and alone itched along my spine all day. The only thing that saved the day was Sky hacking into the camera and uncovering a piece to the puzzle none of us had seen coming. The camera showed that on the night of Euan's murder, Alexandra Pattern had arrived at Fawside Castle—entering via a hidden door leading through the wine cellar—twenty minutes before Bella, and then left at 5:30 p.m.

Alexandra was now our main suspect. She could have been the one sending the blackmail letters, and now we had evidence that she had been there when Euan was murdered.

And that was how we found ourselves at the auction house's charity ceilidh we had seen advertised on Alexandra's pinboard. We were all hoping that she would make an appearance. It was held in a large Victorian hall a few minutes' walk from the Griffin & Thompson saleroom, with a pitched roof covered in snow and large, arched double doors. It reminded me of the village hall back in Little Meddington, although there's usually less dancing there and more yoga.

The sprung-wooden dance floor had a slight bounce to it, and I sensed that everyone there took their traditional dancing seriously. It was a sea of tartan kilts and sashes. I wondered if my 1980s-inspired black velvet dress, a panic purchase, would be deemed acceptable. Sky wore a navy 1950s swing dress—our love of vintage had rubbed off on her over the months, which made me smile with pride. She looked stunning, and my long Georg Jensen Vivianna Torun earrings dangled elegantly at her slender neck, swaying as she laughed.

But mostly, the merriment all around us was lost on me. My mind was still on Bella being held in a police remand cell.

Bella had told Carole to get to Alexandra—and now we knew that Alexandra had been at the castle when Euan was murdered. We believed that Cedric had painted the forgeries listed in Arthur's journal, and we had found them stored in the castle's attic, but we were still unclear who was selling them. My best bet was on Euan, or perhaps Euan and Alexandra together.

"My knees probably won't take the Strathspeys," Carole said as we handed over our tickets. "They're just too fast. I might go and chat with those nice-looking young men at the bar instead. I want to find out who knows Alexandra and what they think of her. Get the gossip on our number one suspect."

I scanned the room, looking for Alexandra. "We need to understand her motive. We are assuming that she knew about the forged paintings in Euan's attic—she was probably verifying them on the side and then helping to ship them to auction houses in the US. She knew the castle well enough to come and go via the cellar door... But why kill Euan, if she was blackmailing him? Why bite the hand that fed her?"

"Maybe he decided to stop giving her what she wanted, or had found something on her," Sky said from behind me. She was unfastening a long tartan sash that swept from one shoulder, across her chest, and down to the opposite hip; Carole had made her put it on. "I'm not sure about this. It's really not my thing. It doesn't go at all with my look."

"Can you see Alexandra?" I asked both of them, wondering if my eyesight was really getting that bad.

Carole, who had moved beside Sky and linked arms with her, was pointing toward the band tuning their instruments at the other end of the paneled hall.

"No," Sky was hissing. "Not on your life..."

I smiled, because there was no chance Sky was getting out of there without dancing for hours if my aunt had any say in the matter.

Carole was always in her element at a party. She had even arranged a hire outfit for Phil and had it placed in his room by housekeeping, as he had still been at the station with Bella when we'd left. Apparently they believed she was a flight risk, and to be fair, they were right.

Sky was being tugged toward the bar but Carole looked back at me over her shoulder and winked. I didn't understand why until I noticed three men in their late twenties... I was quite sure Carole was going to ask them to teach Sky some of the reels.

I was about to step in and rescue her until I recognized that one of the men was a porter from the auction house. Sky's research was, once again, invaluable.

Clever Carole.

Sky was clearly in on the ruse. She smiled along and basked in their attention even though, as we knew, she was head over heels for Owen back in Little Meddington. I stood back against the wall, watching the scene unfold, as Carole drew more and more people into her orbit and Sky giggled at something the young man said. It was quite marvelous to see how accustomed we all now were to covert information-collecting.

The band started playing Scottish folk music, and dancers took their places in a long row down the middle of the room—and then men and women started dancing in and out, around and around. It was mesmerizing to watch, and the music and the pounding of feet on the floor had me smiling for the first time since Bella's arrest.

"You're not dancing?" Phil's voice was soft and his arm pressed against mine as he leaned over to talk into my ear.

"Um . . ." I tried and failed to suppress my widening smile as I looked him up and down. "So, Carole went all out, then?"

He was dressed in a kilt with a sporran and even the traditional *sgian-dubh*, an ornamental knife, tucked in at his lower leg. I became conscious of the fact that I might have been staring at his legs too long and lifted my eyes.

"Like what you see?" He chuckled, and my cheeks heated. "And don't you dare ask . . . Carole already has."

"Ask what?" And then I remembered. "Ah . . . the 'what's under that kilt?' question." He reddened and I laughed, shaking my head. "I mean, I've seen you in gardener's wellies and ripped coat, an officer's uniform, and now this . . . a freshly shaved Scotsman." I pointed my finger in the direction of his new attire. "This is an interesting look. Did you ever think when you decided to join the FBI that this was how you would be spending your time?"

"With you and Carole?" he asked, nudging me in an almost playful way that was entirely unlike him. "You look . . ."

"Scottish?" I finished, not knowing what I would do if he actually gave me a compliment. I tugged at the sleeves of my black velvet dress.

"Carole's in her element, as she was at the Halloween party on the cruise last year." I nodded toward the small crowd that had gathered around her and Sky at the bar.

"I see she's found her audience." He scanned the two-hundred-odd crowd that filled the room. "Have you seen Alexandra? Do you really think she will be here?"

"I've been looking for her. Maybe she's late? She did mention the other day that she wasn't feeling well," I said, pushing myself off the wall. "Shall we get a drink?" That seemed like a better, and maybe more professional, idea than standing in a darkened corner with Phil next to me. The vivid memory of his hand around my wrist as his thumb swept over my pulse was still playing on repeat.

As we moved away, Phil stopped, and I looked up at him. "Phil?" He had locked on to something to our right and I followed his line of sight. Alexandra stood in a corner, chatting to India. They looked relaxed and friendly—Oliver, on the other hand, was standing behind India, his face twisted in a grimace. He didn't seem pleased that the women were talking.

"What are you thinking?" I murmured to Phil. "Because I'm thinking India knows a lot more about what is going on with the paintings, what's stashed in the attic, than she's letting on—and Oliver looks like he either doesn't know, or he does and doesn't like it."

"Time to find out." Phil laced his fingers through mine, and we snaked across the room.

30

Sunday, February 11, 7 p.m.

The beat of the ceilidh band thrummed in my chest and adrenaline swept through my veins as we hurried toward India, Oliver, and Alexandra. I was determined to get the answers we needed so that we could get Bella out of custody as soon as possible.

"They're not just going to hand over the truth. We'll need to find a way to dig it out of them," said Phil.

"Maybe India wants to pick up where her father left off? Take over the castle and become part of the forgery ring . . . ? Euan seemed to make quite a bit of money from it." I kept my voice low and my body close to his, hoping we looked like any of the other couples at the party. We squeezed through the people gathered to watch the Scottish reels and the smell of beer and perfume washed over me. "What else could she do with all those hidden paintings? There would be merit in keeping Alexandra onside now her father's gone."

In mentioning India's loss, I couldn't help but also consider what Bella was now going through. When we were in the attic, she'd seemed as she always did: utterly in control, with unshakable confidence. But was that all just a facade? "Did you talk to the detective again? Is Bella okay?"

"She's fine—more than fine. She's giving them all a headache. That woman is into every aspect of the antiques black market, so I've no idea how she's going to worm her way out of all this, but the lawyer I sent to help her is good. If she listens to his advice." I must have looked concerned, as he continued, "I'm sure she will. She's not saying anything they want to hear, so it'll all depend on the evidence they have on her. I'm no expert in Scottish law, but I think our best bet is to find hard evidence of who killed Euan. A confession from Alexandra would be great."

I smiled. "You *truly* believe that Bella's innocent now."

"Yes. But innocent of this murder doesn't mean she's law-abiding."

I studied India as she leaned in to whisper in Alexandra's ear. "And there's a connection between Cedric James and Fawside Castle because we think those are Cedric's paintings in the attic."

Phil shook his head as we came to stand in front of Alexandra and India. It was time to apologize for our presence at the castle the night before. "Hi, India—I was wondering if I could have a word?" I tried my best to look contrite while the questions I wanted to ask her raced through my mind.

Phil pulled Alexandra aside, and I hoped he would ask her about her relationship with Euan.

"What were you doing at the castle?" India hissed. "What was *Carole* doing there last night? I thought we were friends."

"We're trying to help Bella, who is also your friend. And she's under suspicion for the murder of your father when we both know she didn't do it, don't we?"

"Maybe, but . . ." India gave a small shrug as if she didn't really care, but then she caught herself and said, "I do feel bad for Bella. Being accused of murder is terrifying. Are you any closer to finding out who really killed my father?"

Anger twisted inside me. Did she want us to look into her father's death to throw us off the scent somehow? Was it all an act? I smoothed out my face, relaxed my stance, and channeled my inner Bella.

"I know that it doesn't excuse us being at the castle in the middle of the night, but the back door was open and the alarm switched off. We were only trying to work out what happened that night—study the scene of the crime." I wasn't going to tell her about what we had found in the attic or the camera footage in the cellar. "Is the back door normally left unlocked?" It was probably Bella who had unlocked it, I realized now.

India frowned and shook her head. "No, never. Both my father and Jane have always kept valuable collections in the castle, which is why he had CCTV and a state-of-the-art alarm system installed over a year ago. The police were meant to be keeping an eye on the place too."

I wondered what collections she was talking about. "Are the antiques kept in a secure room within the castle?" I couldn't help but think back to the vaults at Copthorn Manor last year.

"I wouldn't know; antiques aren't my thing. You would have to ask Jane about her collection and dealings. Or ask . . ." She stopped herself and her brow furrowed. "Who's that man talking to Alexandra?"

I remembered that I hadn't introduced Phil to India. "That's Phil. He's with the FBI, and he's agreed to help us look into Euan's death. To help you . . ." I trailed off as I saw India rubbing her hands down her dress as if her palms were sweating, her eyes trained on Phil like lasers.

"But why is he talking to Alexandra?"

I studied Alexandra up close for the first time that night and realized there was something wrong. Maybe it was the way she was gripping her stomach, or the sallow tinge to her skin. "Is Alexandra okay?"

"She's got a cold or something," India said, scanning the room. "Have you seen Oliver? He was meant to be getting me a drink."

There was a large gathering by the bar, and within minutes my aunt would be in the center of it all. As I studied the people around her, my gaze rested on Oliver. "He's being held captive by one of Carole's stories."

Without taking her eyes off Oliver, India strode over to him. When he saw her coming he reached out, pulling her close to his side, and she melted into his chest. They were clearly very much in love, and even though I didn't entirely trust what India was saying to us, I was pleased that they could now pursue their relationship without any objections from her father.

I turned to approach Alexandra and found her glaring at me. "As I've told this FBI man, I had nothing to do with Euan's death. We did business together, but we were certainly not lovers. He sold items through the auction house after I had conducted valuations for him, and that was the extent of our relationship."

The doors of the hall burst open and an icy breeze swept over the dancers. As we turned, Detective Rodgers appeared at the entrance with three police officers behind him. Within moments he had spotted us and was making his way through the crowd, and I wondered if we were all about to be taken back to the police station. Then he nodded at Phil, and I realized that Phil must have told him about the camera footage in the cellar.

I gave Phil a quizzical look. "Bella was being interrogated for the murder of Euan," he said. "I couldn't very well keep it from Rodgers that Alexandra was at the scene of the crime. I had Sky send over the footage she found, and I told them about the box of letters in the attic. Maybe they'll get more out of her than I did."

Rodgers stormed over and Alexandra bristled beside me. "Alexandra Pattern? I'm Detective Rodgers, and I would like to ask you some questions about the night Euan McGovern died."

Alexandra's eyes flicked to India, who was over by the bar talking into Oliver's ear. "But I didn't . . ."

"If you would just come with us." Rodgers lifted a hand to show her the way.

"I'm really not . . ." Her knuckles were white as she clutched at her dress.

"Right this way," one of the other officers said, and Alexandra dropped her head and allowed herself to be shepherded toward the door.

I nodded to Phil. "Did you get anything out of her at all? She said nothing to me."

"Nothing." He sighed. "And I can't say I see a motive for her to kill Euan. How would she have managed to get him out into the garden, in the snow, all on her own?"

We both glanced back at Alexandra moving toward the exit with Rodgers. She seemed unsteady on her feet while they passed through the crowd. As he was pushing the door open, she toppled sideways and fell against him. His officers jumped to her aid as Phil and I surged forward simultaneously.

"Back. Everyone back," shouted Rodgers. A little circle of space opened around them as the nearest dancers scattered. The officers lifted Alexandra up and as we drew closer, I heard one say to another that it would take too long to wait for an ambulance.

We followed them out to the front of the building and watched them help Alexandra into the police car. The wind whipped around us, making me shiver; Phil placed his jacket over my shoulders.

"Thank you," I whispered as the police car sped away. "Do you think she'll be all right?"

"I hope so. Without her, it'll be harder to get all the answers we need," he replied.

Behind us, the music was still beating in time to the dancers' feet. "Beginners, you've seen how the pros do it. Now it's your turn," called one of the musicians from inside the hall.

"Let's see if Carole or Sky have found out anything more about Alexandra from her work colleagues," I said.

As we turned to go back inside, I felt a sense of dread that I couldn't place.

31

Carole
Monday, February 12, 9 a.m.

Carole was very pleased with herself as she strode down to breakfast. She had a date for later in the day.

"Well, that's what George is calling it," she told Freya as they sipped tea. Freya looked as if she might have had a lot of fun last night, but to Carole's deep disappointment she wasn't giving away any details. "George was very insistent at the dance, but I like to think of it as going undercover and having a lovely lunch." She chuckled to herself. "It's undercover fact-finding. Of course, I'm going to wear my fluffy, furry leopard-print coat. And how was your night?" she asked Freya, who looked tired but also had a little spring in her step. Carole was quite sure that had something to do with Phil and the four or five reels they'd danced together.

"I'm worried about Alexandra Pattern. I'm hoping she's better and that the police can get some answers from her," I said.

"Do they really think she killed Euan?" Carole's frown deepened. "And does that mean Bella will be released?"

"It seems that way," I said. "They wouldn't have asked to question her unless they had evidence against her, would they? Phil's talked to the detective and he's hopeful she'll be released soon. Who's George?"

"George Ellis is an estate agent, and he's been acquainted with Euan and Jane for a couple of years. He was pretty cagey when I asked about them. I think he knows something."

Freya paused with her cup halfway to her lips. "You're going on your own? Should I come?"

"Oh, you won't approve of him, so you can't come." Carole lowered her voice for impact. "He's very dashing, but I won't be swayed by a pretty face . . . I'll get all the gossip, don't worry."

Freya sighed. "Fine—but I'm having Sky track your every move."

"Let's get something to eat, and then you can tell me what Phil was wearing under that kilt."

Freya shook her head, but her blushing cheeks told another story.

∼

St Abbs had a charm that was lost in modern developments. Picturesque fishermen's cottages, Victorian houses, and shops swept around the old harbor, and snow had settled on the rooftops; a soft whisper of flakes still danced in the air.

Carole smiled to herself as she walked into the Old Ship for lunch. George had suggested a few different local restaurants, but she'd thought a casual venue was best—she didn't want to give him the wrong impression.

She was mainly here to get some information he had alluded to at the dance last night. George had claimed to have some "interesting theories" about the castle and the McGoverns but didn't want to elaborate with too many nosy people around. Carole had had no choice but to throw caution to the wind and shine all her charm on him until he succumbed and asked her out. He'd held out for a good sixteen minutes, and she'd almost started to wonder if she had lost her touch.

She let the heavy pub door close behind her and waved to Oliver, who was behind the bar. He winked at her and pointed toward a table by the window. Last night he had actively encouraged George's offer to give her lunch on their last full day in Scotland, promising that they could have the very best table.

George Ellis was in his mid-sixties, a little over six feet tall, with a full head of gray hair and a small beer belly that gave him a Father Christmas air. He wore a three-piece tweed suit and well-polished shoes—Carole appreciated that he'd put in some effort. He strode toward her with a smile on his face as if he were about to eat a dozen sugar-covered donuts.

"My dear Carole—I'm thrilled we are meeting again so soon. I hope you slept well. What can I get you to drink?" His warm hand enveloped her smaller one, and he squeezed. "I'm really looking forward to hearing all about your exciting new business venture with your niece. Let's order first, shall we?"

The menu was on a chalkboard over the fireplace, where a newly lit fire crackled pleasantly. "I'll have the winter vegetable soup, please, Oliver," said Carole, looking forward to the homemade roll and butter that would accompany it. "And a sparkling water."

"Fish-and-chips for me, young man, and a pint of your finest local ale."

They settled back in their chairs and Carole began her subtle interrogation. "Terrible about Euan McGovern, isn't it? Did you know him? I thought you mentioned at the dance that you did."

George laced his fingers together and rested his hands on his belly. "He wasn't one of us, and he didn't want to be. Looked down on everyone in the village. In time, we all began to think that things were not all they seemed to be."

"What do you mean?"

George leaned in, and Carole did too.

"Well, I was talking to Alexandra Pattern—do you know her? She works at that big auction house in Edinburgh. I met her at one of Jane's parties a couple of years ago." Carole nodded encouragingly, and

George continued. "Alexandra told me that Euan didn't want to sell the castle, even though it has been quietly on the market for some time."

"The castle is being sold? But there's no sign up to say it's for sale."

"I'm not meant to say. It's all very hush-hush, but it's been on the market for about a year. These big, expensive properties are not always easy to sell. I decided to go and see him and smooth things out, as I had a potential viewing for the place. I thought I'd give him a chance to clean it up a bit. It was a good opportunity to tell him how hard we'd been working to generate interest from buyers. It's on for a lot of money, and that means a lot of commission."

"And what did Euan say?"

"He was a real brute about it, shoving me out the door when I told him that people wanted to view the castle. Told me to take it off the market right away if I was going to go around gossiping with Alexandra about things that didn't concern her. Said she was 'constantly stirring the cauldron.'"

"Euan didn't like her?" Carole coaxed.

"I got the impression that it was more than that. As if she was into his business and he wanted her out of it. Or maybe they'd done business together before, and it had gone badly."

"And then what happened?" said Carole.

"I said that we couldn't sell it anyway without the deeds, and I needed him to find them. Then Euan got even more annoyed and bit my head off. It was all most odd—"

Carole was so engrossed, she hadn't noticed India approaching the table with their food. She flinched as the plates came crashing down, soup sloshing over the edge of her bowl.

"I'm so sorry. I'm horribly clumsy," India said, reaching for the tea towel on her shoulder to mop up the mess. She glared at George, but he seemed unaware of how much his words had upset her, although he looked miffed that some of his chips had fallen to the floor.

"India, dear, are you all right? You look..."

"I'm fine. Fine." But India was still looking daggers at George. Carole rose and took her arm; she was shaking. "Can we find you somewhere quiet to sit down? I think it's too soon for you to be working, don't you?"

Oliver had raced around the end of the bar and was now at India's other side, nodding, with a hand on her elbow. "I did say," he murmured, as if they had already had this discussion.

"I'll be right back," Carole said to George as she walked India away.

"I need to keep busy," India said as they led her toward a door at the side of the bar marked *STAFF*. She glanced back over her shoulder to glare at George once more.

"Not a fan?" asked Carole as they entered a small corridor leading to a flight of stairs. "Oliver, you get back to the bar; I'll make India a cup of tea. Tell George I'll be a little while. If he has to get back to his office, I'll understand." She had extracted a key piece of information from him: it sounded as if Euan had been attempting to sell Fawside Castle before he was murdered, and Alexandra had been interfering. And India seemed as if she needed help.

Carole settled India on an old, worn-out sofa in the flat above the bar and perched on the arm. "Are you going to tell me what all that was about?"

"I'm fine." India tugged her cardigan sleeves over her hands and then wrapped her arms around herself.

"It doesn't look that way to me." Carole stood and made to leave. "Talk to someone, India—you mustn't let it all simmer. Talk to Oliver, or a friend." She shook her head. "Child, grief needs a release. If you don't want to talk, then play out the pain in your music. Write it down, draw it out . . . but find a way to give your heart the space to work through the loss."

India nodded, looking out the window at the snow-laden clouds.

"I thought my dad just wanted to sell this pub because he'd found out about Oliver and me. I didn't think he would sell *everything*. He's always told me that the castle would come to me. That it was my legacy."

"Is that why you were so shocked downstairs? You overheard what George said?"

India nodded.

"Do you know what sort of business relationship Alexandra and Euan had? George mentioned that they worked together," Carole probed cautiously. "Or was it something else?"

India laughed. "You want to know if they were sleeping together. My father could be a monster, but he was a very good-looking man for his age. All those women—Jane, Alexandra... they thought they could change him and live in a fairy-tale castle." She scoffed. "Until he had his claws into them, and then the manipulation started."

Carole wanted to ask more but feared it was too soon after Euan's death.

"I think I'll go and lie down," whispered India, standing up. She drifted out of the room.

Carole pulled out her phone and messaged Freya: *Have you heard how Alexandra is doing in the hospital? Can we find a way to get to her? I have a feeling she's the key to everything.*

She hurried back down to the table, where George had almost finished his fish-and-chips. She beamed at him and he thought she was enjoying his company, but that wasn't it—Carole was proud of herself and her talent for investigation.

32

Freya
Monday, February 12, 2 p.m.

"Alexandra Pattern is dead?" I repeated Phil's statement back to him. It was not what I had expected to hear when he'd asked us all to meet him in the hotel sitting room.

I slumped back into the large tartan armchair and pulled my curls back into a bun. I'd been so sure Alexandra was the key to everything. Perhaps she was, but we wouldn't get any answers from her now.

Carole saw my despondency. "You'll get to the bottom of all this, I'm certain of it," she said sympathetically. "Maybe Sky just needs to hack into Detective Rodgers's computer and see what he knows?"

"No, Sky will not be doing that," said Phil.

Sky shrugged, as if it wasn't out of the question and she didn't need Phil's permission. I gave her a "please don't" look.

"Rodgers told me his theory. Alexandra died two hours ago, from poisoning, he believes," said Phil, picking up his coffee. "And Bella is being released in a couple of hours. Given the timeline, Rodgers thinks Euan poisoned Alexandra when she visited him on Wednesday. As the poison is slow-acting, they're suggesting Alexandra hit him over the head and killed him, stole the Scottish silver, and then fled via the cellar entrance."

"It all sounds very convenient, doesn't it?" Carole sounded as confused as I felt. "And if Euan was being blackmailed, why keep the letters in a box with the paintings? Why didn't he burn them? They're very incriminating, aren't they?"

"I agree," I replied, but I couldn't work out an alternative scenario.

"Rodgers knows what he's doing," Phil said. "I don't have access to the whole investigation, but it's been thorough and swift . . . I like him. Bella is about to be released, and we have the forged paintings and other items from the attic. And the forger, Cedric James, is already in prison. The Lockwood Agency has completed the case, in my book." He leaned forward and placed his elbows on his knees. "I think it's time you all went home—and take Bella with you. She seems to be getting into a lot of trouble up here."

I frowned. "I'm not convinced we have found out who Euan's murderer is or who hit Bella over the head . . . Euan or Alexandra? But why would they attack Bella?"

"Wrong place, wrong time?" said Carole.

We all watched the roaring fire.

Carole nudged me. "Let's go and get Bella."

Sky frowned at Phil as he picked up the cafetiere to top up his cup. "How can you sleep at night if you drink coffee all day long?"

"It's only early afternoon," he replied, taking a sip. "This is important fuel."

Sky and I had peppermint tea, but she was mainly scoffing shortbread like it was about to cease to exist. "I've never really liked this stuff before." She waved around a finger of biscuit. "But maybe it only tastes good on this side of the border? You two don't want any, do you?" It was clearly a rhetorical question; all the available shortbread was on her plate.

"At least Rodgers must see that Bella didn't have anything to do with Alexandra's death. She was in custody at the time," I said to Phil.

"Well, not quite, because he thinks she was poisoned with something slow-acting on the same night Bella was there," he said patiently. "But Bella had no motive to murder Alexandra, so they're favoring other possibilities. Although there's always the chance..."

I glared at him and he winked back. He was winding me up. Carole was watching us, and she chuckled. I changed the subject. "I think we're missing something but I'm more than happy that Bella's off the hook."

Sky nodded. "I agree. I'll dig into Alexandra's background more and see what I can find. There wasn't much the first time I looked. Not married, no kids, lived alone. Oh, but the one other thing I did find out was that the man killed in the car with Cedric James was his son." Sky pulled out her phone and said, "From reading the newspaper reports, he was a forty-eight-year-old man named Christopher James. The crash was just outside Glasgow."

"How is this all connected?" I looked between them.

"More tea will help with cognition." Carole grabbed a passing waiter and ordered a fresh pot, with Sky chipping in that more shortbread would also be welcome.

"We really needed to speak to Alexandra, didn't we?" sighed Carole once the waiter had gone. "But she kept slipping through our fingers. Was she blackmailing Euan because she believed he was an impostor? Sky, let's try and get to the bottom of who he really was. And do we think that India knew?"

As soon as the waiter returned, Sky went in for the shortbread again. I played mother and picked up the teapot. "Perhaps she had an accomplice? Someone who helped her move Euan's body and also knew the same secrets that she did?"

"I think that is a definite possibility," replied Carole. "What about George? He seemed to know a lot about Alexandra and the castle. Maybe he tried to befriend me as a way of learning what we knew?"

"I'll look into him too," said Sky, tapping away on her laptop with one hand and holding a piece of shortbread in the other. We sat in silence as she worked, and then she froze. "This is just some really weird stuff."

"What is?" Carole and I said in unison.

"We've got it all wrong..." Sky looked up at me. "Euan McGovern doesn't own the castle at all..." She was shaking her head. "Do you think Bella knew? Does India know?"

"Know what?" We spoke simultaneously again.

"The castle belongs to *Cedric James* McGovern," said Sky. She started tapping again, her shortbread forgotten. "He legally changed his middle name, which was James, to his last name fourteen years ago—but he didn't change the name on the castle deeds. So... now we need to check who owns the pub..."

"You are so utterly clever, aren't you, darling," purred Carole. Then she froze. "And I'll tell you who probably did know... George the estate agent. I think I'll give him a little call."

"The man we met at the prison didn't seem like the laird of a castle. A convicted forger and driver of getaway cars," said Phil. "Then again, I suppose I don't know what a laird should look like."

"This changes things, doesn't it?" I said. "Do we think Cedric is Euan's father? And it ties up with what happened to Christopher McGovern. He died six years ago, and then Euan came back to run the castle. But Cedric was in prison, and perhaps it wasn't the real Euan who came to claim the castle and the title. Cedric told us that he had two sons. He told us that they were both 'good for nothing' and that they never spoke. And if the blackmailer is to be believed, then it's a fake Euan McGovern who was murdered... So where is the *real* Euan McGovern?" I turned to Sky. "Can you see if there is any documented connection? We need to put together a family tree. Remember what Cedric said—that Bella was asking for a DNA test? Did she believe that Cedric and Euan were related?"

Carole and Sky nodded, but Phil sighed. "We need to talk to Bella about the whole DNA thing and get back to the prison to see Cedric."

He checked his watch; Bella would be getting out soon. "We should leave."

I rose and grabbed my bag. "I think I'll go on my own this time. Even though you and Bella seem to have established a cease-fire, I'm sure I'll get more out of her by myself." I wasn't going to wait for him to object. I needed to spend some time with Bella.

"What about me?" asked Carole as I hurried away.

I turned back. "You stay with Sky and try and get to the bottom of how everyone's connected. Perhaps you could give India a call—ask her if she knew Cedric? After all, she did ask us to look into her father's death."

I could see Carole struggling with the need to be in several places at the same time, but she nodded. "I hope Bella has some answers."

33

Monday, February 12, 3:30 p.m.

It took me over an hour to get to the police station in Edinburgh, and there was a part of me that worried Bella might already have left and disappeared. As it was, I found her sitting on the wall doom-scrolling on her pink phone. A smile crossed her face when she saw me.

I pulled up and put down my window. "Bella?" Her gaze softened. "Want a lift?"

She climbed into the passenger seat and hugged her arms around herself. "I need you to take me somewhere."

"Okay?"

She slumped back in the seat. "Cells... police... I haven't slept."

"I can drive you back to the hotel—we can..." I didn't want to force her to come back with us to Suffolk, but I was uneasy about leaving her anywhere. "There's still an empty bedroom above the shop you can have for as long as you need. I'm sure Sky would like the company."

Bella rolled her head toward me and fixed her tired gaze on me. "I'm not leaving here until I have the answers I came looking for. I haven't gotten to the bottom of what Arthur was trying to show me. So, can you drive me to Leith?" Without waiting for my answer, she plucked my phone from its holder and tapped in the address. "There."

She pointed to the direction. There were deep bags under her eyes, and her wrists had red marks around them where the handcuffs had dug in.

I told Bella that we now believed that Cedric James McGovern owned the castle and that he was the laird. "Do you believe that Cedric James was your grandfather? You asked him for a DNA test. We now know he had two sons . . . Euan and Christopher McGovern. Do you think one of them was your father?" I tried to sound as gentle as possible because Christopher died over six years ago and we had no idea where the real Euan McGovern was.

"I don't know anything anymore. I asked Cedric for a DNA test because I wanted proof that he was my grandfather, but he wouldn't give it to me. My father left when I was little, and I didn't see him much . . . I just wanted to know where he was. My mum told me that he was into dodgy art and antiques, so I asked Arthur for help. Last time I talked to Arthur, it sounded like he had the answers I needed but wouldn't tell me—he just said he had written it down. Then he was killed, and you and Carole inherited everything. Arthur was methodical and diligent . . . he would have written down whatever he had found out."

"Why didn't you tell us?"

She shook her head. "Tell new people who I don't know that my father's side were most likely criminals? I don't think so. That's the sort of information people can hold over a person."

"But now there's a bigger question, isn't there? If the blackmail letters are right, then the man who was murdered last week was not the real Euan McGovern."

"I researched everything I could about the castle before I made the appointment with the person I thought was Euan." She dragged in a long breath. "Can I tell you something?" I nodded, not wanting to say anything that would make her stop talking. "If my father was the real Euan McGovern but Arthur knew that there was an impostor in his place, then I can see why Arthur tried to keep me away. And on the flip side, even if Arthur didn't know about the deception, he was trying to get me to leave the black market, not get more embedded. And everyone in the McGovern family seems to be dodgy in some way. I mean, Cedric is in prison. But I just wanted to know why my father had left . . ." Her small, hushed voice made her sound utterly worn down by circumstances beyond her control.

"Then let's find out. Once and for all."

"You would do that for me? Even after I locked you in a vault?"

"Are you planning on locking me away again?" I joked.

She motioned between us. "It's not me you have to worry about! That FBI idiot is quite protective of you, so maybe he'll lock you up so you don't do anything even slightly dangerous."

"We want to help you. You're our friend, and that's what friends do for each other. I lost my father when I was twelve, so Arthur was like a father figure to me . . ."

"Me too," Bella whispered, looking down at her chipped nail polish. "And now he's gone."

"I'm quite sure Arthur wanted us all working together. And I need your help. There are three more journals that Arthur left me." I twisted the key in the ignition, and the engine purred to life. I started to follow the directions on my phone.

"Phil won't like it. He doesn't want me involved with your agency."

I shook my head. "He doesn't know you, but he's trying to keep a more open mind."

"He's trying for your sake."

"Maybe, but sometimes that's all we get. Try to sleep. I'll let you know when we're in Leith."

"I've worked out one of Arthur's clues," said Bella. There was a glint in her eye that told me we were about to go somewhere Phil would certainly not approve of.

Leith was fast becoming one of my favorite areas of Edinburgh. When we got out of the car, Bella took in a restorative lungful of air beside me, making me think that she felt the same.

After a five-minute walk we stood with our backs to the docks, looking up at a red-brick warehouse conversion with a café on the ground floor.

"They have great coffee. Let's get some, then we'll go inside."

We ordered coffee to go and then Bella led me to a door between two shops.

"You lived here?" I asked, remembering that Bella had lived in Edinburgh for quite a while with her ex Chris Prince.

There was a keypad beside the door. She tapped a number in. "Yes—I used to live in this building. I loved it here. When I got out of the police station, I called the building manager and told him that I needed the code to check for post that might have still been sent here. Andy always had a soft spot for me. You know, it was Arthur who told me there was a flat for rent. Chris moved in not long after the Copthorn Manor case was solved. You can get the tram into the center. Chris and I used to do that... But all of that fell apart." Her brow furrowed.

I reached out and patted her arm until she flinched away. She wasn't one for affection, but the vulnerability in her slumped shoulders made me think she needed someone to lean on. "In all honesty," I said, because utter honesty with Bella was the only way to build trust with her, "he wasn't a great choice. But we've all made those mistakes. I made mine by marrying someone else after the man I truly loved died."

Bella pushed open the door and we stepped into a small hallway with post boxes along one side, a lift, and stairs. "It's only one flight, and I don't like lifts," she said, striding up the stairs without looking back.

I caught up with her. "So we're going to your old flat?"

Bella tried the handle on a navy-blue door. "Nope. Do you remember what Arthur wrote at the top of the page with the paintings on?"

"'Man Alive'?" I didn't understand where this was going.

"While they were holding me at the station, that detective mentioned my old address here. Chris and I lived at number four." She pointed across the corridor. "Arthur and I used to go to a bingo hall not far from here. He always said that it was a place where we wouldn't be noticed, but I suspect he just wanted an excuse to play. He found it charming that many years earlier, when I was little, I used to go along with my gran every Friday night to the bingo while my mum was working at the restaurant. We always met at my flat before heading off together, so he'd greet me with the bingo call: 'Knock at the Door—number four.' I know all the rhymes used for the numbers now. Do you have that lock-picking kit in your handbag?"

The answer came to me. "Man Alive—number five. And Arthur knew that 'number five' would mean something to you. He trusted you would put the pieces together." I opened my bag and pulled out the roll of locksmith's picks. "What's behind this door, Bella? And are you sure there's no one home?"

"No one is home but . . ." She tilted her head at the door. "This might take a minute. There are four locks here. A bit excessive for an apartment block like this, isn't it?"

"Someone wants to make sure the apartment isn't broken into." The locks looked new.

Bella smirked. "I haven't met a door I couldn't get into."

She had plucked the picks from my hand and placed them in the first lock. "The security was bad here . . ." Soon we heard the first lock click open. "Arthur's brain was always working overtime, always seeing how things would play out. He saw the small details. Just like you do." I watched as Bella skillfully opened one lock after the other.

She pushed the door open and stale, dust-clogged air reached my nose. "I think he knew Euan was an impostor and didn't want me getting involved."

I understood what she was getting at. "He left the journals for us and knew we would come looking sooner or later. He didn't want you on your own, Bella." I reached out again. "You're not on your own." I would say it as often and in as many ways as possible until she believed it.

"The most infuriating thing is that I think Chris was the one trafficking the art to Boston. Moving art, antiques, and antiquities isn't easy. It takes a network, and Chris had one. Alexandra could help forge the documents, but I've seen nothing to suggest she had the expertise to fool border control."

"Chris Prince, your ex? He was in on this too?"

Bella told me about Arthur finding flat number 4 for her, and how Chris had later moved himself in.

"... At least he's in prison now." Her eyes clouded and she shook her head, trying to regain the control she craved so much. She knew that Chris was a piece of work, but the realization that her ex had been using her from the very start was clearly a whole new level of pain.

I opened my mouth to say something, but she continued, "You know, one of the very first times I met Arthur was on a train to Edinburgh. We sat next to each other in first class and realized we were both going to attend an auction the next day. But really, I wasn't—I was only there to see who bought some of the jewelery. Then I planned to steal it."

"Let me guess: you stole the jewelery as it was being sent to the new owner, and Arthur was put on the case by the insurance company to find it."

"Yes, and he did. We had a great chat, and I gave up a few of the jewels . . . Arthur was always so interested in everyone, wasn't he? Got you talking about yourself without realizing you were telling him everything. Just like Carole." She smiled wryly. "Arthur had been at the auction to view a Raeburn portrait of a young boy. I told him that it was strange because my mother had had the same painting on her wall, and it had been given to her by my grandfather. Arthur was shocked. I explained it was one of the only heirlooms I'd had left when she died, but I'd had no money and so I had tried to sell it . . . and that was when I'd found out it was a fake."

"And the one at the auction house?"

"Also a fake, according to Arthur. This was six years ago. Arthur told whoever needed to know, and the painting was withdrawn. Anyway, that's how all this started, our friendship . . . me looking for my family, and Arthur promising to help. When I lived here, I never saw anyone go in and out of this flat. The estate agent told me the owner lived in Australia or New Zealand. But the layout is the same as my old flat."

We stepped inside, into a narrow hallway. Bella reached for an internal door and smiled broadly at me. "Ready to see what's really in here?"

"Nothing like the hunt, is there?" I replied as she turned the handle and pushed the door open.

34

Monday, February 12, 4:30 p.m.

The mystery Leith property was a small, barely furnished two-bedroom flat with high ceilings and three large windows in the living room overlooking the docks. The main living area had a dark brown leather three-piece sofa and chairs, a coffee table, and a bookcase. I sneezed as dust motes danced in the afternoon sunlight; they covered every surface.

I stood in front of the bookcase and ran my fingers over a large collection of old Griffin & Thompson auction catalogues. I wiped the smudge of dirt on my jeans before pulling one out and opening it.

"Alexandra Pattern worked at Griffin & Thompson. There were auction catalogue cuttings stuck to the backs of the forged paintings in the Fawside Castle attic. It can't all be a coincidence," I said to Bella, who was hovering over my shoulder.

"Let's work backward." She plucked the catalogue out of my hands. "The dead man you found was calling himself Euan McGovern, and he started living at Fawside Castle around six years ago. I didn't tell the police about the blackmail letters in the attic, but I'm sure they have them by now and are running a DNA test on the dead man. Around the same time impostor Euan moved into the castle, Cedric was sent to prison, and Christopher McGovern was killed in a car crash. And Alexandra Pattern started working at the auction house."

"It's not a coincidence." I pulled out another catalogue.

"From what I learned, when Euan McGovern left boarding school at eighteen, he also left Scotland—which would make it easy for someone else to assume his identity, wouldn't it?"

"Do you think Cedric knows?"

Bella shrugged. "He didn't say anything to me about his sons when I went to see him. If he didn't want a DNA test because he was worried I would check it against the dead man, that means he did know. Maybe he's the one who placed an impostor there to look after the place while he was inside?"

I scanned the bookcase. "These old catalogues were used to establish provenance for the forgeries. And by the looks of this place, they've been here quite some time."

Bella pointed to the floor, where footprints other than our own were imprinted in the dust. "Someone has been here more recently than six years ago. If Euan and Alexandra were keeping the forgery ring alive, they probably came here to match the sales in here to the fake paintings."

"Do we think Cedric owns this flat?" I picked up another old catalogue. "These really go back a long way." I flicked through black-and-white pages that looked ready to come apart in my hands. "This one's from the sixties. How long do you think this has been going on?"

There was no reply. Bella was opening another door off the small entrance hall and I jogged a couple of steps to follow her.

"What are we looking at?" I asked.

She was standing in front of two easels holding two identical paintings. There were eight more paintings on the floor.

"We are looking at the base for the forgery operation. This is his art studio," Bella whispered, even though there was no one around to hear us. She pulled out her phone and started taking photos of the paintings—mainly landscapes in a Victorian style. I recognized a few from Arthur's journal, and I was quite sure that was why Bella was taking photos of them all.

I placed a hand on her shoulder. "Shall we go and sit in the kitchen? Drink our coffee, and you can tell me how this all started?"

Bella paused as if considering how much she was willing to tell me, then slowly nodded. "Sure." We went back into the open-plan kitchen and sitting room, where she headed directly to the window and stared out over the docks.

"When I was clearing out my mum's flat after she died, I discovered an old tenancy agreement from the very first place we lived after I was born. It was in the name Lester White. In another drawer, there were a couple of letters to Frank Sargent. For a long time, I thought one of those names belonged to my father. Then, as you know, I asked Arthur for his help."

"Ah yes, and then you got Sky to investigate?"

"It was very convenient of you to employ a hacker. She is bloody brilliant at her job, you know. She needs a pay rise." She watched a couple of dog-walkers stop and chat. "What Sky found was my grandfather, Cedric James, in prison. He was the one who had been helping my mother out twenty years ago but she had never told me."

"And you found impostor Euan through Alexandra Pattern. Did you suspect that the real Euan was your father when you made an appointment to see him?"

"No, I just thought it was a lead. That . . . maybe . . . he knew my real father. I didn't know that Cedric owned the castle or anything like that. If I had, I would have showed up to the castle as myself and asked some questions. But then I turned up and nearly got killed . . ." Bella paused and slumped against the window frame. "What did Alexandra say? Because she's up to her neck in this."

"We didn't... couldn't ask."

"Why? Has she been arrested?"

"She was... but she died in hospital. Of poisoning. The police think that she killed the man who was impersonating Euan. That they were working together and perhaps romantically involved, and at some point she started blackmailing him. He might have asked her over the night you were arriving and given her the poison. He definitely wasn't the type of man who would deal lightly with an opponent. An impostor has a lot to lose."

Bella shook her head, face creased in disbelief. "I don't understand... I never saw her at the castle that night."

I explained about the hidden passageway and camera.

"That's it? They killed each other?" She rested her forehead against the window, defeated. "That can't be right."

"It's all rather convenient," I admitted.

Bella lifted her head and let her gaze drift around the room until she paused, looking at the floor. "The dust..." She ran back into the art studio and opened the wardrobe. It was empty.

I followed where she had been looking and saw what we had missed the first time—other footprints in the dust leading to the wardrobe, and inside, there were indentations where a long object must have been stored until quite recently. "I think there were paintings stored in here. And I think the ones in the castle attic might have come from here... Dolores said paintings were moved up to the attic when Christopher McGovern died, because they were his paintings. We thought she meant the paintings were already in the castle when he died. But what if they were always stored here?" I asked.

"You think someone came and took them from here and placed them in the castle? Why? And who would do that? Impostor Euan?" It would make sense that Cedric had a small, inconspicuous flat in Edinburgh. Why move the paintings to where they could easily be associated with the McGoverns?

Then it hit me. "It's more likely that someone has been setting the scene. Surely there was a spare key to this flat, and maybe the address was written down somewhere in the castle. Cedric has been away for six years. If in that time someone uncovered the location of this flat and what was hidden here . . . Taking items from here to the castle would give the police something to find . . . paintings, the blackmail letters . . . and then there was a hidden camera showing Alexandra coming and going, with a time stamp. Maybe everything is too convenient. A long-standing forgery ring wouldn't be that sloppy."

"The only thing that they didn't account for was me turning up that night," said Bella. "And I looked like Alexandra—I wore a wig that matched her hairstyle. It was a stupid decision, but if there were cameras, I wanted people to confuse me with her."

I put my empty coffee cup down on the kitchen counter. "If it was all staged, it can't have been done the night of the murder, could it?"

"I'm not sure. But it has to be someone who knew the castle well. The attic wasn't easy to find," she replied. "We need to question them all again, try and get someone to slip up. It would be good if we could get them all together and . . ." She paused as she saw my smile. "What?"

"You'll stick around and help?" I was thrilled, but I needed to temper my excitement, because it could make her think twice.

"You don't trust that I would?" The deep frown across her forehead gave away her disappointment in me.

"No, that's not . . ." I stepped toward her, not knowing what I should say. "I do . . . it's just—" *You never seem to want to fully commit to the Lockwood Agency . . . to us.*

Bella huffed as if she knew what I was thinking. "Don't worry, Phil gave me no choice." When I frowned in confusion, she continued,

"He's got his hooks into me now after helping me get a solicitor. Said I'm to be his informant." She sighed. "So, for now I'm along for the ride . . . until I can get myself out of his clutches. Unlike you, it's not where I want to be."

My cheeks started to heat. "I never said . . ." This was all going horribly wrong.

She held up her hands in surrender. "I know, I know, it's purely professional. Honestly, I wish I'd never gotten involved with all of you last year. It's become nothing but trouble."

"Bella, I want you to be part of the team, but I don't want you working for the agency out of obligation." Phil had a way of totally messing up where Bella was concerned.

"I don't need a *team* of people that don't trust me. I'm good on my own. And the one time I did let someone . . ."

Annoyance prickled inside me. "Come on, Bella. You can't let Chris bloody Prince stop you from ever trusting anyone again. Maybe take a break from dating if you want, but that doesn't mean you isolate yourself from *everyone*. You were right when you said that you saved us back in Jordan—you did. You told yourself that you were only helping us because of the deal we struck to give you access to Arthur's journal, but you helped us long before that too. And now we can try and repay the favor. Let us all help you find your father."

"You never thought that I killed that guy impersonating Euan, then?" There was a challenging glint in her eye.

"Never. Carole and Sky never did either. We were worried about you."

"So, who's looking after the shop?"

I winced. "Sky left the shop in Agatha's hands."

"God help those customers."

We both laughed. "I'm quite sure my profits are going to go up considerably. No one is getting out of that shop without buying something."

We let the laughter settle and looked at each other.

"We should get back to the hotel before Phil sends out a search party for us ... or maybe just for you ..."

"You and Carole need to stop winding us both up."

"Perhaps you should both stop looking at each other the way you do. You think the FBI just goes around handing out consultancy opportunities to anyone? And before you say it, I know you're more than capable, and it's a good way for Phil to get all the information Arthur left you no matter how valuable they are turning out to be. He definitely wants more." When I opened my mouth to protest, she continued. "Even if he hasn't said anything ... yet."

I needed to change the subject as the image of Phil and me in the castle cellar came rushing back. "Let's photograph everything in here before we leave." I pulled out my phone and entered the studio to start taking photos.

Bella leaned against the door frame, taking in the scene before us. "Someone's been lying from the beginning, haven't they? Searching for my family only turned up a forger and a thief in prison who got his son, Christopher, killed when he was fleeing a robbery in Glasgow. And an impostor laird who was killed before I even had a chance to talk to him." She rubbed her forehead, and I realized we needed to leave so that she could get some sleep. "I wonder who India really is. I thought for a moment that I had found a half-sister. But does she really know who the dead man was?"

Poor Bella—she had allowed herself to believe, just for a moment, that she might not be alone anymore. Putting my phone away, I pulled her into a hug, and she relaxed against me. I could feel the fight leaving her.

"I thought I might die," she whispered. "While I was in that holiday rental with a concussion. And no one would find my body for days, or weeks ..." Her voice cracked, and I squeezed her tighter as my heart ached. "It's been a bloody terrible week."

"I know." I kept my voice low and soothing. "Let's get back to the hotel and you can have a nice long, hot bath. And sleep. Then we're going to find out who the dead man was, who killed him." I pulled back from her and rubbed her arms, trying to bring warmth back into her cheeks.

Bella stepped back. "A bath sounds amazing." She gave her armpits a sniff and wrinkled her nose at the sour stench. "Wait, you let me walk around smelling like this? You let me walk into that café!"

I chuckled as she fled toward the front door. "I didn't notice until I hugged you, and it's not that bad."

"And here I was thinking you might be friend material," Bella called over her shoulder, but she couldn't hide the smile that transformed her entire face. Guess she really had needed that hug after all.

35

Monday, February 12, 6 p.m.

"And here we are, all together again!" said Carole as we settled around the sitting-room fire at Kelmore House Hotel.

But we weren't, not really.

Phil and Bella were sitting as far away from each other as possible, not making eye contact. She was clearly not happy about being coerced into working as his informant, and I was going to have to talk to him about that—there were better ways of getting Bella to help us. *Making* her do it wasn't going to work. Sky seemed hurt that Bella could have called her for help while she was on the run after the attack at the castle, but didn't. Carole was trying hard to bring everyone together with tales of her time in Scotland with Arthur, but for once it seemed forced—even she couldn't hold all of us together on her own.

And yet, after spending time with Bella in the Leith flat, I felt I understood her better than ever before. She was just like me in my early twenties—sure, she worked on the other side of the tracks, making money from the black market, and I had earned my wage trying to bring it down. But that world had broken both our hearts. The only difference was that I'd had Carole.

My gaze rested on Bella as she held her coffee cup to her lips and watched the flames flicker in the hearth. Snow fluttered down outside the window. She was hurt and lost and determined to fight through it alone. But Carole had never allowed me to shut her out, and that had taught me that sometimes all you can do is show up and offer a hand, over and over again. I didn't want Bella to follow the path I had—allowing my pain to dictate my actions. Getting married and pregnant had seemed to be the only option for me then. I very much doubted Bella would choose the same route, but the direction she was going in was guided by fear, not hope. And I wanted more for her. I was determined to try to make her see that.

The black-market art and antiques world was attached to almost every other criminal activity. Every spoke of the criminal underworld was connected to the same wheel. Our little group, sitting around a fire while winter lashed the countryside around us, could change so much for the better if we could only learn how to pull together and combine our skills. But first, we needed to build some trust.

"Bella, maybe you should tell everyone what you've told me."

"It's my business. Not theirs."

My theory was that after Bella had lost Chris last year, it seemed to have pushed her over an emotional ledge, making her seek a lasting connection. Did she really believe that finding her biological father would give her that?

"And Chris?" I coaxed. Inwardly I was worried; maybe I was wrong to make her tell everyone.

She huffed and looked at Phil, and I understood that she feared his judgment.

"All right, then—why don't I fill everyone in?" I asked. She shrugged in reply.

It didn't take long to tell everyone what we had found in the flat and who Bella was searching for. Silence was thick in the air after I had finished, but there was nothing but empathy in everyone's eyes. I was about to say I was going to my room to rest and regroup, and suggest that we let Bella do the same, when Phil's phone pinged. He took a moment to read the message and then looked over at me.

"Rodgers says they've identified the poison that killed Alexandra. It seems it was a type of mushroom that can take three or four days and up to a couple of weeks to kill a person. But there's more... The person impersonating Euan McGovern also had this poison in his system, but far less. They are assuming that he ingested it when he gave some to Alexandra, but... I'm afraid they're not ruling out the involvement of a third party. Euan never cooked, and there's no evidence that anything was cooked in the castle on the night he died." His gaze flicked to Bella.

"I thought I was off the hook?" Bella said.

"Death cap?" interrupted Sky, leaning forward. "Is that what they're saying?" I gave her a quizzical look. "What? I like watching murder mysteries. Also, just saying, that poison is a very female method of murder... very Agatha Christie."

"Alexandra had extensive liver and kidney damage. Not a nice way to go," said Phil.

"And this third party the detective mentioned is me, is it?" Bella stood up and pulled on her coat. "I didn't really like Alexandra, but I didn't want her dead. And I never even met the man impersonating Euan... I'm going to get some air."

"You can't go out in that, darling." Carole pointed to the window as snow pelted the glass.

"I'll go to my room, then. To sleep this fiasco away. Someone tell me if the police show up so I can make a run for it." She seemed to be trying to make a joke, but she wasn't smiling. Clearly she was barely holding on.

I nudged Phil with my foot as she walked away. "Do they think the case is all tied up? Or do they really still consider Bella a suspect?"

"I'm not sure," he replied.

"This is just getting worse," groaned Sky. "Bella had no motive to kill either of them."

"What we haven't found out is the real relationship between impostor Euan and Alexandra," said Phil, sitting forward and lowering his voice. "How they met. And where is the real Euan McGovern?"

"There's something else," said Carole. "We know that Alexandra was a regular guest at the castle—so regular that she struck up a friendship with India and knew about her 'secret' relationship with Oliver. I think we need to talk to Jane and see if she was in on the whole impostor thing. Also, how can we check whether or not India is a McGovern?"

"And remember the paintings in the attic. You think they were moved from the flat—so who did it? Who had keys?" asked Sky.

I shook my head. "It doesn't add up."

"And who put the blackmail letters in the attic? It can't have been Alexandra. Why would she incriminate herself?" said Carole.

Sky's mouth tipped up into a curl. "That's a genius setup, isn't it? And it would take some planning. The blackmailer and the victim look like they both killed each other, while the real murderer gets away with it. Maybe the *real* Euan came back into town and realized what was going on and took his revenge."

Carole and I slumped back in our chairs at the same time. Sky was right: it seemed like there were some massive holes in the police's theory.

We have no clue what went on that night.

Bella isn't in the clear.

But I couldn't say that out loud. I needed everyone to focus, not be as filled with despair as I was.

"I still think this is worth looking into, but goodness—if there's poison somewhere in the castle, we need to warn India and Jane," said Carole.

"Alexandra could have been poisoned anywhere. As could impostor Euan," replied Phil.

"Feels like we're at a dead end . . ." I whispered to myself.

"There is something else we haven't yet broached. India hated her father; he was planning to sell the pub out from under her boyfriend. A lot of things became easier for her after Euan's death and, according to this . . ." Sky showed us Alexandra's calendar on her laptop. "Alexandra had lunch with India three days before Bella was due to meet with fake Euan."

Phil huffed. "There are too many people who wanted that man dead, and yet it's only Bella and Alexandra who we can prove were there that night. Bella's tenuous association with the FBI will only go so far in fending off the police."

"Bella didn't do it," said Sky. "She's a victim of bad men. A survivor of them."

As is Sky.

As is India.

These women were so much stronger than the men who mistreated them realized.

"There's more bad news," said Carole. "We have rooms for tonight, but the hotel is full tomorrow night. They can't extend our booking any further because they're holding a three-day gin festival, and that means all the other local places are booked up too."

"I guess by tomorrow morning it's time to go home?" asked Sky, sighing. "We have found the paintings in the journal. The FBI contracted us to find out where the paintings came from, who the forger was—and we have. Bella would probably be better off coming back to Suffolk with us. Maybe it's best we get away from here."

But I couldn't let it go. I needed to find out who had killed impostor Euan and get to the heart of the forgery ring—I couldn't leave with so many unanswered questions.

"Did we miss something when we were inside the castle?" I wondered, scanning the faces around me. "There must be some evidence pointing toward who Cedric's sons were. Photographs showing the *real* Euan McGovern, and maybe documents indicating where he is now." I turned to Phil. "And we probably need to go and pay Cedric another visit too."

Phil pulled out his phone and started typing. "I'll see what I can do."

"When we first looked around, I remember mentioning that there were no family photos except for one on Euan's desk . . . I didn't think much of it at the time. But as the dead man pretended to be Euan McGovern, it's reason enough for him to hide all evidence that he was an impostor."

"I hope he hasn't destroyed everything," said Carole.

My phone rang in my pocket, and I saw a number I didn't recognize. "Hello?" I said.

"Freya? This is Oliver, India's boyfriend. There's been an accident."

36

Monday, February 12, 6:30 p.m.

The drive to Borders General Hospital took over an hour. There was a huge debate about who would go in which car, but in a moment of madness I decided we were all going together "as a team." Therefore, everyone was packed into Carole's car, and I was driving. Phil and Bella were sitting in the back seat together. At first, crackling tension filled the space between them. I had wanted Bella to stay at the hotel and rest but she'd refused to be left behind. As she pointed out, India might be her half-sister.

It only took one look in the rearview mirror to realize that I probably shouldn't have pushed it. Bella was slumped against the window, asleep but still frowning.

The snow was coming down in sheets and I checked on Bella in the mirror again, wishing she had stayed behind.

"What went on between you two?" Phil whispered as he leaned forward between the front seats.

"We talked . . . I understand a bit more about where she's been and what she's been through," I said, shifting in my seat. I felt uncomfortable talking about Bella while she was asleep.

"Okay, but you can't change her. You can't make her join a team she doesn't feel part of. It won't end well. She won't toe the line because she doesn't see one."

"And what about you? I hear you're forcing her to be an informant," I huffed out in objection, but his words stung because I knew he was right. I'd been trying to make Bella work like we did—attending video calls and updating everyone else weekly—but she was never going to be open like Carole or Sky.

"I'm not *making* her. I suggested it ... and it suits her better. She can still swim in the murky waters she so loves."

"She doesn't love it; she doesn't know any other way," I hissed back and then clamped my mouth shut, not willing to talk any more about Bella while she slept behind us.

Carole shot between the seats and poked Phil in the shoulder. "No one is changing anyone. We're being supportive, and you need to get on board or we stop the car and you can get out."

"Fine, but you've been warned."

~

There is a certain smell to hospitals that turns my stomach, and the sage-green paint on the walls makes my head hurt. I had spent time in hospital after my parents' death, Carole at my side the whole time, and I hated crossing the threshold of one again. It was one of the only places that could bring back the gut-wrenching pain of the burns on my hand and the grief in my heart.

Carole linked her arm through mine and squeezed. "It's not then." She knew what I was thinking.

"I know." But the twelve-year-old that still lived inside me didn't. "Let's find India and Oliver."

Bella was already at the reception desk, getting directions, and she waved us over.

As soon as India saw Carole walking down the corridor, she flung herself into my aunt's arms. I would have done exactly the same in her place. "Is it terrible of me to have wished so many times that Jane would leave my life and never come back? And then when I heard it might have happened, I just went numb."

Carole gave her a quick hug and then pulled back to look at her. "Why don't you tell us what happened? Oliver was very vague on the phone."

India gave Bella a small wave but didn't reach out to her, heading back to her boyfriend, who was leaning against the wall with his arms folded over his chest. He looked worried, even though he wasn't close to Jane. It made me wonder what was really going on.

"Jane said she had some business to do in Edinburgh . . . but the car crash was near here, and that's not on the way to Edinburgh at all, so I don't . . ." said India.

"She was probably going to see one of her many lovers," Oliver said between clenched teeth. "Although I thought that she was into that estate agent."

India shook her head. "No, that's not it. The doctors said that some of the cuts had come from the pottery in boxes on the back seat. I think she was taking some of her Wemyss Ware collection to someone. Probably moving her collection out of the castle."

"If the estate went through probate, all those items she had removed wouldn't be logged and valued," said Carole. We had been through the whole process when Arthur had left us the shop in his will.

Or if they were stolen, then she didn't want anyone to look too closely at them.

"How is she?"

"She'll live. No concussion or anything and she's in there ordering everyone around like always. She was just lucky that there was a truck following behind her when the car landed in a ditch—the driver saw and called the ambulance. Do you know that they had to cut her out of the car?" India shook her head.

"Do you want to see her?" asked Oliver, his tone impatient. "Because only one of you can go in at a time."

Everyone looked at me. "I mean, Carole is the one who knows her." Carole was shaking her head because she didn't like Jane one bit. "Okay... I'll go in, then."

Phil nodded in agreement and went to stand beside India; it was clear that he wanted to ask her some more questions. But India stepped away from him and met my eye. "I'll take you."

The ward held six beds and they were all occupied. India pointed me toward the far right corner by a snow-covered window. "She's fine," she said, before fleeing. I wondered why she had even bothered showing me in.

Jane was sitting up like a queen awaiting her audience. It was honestly impressive given what she had been through, but I felt a twinge of sympathy for the nurses who were tending to her.

"Hi, Jane, how are you?" I said in my quietest hospital voice.

"Oh, you're that friend of Carole's, aren't you?" she called as if I were ten feet away. "What are you doing here?" She arched her neck to see around me. "Where's everyone else?"

"We're only allowed in one at a time. What happened? Is there anything you need?"

"Oh, how very lovely of you to be thinking about me. The car is a total write-off. I'm so lucky that I wasn't too badly hurt, and that I had left my beautiful baby pups with a friend to look after. They were barking too much to stay in the pub with me. I was on the way back from settling the dogs... when I skidded on the road. Have you seen India?" She looked past me once more. "Has she left already?"

"She's outside." I walked over to sit on a chair next to the bed, making it clear that I wasn't ready to be dismissed just yet. "Did you hear about Alexandra Pattern?"

"What?" Her eyes snapped to mine. "What do you mean?" She gripped the white hospital sheet and then, when she saw me looking, stretched her fingers out and smoothed down its edge.

"She died last night, and the police believe that Euan poisoned her. Do you think Euan would do such a thing?"

Jane flicked her hand around as if she were swatting a fly away. "That irritating detective man was here, asking all his useless questions again, and I told him the same again. I. Know. Nothing. I was in Edinburgh when Euan died . . . If they think that Alex did it, then maybe she did. Maybe it was a lovers' tiff. He did like his lovers, but I'm the one in the castle."

"Other than Alexandra, was Euan seeing anyone else?"

She shrugged. "I don't care." The bitterness in her tone told me that wasn't the whole truth. "You know that not everything Euan did was aboveboard?" Her voice had dropped an octave. "There was some argument going on over a few paintings. Although they were like that, Alex and Euan, always squabbling like an old married couple. I never saw what paintings they were talking about, as Euan was always very careful to keep me out of it. But every so often I would see a wrapped one in his car. I asked about them, of course, but he just said he got them from auction and was selling them on to a client." She straightened herself on the pillows. "Are we allowed back into the castle yet? I would like to be in my own bed."

She was trying to change the subject, but I wasn't going to allow that. "Euan and Alexandra worked together? In what way?"

"Alex knew some guy called Chris Prince who could send anything anywhere. I never got too involved, but I know how expensive it is to keep the castle lights on. India thinks she's inheriting a fairy tale, but really, only a villain can make the sort of money you need to keep the place going." The venom in her words was biting.

Chris Prince! Jane had confirmed Bella's suspicions. Her ex-boyfriend was involved in trafficking the forged paintings to Boston. But Chris was in prison, so it couldn't have been him who killed Alexandra or Euan. And then there were the blackmail letters . . .

"Apart from Alexandra, do you know of anyone who had ever threatened Euan?" I still wanted to know who had sent the letters.

Jane met my eye. "India could have done it, you know. She could have walked from the village over the fields and bumped him off so that she could get her grubby mitts on the castle with her fake Prince Charming." It struck me once again how little grief Jane exhibited over her partner's death. She faked a yawn. "I'm ever so tired," she said, trying to smile.

"Then I'll leave you to rest." I returned the disingenuous smile.

The rest of the group stood silently waiting for me in the sterile corridor. They all looked at me with questioning eyes, but I didn't want to talk too candidly in front of India and Oliver—not after Jane had just suggested India could be the murderer.

It was Carole who broke the silence. "We should really get back to the hotel to pack and try and find somewhere to stay tomorrow night. India, dear, I do hope you're holding up all right."

"I am, but . . ." India looked up at Oliver, and he gave a nod of approval. "I was wondering if you would like to come and stay at the castle with me? There is a good chance that it will all be mine at some point, and there are so many antiques in the place. It would be good to get an idea of what they are all worth. And . . . well, there is another blizzard coming in, weather warnings are all over the news, the roads will be impassable come nighttime. Oliver wants to stay with me, but with the weather the way it is, it's best for him to stay above the pub on the nights he's working late. It's just, the castle is so big..." She reached out for Bella, who tried not to flinch from her touch. "I would welcome the company."

Carole placed a hand on her arm to stop her rambling. "We'll all stay. The only good thing about him..." She pointed her thumb over her shoulder at Phil. "Is that he has a gun and knows how to use it. It'll be like a lock-in at a pub, but far better."

Bella pointed to the muted TV down the hall in the waiting room, where a young reporter stood in front of a large window as snow battled against it. *Weather Warning* was flashing in the top right-hand corner.

"I don't think..." Phil began to protest, but Bella silenced him with a side-eye. Getting back into the castle again wasn't a bad idea. It would give us more time to talk to India about the paintings in the attic and the contents of the blackmail letters. Did she know that someone had thought the dead man wasn't really Euan McGovern?

"We would far rather stay with you for the night than at a hotel." Carole pulled India into a hug. "Perhaps there are still answers at the castle we could uncover. Find out what happened to your father once and for all."

India beamed at her.

The plan was set. "I'll message Sky, and we'll go back to the hotel and pick up our cases. Oliver, you drive India to the castle, and we'll meet you there. How does that sound?"

Everyone looked around, waiting for someone to object, but it seemed that for once we were all in agreement. We stepped into the lift and the others filed in around us. I told them what Jane had said and that Bella was right about Chris Prince.

"One night left to solve this case," said Carole. "We're just the team for the job."

"I think 'team' might be stretching it," Bella quipped.

Carole chuckled. "Maybe this is the perfect time for some team-building."

I couldn't suppress a smile. "I'm just hoping we all get through the night in one piece."

37

Monday, February 12, 9 p.m.

And that was how we all found ourselves back at Fawside Castle with another driving blizzard about to set in.

"Would you be in the will? If the dead man wasn't Euan McGovern, and your biological father was the *real* Euan McGovern?" Sky whispered to Bella as India led us around the corridors, allocating bedrooms to each of us. "And when are you going to talk to India about *maybe* being her sister?"

"This wasn't what I came here for . . . I was looking for my father, not a damn building." Bella cast her gaze around the long hallway on the second floor with their rooms down one side. "I think everything depends on Cedric. He owns the place, and he isn't dead. There's no inheritance while he's alive." She tightened her ponytail and rolled her shoulder. "I need to ask India if she knew Cedric. I've tried a few times to talk to her . . . tell her I might be her half-sister. But until I know the truth, I can't bring it up again. We need to keep it to ourselves."

I nodded. "I'll let everyone know to keep quiet."

Bella slumped against the door frame of her bedroom. "When I confronted Cedric in prison, he told me to keep away from his son. That he didn't even talk to him anymore, and that I needed to wait . . . but he never said what I was meant to wait *for*. If Cedric was laird and owned the castle, how could he not know that there was someone impersonating his son? Even being in prison, that's a hard thing to be kept in the dark about."

"What's your theory?" I asked, agreeing with her.

"Perhaps impostor Euan and Cedric were working together?" said Bella. Her voice was low and even but stopped abruptly as India came out of the room next door that she had just allocated Phil and walked toward us. ". . . Perhaps Cedric knew all along." Bella shrugged and entered her room.

Carole waved India over and I followed. "The beds have heated blankets, as the central heating is really bad," said India as I stepped into Carole's fridge-like room. There was an impressive four-poster bed covered in 1980s chintz, which made Carole beam with joy. "I'll leave you to get settled in. Shall we meet in the drawing room in half an hour?" She closed the door behind her.

"George told me Euan was livid when he found out that the castle was being sold," Carole said. "But the way he said it made me think that George believed Euan was the legal owner—and an estate agent would have checked that detail, wouldn't he?"

"You think he knew and didn't tell you?" I asked.

Carole frowned, deep in thought then replied, "He asked me to lunch right after I had introduced him to Phil. Perhaps he wanted to direct some blame the wrong way . . . toward Alexandra Pattern."

"And if he was Jane's lover, then I bet he told her everything he knew," I said. "Would Jane write poison-pen letters to her own boyfriend? Was impostor Euan paying for her silence?"

We frowned at each other.

"Get settled in, and I'll find some food for dinner."

I left Carole to unpack and started to head downstairs after dropping my suitcase off. Phil caught up with me. "About to start snooping?" There was a glimmer of mischief in his words.

"We don't snoop." I pretended to look shocked. "I'd like to remind you that we're here on *your* case, and India has given us permission to look around the house. She told Bella that she had no idea about the paintings in the attic or the silver in Euan's office."

"If you're not snooping, where are you going?" he asked.

"I was going to look for some food. With all the packing and getting here before the snow set in, no one has had time to eat."

We reached the kitchen. I scanned the store cupboard for pasta or something I could make in bulk for everyone for dinner.

I put a pot on the hob to boil some water as I tried to map out the McGovern family tree in my mind. "I've been wondering..." I stopped when I sensed Phil stepping up behind me.

"Yes?" His voice was warm and low.

Over my shoulder, I saw a glint in his eye, and my breath hitched.

Just be professional and concentrate on the case. The agency can't afford to lose the consultancy job if feelings get involved.

"It seems like a very... disjointed family, doesn't it? Cedric implied that he hated his son, Euan McGovern. What if he hated his biological son so much that while he was in prison, he put someone else in his place? India says she didn't know anything about Cedric. What if the dead impostor was her real father? Then it would make sense that she wasn't told of Cedric's existence." I tipped an entire bag of pasta into the boiling water. "If Jane found out about the impostor not being the real Euan McGovern, that would explain why she questioned India being owed an inheritance. Alexandra seemed to know quite a lot about all of this, and is now dead... It's the motive that we're missing." I had found some vegetables and started to chop an onion. "Because even the blackmail letters don't seem right." And that's when I remembered. "And what happened to the Scottish silver?"

Phil had picked up his phone and was scrolling through his emails. "I see it in the report here, but the police have had no leads. The silver could all have been melted down by now."

"If Alexandra stole the silver while she was here, where would she have taken it to be sold?" I thought back to my antique-hunting days with Arthur. "I need to get Sky to dig more into Alexandra's associates. I'm assuming that by now the police have searched Alexandra's home and other places she might have stored it. Bella says that she was quite sure it looked a lot like the silver from Arthur's journals. If Euan's and Alexandra's murders are linked but they didn't kill each other . . . then why did the murderer take the silver that night?"

"The Scottish silver is the key." Phil was leaning against the kitchen counter.

I pushed a box of mushrooms over to him. "Chop."

Phil picked up a knife and then paused. "I'm not sure adding mushrooms is a good idea."

I started at the box. "Good point. Didn't the police take all the food from the fridge to examine it? So where did all of this come from?"

"Maybe India stocked the kitchen before we arrived?" His phone pinged. "Sky says she already checked all the pawnshops and dealers for the silver and they're a dead end."

"There is another angle we have to consider. Cedric James could have had a motive for killing both Euan and Alexandra. What if Cedric allowed Euan to live in the castle and look after things, and then Euan and Alexandra found a way to make some more money selling off Cedric's forgeries behind his back? The only problem is, Cedric had no opportunity. He is the only person who has a watertight alibi in prison . . . Unless . . ." I trailed off, but I could see that Phil understood what I was thinking.

"Cedric had an accomplice on the outside, doing all his dirty work for him? But who? Jane? India could have lied about knowing him, and she could have enlisted Oliver's help. George could have had dealings with him because of the castle's sale," said Phil. "I'll see if I can get a look at who visited him in prison recently—that might give us a clue."

"And do we think what happened to Jane was really an accident?" I asked, starting to cook off the onions. "Was it just a coincidence? Everyone thought that Alexandra was just sick until we found out she was poisoned."

"It's what she said. But if she too knew what was going on, one could surmise that someone is busy tying up loose ends. Getting rid of everyone involved in the forgery scam. But unless someone checks the car over then no one would know if it was tampered with."

I agreed. "I wish I'd been able to get more out of her in the hospital. She is definitely hiding something, but I would guess that it's because she knows Euan wasn't really Euan. That's why she's started moving her collection out of the castle—in case the real Euan shows up."

The pasta was at a rolling boil when Oliver came in. "I've got to get back to the pub to check in on everything and close up. Are you all settled?"

"We are, thank you." My gaze fell on a mop and bucket in the corner and I asked, "How is Dolores doing?"

Oliver ran a hand though his hair. "I'm honestly just glad she wasn't the first one who found Euan's body. I'm grateful that you and Carole were there. Euan could be an asshole, but Gran was very fond of him, and he of her. She ran this place, so she's understandably shaken by the whole thing."

"And she knew about you and India?" I asked. "Is that how Euan found out about you two?"

"Look here." His nostrils flared. "Gran didn't mean to say anything . . . only that India had been into the pub. But that's all it took for Euan to become suspicious. India and I were already talking about moving away . . . We were going to start a new life." He sighed. "I need to get back to the pub." He turned and strode out of the kitchen.

Phil shook his head, watching him go. "Perhaps this evening we can get to the bottom of what really went on between India and impostor Euan."

～

We served up the pasta in bowls and all huddled around the fire in the drawing room with the telly on, watching old episodes of *Gilmore Girls*. Carole wanted to watch some sort of dating show, but there was no way I was going to give her any ammunition while I was sitting on a small sofa next to Phil.

"I think we should try to do some antique hunting stateside, don't you?" She nudged me with her foot.

I chuckled, thinking that Rory Gilmore's childhood and mine had a few things in common. "I think we need to stick to the case we currently have."

"But *I* think we need to plan the next one. *I* think New England in October would be prime hunting time, all the leaves on the ground, with spiced pumpkin lattes and all the Halloween costumes . . . I still have that one I got for you for the cruise that Phil liked so much."

"I . . . what?" Phil looked up from reading emails on his phone. "What do I like?"

"Not *what*, darling, but—"

"Nothing!" I glared at Carole, needing us all to get back on topic. "Nothing has been stolen in New England as far as we know."

"Actually, there's been a spate of gallery thefts—" Phil began. I cut him off with a stern look. *Not. Helping*, I mouthed as my gaze caught India, who was picking at her food. "Why didn't you tell us that you knew Alexandra Pattern?"

India put her bowl down on the coffee table. "What does it matter now? I didn't want to get involved with all the stuff she was into. And I wanted to keep Oliver as far away from it as possible. The police are looking into him as well, did you know that? They've been to the pub a few times and it's got the gossip mill going, given his history. I didn't want Bella to be involved either. But Alexandra knew of Arthur Crockleford, so it didn't surprise me when Bella went to see her."

"Because you didn't tell me the truth, I showed up to an appointment with Euan wearing a wig that looked like Alexandra's hair. And I nearly got myself killed. That's not what—" Bella broke off, not willing to say the word "family" or "sister" out loud. She looked at Carole, then me, then Sky, and there was a flicker of pain in her eyes.

"I don't understand why you're this angry," said India, frowning at Bella. "What's going on?"

"I'm going to start clearing up in the kitchen. You both relax," said Carole, standing up to collect the plates.

"I'll help you," I said. "Sky, Phil—I'm nominating you for dishwashing duties."

You would not have thought it possible for such bone-tired people to move so quickly, but everyone understood that Bella needed space to tell India about her real reasons for coming to Scotland.

A few minutes later, as we were setting the kitchen to rights, we heard raised voices.

"What do you mean, *maybe* I'm your *half-sister*?" India's voice was strained and high-pitched. There was a low mumble in response, and then, "You're telling me that Euan and Alexandra were in on the scam of selling fake art in the American market? That you think I have a *grandfather* who's in prison . . . ?" India was almost shouting now.

Carole and I exchanged glances with Phil and Sky. My chest tightened. India was right. We had said that we would help her find out who had murdered her father, but was impostor Euan really her father? The crimes were piling up, and we had no answers to give her.

A door slammed. I winced.

"We'll be the judge of that," Bella shouted back, and a second later the kitchen door crashed open. "Hey, Sky, fancy a drive? I think it's time to go through Alexandra's flat for ourselves. See if we get lucky and she's stashed the silver in her flat. Or if she was the one blackmailing Euan, which the police assume, then she must have some concrete evidence hidden somewhere. Alexandra must have known who the impostor really was." Bella held out Sky's coat; Sky was already pushing past me to reach her.

"Wait. A storm's coming in," I objected.

Sky ignored me, pulling her car keys out of her pocket. "The WiFi's shit here anyway."

"Wait," I called again. It made no sense for them to drive all the way to Alexandra Pattern's Edinburgh flat in these stormy conditions. But neither of them stopped.

"We'll be late; don't wait up," called Sky as they hurried off.

Carole put a hand on my shoulder to stop me. "Must be lovely to have all that get-up-and-go."

Phil shook his head. "If they're caught . . ."

I was about to object, until I remembered that most of the time Bella was better than any of us at evading capture. Still, worry gnawed in my gut, but there was nothing I could do to stop Bella when she'd made a decision.

38

Cedric
Monday, February 12, 9 p.m.

Cedric James stood outside in the freezing cold, but he didn't mind it one bit—it was the icy breath of freedom that he'd waited years to feel. Neither his snooping granddaughter nor those FBI people had asked when he was being released, and he liked the idea of surprising them.

He had bought a winter coat at a charity shop near the prison. He was braced for the oncoming storm.

A taxi pulled up in front of him and he opened the door. "There's a massive blizzard coming in from Scandinavia across the North Sea," the driver said from the front seat as he climbed in. "You're my last job, and I'm only going your way as my gran's over Kelso way."

Cedric grunted. He didn't want chitchat, he wanted revenge. It was an hour's drive to Fawside Castle and the road would be impassable soon.

It wasn't easy to see out of the front window; the snow was coming down hard. It had been years since Cedric had been in a car. The last time, he'd been rushing to get away from a screeching house alarm and the blare of police cars chasing them. Then he'd taken a corner too sharply while the rain beat down. The car had flipped over. There had been a loud thud, a crunching of metal ... and then nothing until he woke up in hospital.

Prison was the punishment he deserved, but he'd been away too long—wallowed in grief—and ignored the world beyond his paintings. And while he was incarcerated, he'd been dealt blows that he never saw coming.

He gripped the door handle and tried to still his thrashing heart. His sweaty hand slipped as the car swerved to the right and stopped.

"All right back there?"

Cedric couldn't breathe; he couldn't get the words out. The world spun as his horrific past came beating down on him. And then he remembered his castle and what had been taken from him. He knew that he just had to get there. No matter what.

"Is the car all right?" he croaked out. "Can we ... go on?"

"It's fine, just a bit of black ice. I'll go slower from here, but we should be there in fifteen minutes or so." The driver looked at Cedric in the rearview mirror. "You sure you're okay? You look like death warmed up."

"I'm fine. Just drive."

He wasn't okay. Far from it. When his son had been killed in the accident, his world had crumbled. Now he was going to set it all right. Revenge was the only thing that had kept him going over the last six years, and now he was ready.

39

Bella
Monday, February 12, 9 p.m.

It felt good to be doing something. Sitting around in a drafty old castle wasn't Bella's idea of fun, and India's venomous words were still running in a loop through her mind. She'd thought India might be glad to learn that she might have more family, because she was an only child, like Bella. It was clear from her angry reaction that she didn't see it the same way at all. They'd gotten on really well when they had met, so it had been hard to see the anger on India's face when Bella tried to explain what she was really searching for in Scotland.

Beyond the windscreen, the snow fluttered down—no sign of the storm that the news warned about. She had spent so many nights on her own over the past few weeks that seeing Sky sitting behind the wheel beside her was oddly comforting. When she'd asked Sky to come with her, Sky had jumped into the car without a second thought.

Bella feared that if she ever met her real father, his reaction would be exactly the same as India's. She had asked the solicitor to get the police to do a paternity test on Euan—then she would have the proof she needed. If the dead impostor wasn't her real father, then who was?

Bella met Sky's soft yet troubled gaze.

"You doing okay?" asked Sky, turning back to the road. "You've had a shit time of it."

That was an understatement, but Bella didn't want to talk about the mess that she had found herself in, so she changed the subject. "I forgive you for telling Freya and Carole all my personal stuff." She focused on the snow-laden hedgerows outside her passenger window.

Sky sighed. "I am sorry. Really. I'm sorry I didn't say that sooner. But all you had to do was call me and not make me so worried that I drove across the country to find you. And now we know it's all connected..." Her tone hardened. "I'm not sorry I told the rest of the team."

"*Team*," Bella huffed. She hated that word. It implied that she was responsible for Sky, Carole, Freya, and even Phil. But Sky had just jumped into a car with her without needing an explanation, and the memory of Carole finding her in the castle and pulling her into a hug still warmed her like a spring morning. They had all wormed their way in. She would need to work harder at pushing them away. That's what she kept telling herself.

"Yes, *team*. That same team saved the day when my crazy ex had me locked in the shop last spring," said Sky. Her tone was light but her words dug deep.

"Has the team expanded to most of Little Meddington? Wasn't it Agatha who got your ex out of the village?" asked Bella. But she knew that wasn't the whole truth. It was Freya who had told Agatha, who had told the village. Sky had been saved because of the Lockwood Agency *and* the wider community they belonged to.

"Okay, how about we use the word 'friends'? We're all friends, and we look out for one another. You're my friend. Like it or not." Sky's lips tipped up. "So, you gonna tell me how you are?"

Friends. It had been a long time since Bella had had any real friends. Her line of work demanded distance—that was how she kept herself safe. But that night at the castle, she hadn't felt safe on her own, which was why she had called Carole. She had known that if something were to happen, they would come running; they would find a way to keep her safe just as they had done for Sky.

Friends.

The truth she didn't want to acknowledge crawled up her throat, because Sky was someone who never judged. And after the conversation with Freya, she realized that she trusted Sky.

"Honestly, it's been a lot. The argument with India tonight . . . I didn't see it coming. Was I really so naive to think she might be happy about having a half-sister?"

"No. You were hopeful . . . and hope is a flighty thing. I think this was the first time in a long time that you had let yourself believe that Arthur had found your father. Had found your family. It's okay to be disappointed. But did you ever consider, that wasn't what Arthur was leading you toward? Maybe he saw the truth about Euan, so he sent you to the people *he* considered family . . . He put Carole and Freya in your path for a reason." Sky started reversing the car into a parking spot. "My dad was a nightmare, and I didn't know my mother . . . Living above the shop is the first time I've felt at home."

Bella folded her arms over her chest and gulped down the lump that was building in her throat. It had been a long time since she had believed she belonged anywhere.

"I brought Freya's lock-picking kit, but I've only just started learning . . ." said Sky, pulling on her coat.

"Don't worry, I'll get us in. Before I went to see Alexandra last week, I did my research and watched her for a day or two. Got familiar with her building and all of that."

Sky reached for the car door. "Who would hate Alexandra so much as to poison her with those mushrooms? It seems like a nasty way to go. You'd have to really have it in for someone to do that to them."

Bella didn't have the answer. She stepped out into a freezing wind that burned her cheeks as her boots crunched on the snow. "All I seem to be doing lately is hanging out in Leith." She had loved living in Leith, but it was still a source of painful memories.

"Is that where Alexandra lived?" Sky looked up at one of the large red-brick warehouse conversions. "Does working at an auction house pay that well?"

"The black market pays well," replied Bella. "The forgery ring would give her a good income . . . And if that were the case, does it make sense that she would blackmail one of the other members?" She took in a long breath. "Alexandra knew my ex, Chris . . ."

Sky stared at her. "How?"

As they walked toward Alexandra's building, Bella told her about Chris and how he was one of the best at trafficking black-market items all over the world.

". . . Chris would've killed Alexandra if he'd found out she was blackmailing anyone close to him. But he's being held on remand, so it can't have been him. I'm sure of that." Bella pressed the buzzer for number eight.

"Hello?" an old, quivering voice answered.

"Is that Jack? This is maintenance. I'm back again to check on the lights in your corridor. We've had a complaint that they still aren't working."

"Oh—well . . ."

"I know it's late. I'm sorry for the disturbance. It's been a long day; you know how it goes. We won't disturb you or come to your door. We just need to check the corridor, if that's okay? Just like before."

The door buzzed, and Bella pushed the door open.

"Done that before?" asked Sky.

Bella shrugged. "I told you that I did some research on Alexandra."

"I didn't know you went digging around *inside* her building."

"You dig around on the web and I dig around in person." Sky

laughed, and it struck Bella that they would make quite a pair with all the information they could gather together.

Alexandra had a sprawling studio flat in the eaves of the building, which meant that all the ceilings were steeply pitched toward the middle. There was a small all-white kitchen and a shower room off the large living area. "It's all very . . . white, isn't it?" said Sky.

"I thought we should come back here. It struck me that there's nothing personal in this place at all. Last time I was here, I was looking for documents or a laptop, so I didn't pay much attention to the decor. But look . . ." Bella pointed at a potted plant in the corner.

"What's wrong with it?" asked Sky, walking over to it. She looked closely at the rubber leaves. "It's fake but a lot of people have fake plants in their homes."

"Do they?" Because Bella didn't think they did. It was the sort of thing you had in an office building. "Do you know what I've been thinking since the last time I was here?" She didn't wait for an answer. "This is all staged like a lived-in home. But I don't think anyone lived here, or if they did, they hadn't lived here long." She pulled a pair of latex gloves from her pocket and started pulling drawers out from a chest, running her hand around the inside of the frame.

"Maybe she's a neat freak or something?" Sky shivered, watching Bella pick through Alexandra's flat. She was standing in the middle of the room with her arms folded, clearly not wanting to touch anything.

"Put these gloves on and start searching for papers, books, or letters."

Bella threw another pair of gloves at Sky, then replaced the drawers and headed to the kitchen. "Check all the food boxes and the space behind the fridge. It's an obvious place, but we'll see how devious Alexandra was when we find whatever she was hiding."

Sky started opening the cupboards, but they were bare.

Bella opened the spotless oven. "Guess she lived on takeaways."

Sky closed the last cabinet. "There's nothing here apart from some plastic cutlery and paper plates."

Bella walked into the center of the room and looked around. What was she missing?

"How about we come at this from another angle? Say Alexandra Pattern was exactly like you. You know, all criminal," Sky said. "If it were you, where would you hide important things?"

And that was the right question—the one Bella could answer. Sometimes it was useful to have the mind of a crook. "Not in here." She strode toward the door.

"How are we going to find her other home, if she had one?" Sky followed close behind.

"I don't mean not *here*—just not in there." Bella paused at the door of the flat. "I wasn't lying about the light. It has been faulty. There were repairmen here last week and that's how I got in." They stepped out into the corridor, which had ceiling tiles like the ones in offices. Bella reached up and started pushing them up, one by one. She was about to give up when one of the recessed lights moved with ease. She pushed it higher, inward. "Will you grab a chair?"

Within moments, Bella had her head through the hole in the ceiling as the light flickered. She was focused on a pink plastic folder concealed on the grid supporting the tiles. She reached up, got hold of it, and handed it to Sky as she climbed down. Pride swelled in her chest—she really did love the hunt.

Sky opened the folder and pulled out three passports.

They took the chair back into Alexandra's flat and shut the door. "We've probably been here too long," Bella said, checking her watch. "We need to get back. I have a bad feeling about tonight. I think Freya and Carole are in danger."

"What do you mean, a *bad feeling*?" Sky called after her, but Bella was already hurtling down the stairs.

40

Freya
Monday, February 12, 11 p.m.

"Where are Bella and Sky? It's getting bad out there. I'll call them again." I stood by the castle's front window watching the snow-covered drive until I saw headlights racing toward the castle. "Someone's coming," I called out to anyone who would listen, hoping it was Sky and Bella but knowing they couldn't have made it back so quickly.

India pulled a large cream Aran cardigan around herself and sighed. "I couldn't stop them." Oliver walked down the stairs and stood behind India—it was clear that he had been upstairs somewhere and had never left the castle when he said he was going to.

Phil and Carole walked into the hall.

"Who?" I asked, straining my eyes as India switched on the outside lights.

"Goodness, I didn't expect a crowd." We all spun around to see Dolores coming down the corridor from the back door. "Oliver said Jane had discharged herself from hospital and George was bringing her back here. Oliver didn't want India to be here alone with her . . ." Dolores's gaze jumped between us. "I didn't realize everyone was here."

"Why is George coming here?" asked Carole.

"Didn't you know?" India snorted. "George and Jane are... at it."

I scanned Carole, checking for signs that she was hurt by the knowledge that George, the estate agent, had taken her out to lunch while seeing another woman. She winked at me.

Carole stepped forward. "More the merrier, then. But you needn't have come out in this weather, Dolores. India asked us to stay with her." She reached out for Dolores. "You're shivering. Let's get you by the fire." As she was walking Dolores to the drawing room, she said, "Seems like we're all having a bit of a party... Do you play poker?"

"This is not the place to fleece everyone out of all their cash... It's late," I called after her.

"I would never." Carole looked over her shoulder, Dolores still in her grip. "I don't really know how to play, but I find card games a wonderful way to really get to know people. And I'm not sleeping until Bella and Sky are back."

I laughed at the lie—Carole was very good at poker because she was spookily good at reading people.

The front door opened and George stepped in with his arm around Jane. Jane's two dachshunds trotted inside and headed for the drawing-room rug by the roaring fire. I realized that George was probably the "friend" that had been looking after the dogs.

"Good evening." He didn't look too pleased to see any of us, until he saw Carole and his frown morphed into a smile.

Carole spun around and planted a wide grin on her face, giving me one of her insincere acting faces. "George, darling, are you staying? We were thinking of playing strip poker."

Phil groaned and sped past Carole into the drawing room. "I'll come and get you when I've found some cards," Carole called after him, and then said to me, "Don't blush—you want to see what's under that chunky jumper as much as I do."

India started laughing. George's face was unreadable—somewhere between wide-eyed disbelief and amazement.

Jane was still hanging off George's shoulder. Her eyes were glassy and vacant with bags underneath them, and her ankle was in a cast. The bravado seemed to have drained out of her. "I didn't realize . . . I just wanted to get home." Dolores left Carole's side and hurried back to Jane. She might be elderly, but she seemed more than capable of taking some of Jane's weight.

"Of course you did. Come on, let's put you to bed, and I'll make some soup for your supper," said Dolores. "This way." She tilted her head toward the stairs. She might have told us how much she disliked Jane, but she was very good at acting the concerned employee.

Carole and I watched them go and I pulled out my phone to text Sky again, asking when they would be back.

The message I got back was not one that I was expecting. "Sky is saying that they found passports at the flat. She's bringing them to show us," I whispered into Carole's ear.

"I can't live with the suspense. Tell her to tell us what they found and send photos." I did, but the message went unread.

"They must be in a dead spot."

Carole sighed. "Very well, let's go and have a little hunt around the study in the guise of looking for playing cards, shall we?"

And then I realized what she'd been getting at with all her talk of playing poker. It made me remember why Arthur had liked to take Carole along on his hunting trips. What she purported to be wasn't always what she was. Together with her flair and exuberance, which was one hundred percent *her* all of the time, there was also true mischief.

The large study made me shudder as I remembered what Bella had told me about the night she'd entered the room nearly a week earlier.

"This is where Bella was attacked. It's no wonder she couldn't wait to get out of here tonight."

Carole shook her head. "That poor girl. After this we're going to help her, aren't we? Take her home and give her some time to relax around friends."

"This all started because she asked Arthur to help her find her estranged family. I'm not sure any of this mess was what she hoped for. So, yes, we're going to make sure that she never has to go to such lengths again."

"Show her what it truly means to be a family."

Like Carole, Arthur had showed me what that looked like when I was a child, after my parents died. He had become part of my family and shared his love of antiques with me, but it wasn't just me he had taken under his wing, it was Bella too. It was Arthur's legacy, just like bringing me home and getting Phil the answers he needed about his FBI partner's death.

I went over to the heavy mahogany desk and started pulling out drawers. None were locked, which made me think that nothing of value would be found inside.

"Isn't it funny that there are old photos of children on the desk, but nothing recent?" I looked up at Carole. She was holding up a photo of two small boys—it reminded me of the photo in Dolores's house.

"Do you think that they're Cedric's sons? Euan and Christopher?" I said.

"I suppose India wasn't fond of impostor Euan enough to want to be in a photo with him, and the feeling, I believe, was mutual." Carole crossed to a Victorian bureau that sat in the corner beside the unlit fireplace. "I have always loved the idea of a Victorian or Edwardian lady sitting at one of these desks writing letters to her lover. Quill and ink in their rightful place . . . and . . . eureka!" Carole held up a boxed poker set that was brand-new and still wrapped. "I bet someone gave him this for Christmas once and he never used it. Have we searched everywhere here?"

I nodded. "I've opened all the drawers and there's nothing of any use. No bills or anything. All the important documents must be somewhere else in the house."

"I'm going to get everyone I can to play poker. Jane is in bed, so that's not an issue, and you and Phil can go search Euan's bedroom for evidence of who he is. He must have kept something on him."

We left the study and hurried back to the drawing room. Phil was placing more logs on the fire while the two dachshunds were sprawled out on the rug. Oliver and India were huddled on the sofa, and George was on the chair next to the fire.

India smiled at me as I entered. "Dolores is making Jane some soup and cheese scones if you want any?" Yet more indication of how well Dolores looked after the members of the household.

"I'm fine." I motioned to the box Carole was carrying. "But Carole did find the poker set—who's up for a game?"

Phil sighed but I gave him a "play along" look that silenced him. He knew that we were up to something, and he now stood quietly, leaning against the fireplace, watching Carole scour the room. "Can I help?" he offered.

"This . . ." She pointed at a card table in the far corner that was piled with old magazines and books. "We can clear it and move it into the middle."

Phil was with her in an instant, and then Oliver, India, and George were drafted in to help move the furniture around. As the clock ticked toward midnight, the game began.

41

Monday, February 12, 11:45 p.m.

The dimly lit drawing room was hushed with the poker players' concentration. The fire crackled and popped as Phil placed another log on its glowing embers. Wind seeped through cracks in the windowpane and made the curtains ripple as sleet hammered on the glass. The wooden floorboards creaked underfoot as I joined Phil by the mantelpiece.

Carole and I had come up with a vague plan to keep everyone busy while I searched the castle again, but I wasn't the actress she was. It made me cringe inwardly as I tried to look as if I was flirting and wanting some alone time with Phil—although if I was honest with myself, it wasn't entirely acting.

"Ready?" I asked him, knowing full well that I hadn't told him the plan. I stepped close to him and ran a fingertip down the buttons of his black Henley shirt. "Play along," I murmured. "We need to search the other rooms." I motioned toward the door.

He looked down at my hand and then quirked an eyebrow. "If you insist." But he didn't move.

I stepped back and scanned the room—it was too hard to keep things professional when he was looking at me that way. The poker players around the table erupted with laughter as Carole continued her story of running out of petrol, walking to a petrol station, and being saved by a local van driver, only to forget where she had left the car. I hadn't believed that anyone would take the game seriously, but then I'd underestimated how hard it was to say no to Carole. Now four people sat around the circular table, their faces bathed in the soft glow of the floor lamps arranged around them.

The fire danced in the corner and the candles on the mantelpiece flickered. Phil leaned toward me and whispered, "Are they really playing *strip* poker?"

His closeness was distracting. I focused on the table. "I think they think Carole was joking about that."

"Then they don't know her very well, do they? She's in her element right now."

My focus narrowed in on Carole, who had reapplied her bright lipstick and was now murmuring to George, who sat on her right.

Time seemed to slip by as we watched the game. George had lost his jacket. India had taken off a shawl; Oliver was unscathed, as was Carole.

The round progressed quickly, with chips and clothing exchanged in a blur of strategic bluffs and nervous laughter.

"Full house," purred Carole, sliding her cards onto the table with a wicked grin. "Let's see what you've got, darling." Her voice dripped with a challenge as she laid down the cards.

"Four of a kind."

Oliver beamed. "Straight flush beats that." He revealed his hand and whooped.

George's expression soured as he leaned back in his chair, exhaling sharply.

Across from him, India groaned, tugging at an earring with a smile— there was something different about her now. A shrewd glimmer to her eye as she surveyed her opponents.

"How are you bearing up, being back here?" Carole asked her. "It must seem strange, painful... after your father..."

"It's weird... but it's also peaceful. That's probably terrible of me to admit, isn't it?" said India. She tried to force another smile, but it came across more as a wrinkled nose.

"This game is getting interesting," muttered George as he pulled off a sock, having lost another hand. "Maybe we should call it a night?"

"No one is sleeping until Sky and Bella are back," said Carole. "This is fun. All we need now is some whiskey."

Oliver nodded. "Where did Euan keep the good stuff?" he asked India as he lost a hand and pulled off his jumper.

Carole glanced toward the doorway as though she half expected someone to emerge from the shadows. "Well, none of us can leave in the middle of a game." Her fingers innocently brushed her hair aside. "Phil, Freya—why don't you go and look for some whiskey in the wine cellar?"

That was our cue to leave.

"And this is *not* the time for you two to sort out all that sizzling chemistry." Carole's smile was knowing, buying us time as she seeded a plausible reason why we might be absent for a while.

I linked my arm through Phil's and pretended to be unsteady on my feet from the wine. We had only taken a couple of steps when a clatter came from beyond the door, and we pivoted around to face it.

"What was that?" India rose to her feet.

Phil was already opening the door. "Are you okay?" he called.

The room fell silent as everyone waited for a reply. "Just the spoon falling from the tray," Dolores called out.

Behind me, Carole leaned toward India and placed a hand on her arm. "Anything the matter? You've gone very pale." Then, with deliberate precision, Carole shuffled the deck and dealt the next hand.

I gave Phil a look; it was time to go. "India, where do you think the whiskey would be?" I asked.

"Probably in the cellar—but you don't want to go down there. It's all damp and creepy. There's probably some white wine in the fridge." She didn't look up from her cards as she said it. "Get some of that instead."

Oliver was frowning at his cards, but every so often his gaze flashed to India and something unspoken passed between them. "I think a glass of wine as a nightcap is a good idea," he said to Phil.

Of course, they didn't know that we had been down to the cellar already—and now I was definitely going down there again.

"Shall we?" Phil asked me as he strode toward the door.

"Time to pay up," Carole added, placing her cards on the table.

Looking back over my shoulder, I saw Oliver smirk at her, his heavily tattooed arms reaching to undo his belt. I had never seen Carole look more thrilled as she shooed us away with a wink.

42

Tuesday, February 13, 1 a.m.

The lights flickered as Phil and I stood in the large main hall. Were they about to cut out? Because that was the very last thing we needed—to be stuck in a medieval castle with no electricity. I studied the nearest light bulb, hoping it was just a blip. When the flickering had stopped, I realized Phil wasn't looking at the lights at all. His focus was on me.

"India doesn't want us anywhere near the cellar, did you get that?" he asked, averting his gaze to the stone arch with its three steps leading to the cellar door.

"Maybe she's the one who put the camera down there?" I frowned. "When Sky reviewed all the motion-sensor footage, she said the only person it showed was Alexandra."

"But whoever put it there could've switched it off when they went into the cellar themselves," Phil replied. He reached toward a threadbare tapestry by the arch. "Here's the light switch; it's nearly covered by this . . ." He pushed the tapestry aside. "Probably why we couldn't find it last time." He flicked the old-fashioned switch and light spread out from under the door.

Jazz started pumping from the direction of the drawing room, and I imagined that Carole had decided to get everyone dancing—probably seminaked. One more distraction to give us some time so that we could find evidence of who had hurt Bella, killed impostor Euan and Alexandra, and stolen the silver before the night was through. It had all started at the castle, and I was desperately hoping that we could end it there.

Phil opened the cellar door and crossed the threshold; I followed him, closing the door behind us.

"We should grab a bottle of whiskey while we're here. In case anyone comes looking for us," he said as we descended the spiral stone stairs.

I hurried over the concrete floor, the odor of dirt and mold hitting the back of my throat once more. I shivered but didn't stop. Arthur had trained me well; the only thing I needed when on a hunt was logic and instinct, the critical judgment that enabled me to discern a fake antique or the small inconsistencies in a person's story. We needed more proof. More clues needed to be unlocked if we were going to find out what had really happened the night impostor Euan died and locate the stolen silver.

"The padlock hasn't been replaced." I stepped through the open iron gate and passed the racks where we had found the camera, which had now been handed over to the police. "We didn't get to look further last time." I pointed to the far end of the cellar, where there was another door, and reached for my bag with my lock-picking kit inside—but it wasn't there. I groaned as I realized I had left it on a sofa in the drawing room.

Phil stood beside me. "Let's hope it's unlocked."

We had only taken a few steps when the lights went out and I spun around, reaching instinctively for his arm. "Has the electric cut out?"

My heart hammered in my ears as my eyes tried to adjust to the darkness that was reaching down the stairs. Long shadows filled the cellar.

It wasn't the electricity; it was the cellar light bulb. The weather hadn't plunged us into darkness. A person had.

There was a distant jangling of keys, and then a lock clicked. My stomach knotted. My legs were moving before I had a chance to think about our options.

With my hands outstretched on the rope banister, guided by the slip of light from under the door, I hurried back up the steps and gripped the door handle. Locked. I pounded my shoulder into the wood. I had never tried to break down a door before, and it wasn't as easy as it looked on TV.

"Easy," Phil murmured, placing a hand on my shoulder. He guided me away from the door, and my back pressed against his chest. "Let's try that other door beyond the wine cellar and see if we can figure out what's going on while someone thinks we're locked away."

"Okay . . ." I was worried about Carole up there on her own.

"If not, I promise I'll break it down," he whispered.

I tilted my chin to peer up at him, but it was too dark to see the promise in his eyes. "Do you have your phone? I left mine in my bag."

Phil patted his jacket pocket. "It's charging in the drawing room. Come on." He laced his fingers through mine and tugged. "Someone wants us out of the way, and we need to find out why."

I pulled my hand back and ran my index finger over the burn scar on my palm, an old tic that resurfaced when I was nervous. "And Carole?" I couldn't look away from the door. "We're locked in here and she's on her own."

"We won't leave Carole for long. And you know she plays the dumb blonde very well." The jazz boomed from above as Phil walked back down the stairs. "We'll get out of here. You got yourself out of the Copthorn Manor vault, and this time there are two of us."

He was right; this wasn't like being locked in the vault—not because the fear of being caged was any less frightening, but because this time I wasn't alone. Phil pulled out his torch, and we hurried through the cellar to the door at the far end.

"Stand back at the entrance and cover your ears." Phil raised the gun and waited for the beat of the jazz to come around again. Then a loud bang echoed around the space.

"There's no way they didn't hear that," I said as my ears rang.

He kicked the door and it swung inward as I caught up with him. It opened into a small, turret-like space—I ran my hands over the walls and found a light switch. A sturdy wooden ladder led up to a door above us, which, I guessed, led to the gardens at the left-hand side of the castle. The wood was well worn and free of dust.

"Do you think Alexandra was the only person to use this entrance? Back in the day, it must have been a coal chute or something," I said.

Phil started to climb and I followed, eager to get back to Carole.

"Someone knew this wouldn't hold us for long, so why bother?" Phil reached the top and pushed the unlocked outside door open.

I was halfway up when I noticed an opening in the brick wall to my right. "Can you give me the torch for a second?"

He stepped down and passed it to me, and I shone the beam into the hole. "There's a bag in here." I reached over to grab it; the ladder wobbled. I shuddered and flattened myself against the wooden rungs.

"Freya?" Phil's voice was hoarse. "What are you . . ."

"I just want to . . ." I leaned forward again and gripped the large duffel bag with one hand while looping my other arm through the ladder and holding the torch. It was precarious at best.

"I don't think you should . . ."

I heaved the bag out of the hole and a metallic clattering sound echoed in the turret. "I think we've found the missing silver."

"Let me help." Phil reached down and pulled the bag onto his shoulder as I climbed up.

Back on solid ground, I huddled my arms around myself as we stepped out into a foot of snow, my jeans instantly soaking through. Icy flakes drove into us.

"The door to the ladder was locked," I said to Phil. "And without seeing the blueprints, no one who didn't intimately know the castle would realize there was another exit." I studied the bag on his shoulder. "The silver was never stolen... it was hidden, to make the police believe it had been taken. Everything that happened was all planned, down to the smallest detail."

Phil pulled me closer and tucked me into his arm. "We'll be out of this soon. Let's head all the way around, go in the back door. Quietly as we can."

My mind was still sifting through new information. "The only thing that nobody could plan for was Bella. She made the appointment with Euan the day before she turned up."

"Ever the wild card," said Phil.

"She's the reason we looked into this far more than anyone was meant to. We don't need to make her toe the line and fit in."

The cold dug deep into my bones and I was desperate to get back inside, but Phil paused before we reached the front of the castle. In the dim light of the torch he opened the bag, and I noticed two silver-and-agate stag menu holders.

"I think those are the pieces from Arthur's journal that were in Euan's cabinet."

Phil closed the bag of silver. "Whoever is behind this must have known these items were stolen. They didn't want the police to see them and start investigating further."

"If they were ever discovered, I imagine someone hoped the police would assume Alexandra stashed them as she left and never got the chance to retrieve them. But what if that isn't true? The only other people who could have left them there are Jane, India—maybe with Oliver's help—or Dolores."

"Or George. An estate agent could have a set of keys, and he would have access to a floor plan," said Phil. He frowned. "Why would someone lock us down there? We're missing something."

The wind hurled snow at my cheeks, making my teeth chatter. My breath fogged out in front of me. "We should get back inside before this weather really turns."

The snow crunching under my trainers had seeped through to my socks by the time we reached the main drive, where we were met by a car speeding toward us. The glare of headlights was blinding—I held up my hand, and Phil pulled out his gun.

"Maybe that's overkill." It only took a few moments to realize it was Sky's car. "It's Sky and Bella." I took another breath, and the freezing air stung the back of my throat.

They pulled up, and Bella got out first. "What are you doing out here?"

Phil holstered his gun as soon as she stepped out of the car, and relief made me smile—that was progress. Bella shook her head at me as she pulled off her puffer jacket and handed it over. "Put this on." I took the coat; I was shivering hard. "You look frozen. Why are you out here at this time of night?"

"Did you see that taxi leave?" said Sky, getting out of the car behind her.

"Taxi? No—we were locked in the cellar. We've just got out," I said.

"It. Wasn't. Me," Bella said, instantly defensive.

"She was driving a car in hazardous conditions. Bella's good, but she's not that good," Sky said.

"Who could have been in the taxi?" I asked. They both shrugged in reply as we walked around toward the back entrance.

The back door was wide open once more, light streaming out and making the fallen snow gleam. It was like a beacon of warmth, and Bella jogged around me in her haste to reach it.

"Was everyone in this part of Scotland born in a barn?" I asked. Phil gave me a quizzical look. "Don't you have that expression..."

"If the two of you are done flirting, you need to see this," called Bella. She had stopped on the threshold and was clutching her arms around herself, staring down at something.

I sped up to reach her, stopping short as I followed her line of sight. A body lay on the dark-red tiled floor of the boot room.

"Oh, hell," said Sky, coming up behind me. "Who's that? Is he *dead*?"

Phil handed me the bag of silver and bent down to the man on the floor to check his vitals. It took me a minute to recognize him, but Bella was already shaking. The man was wearing a jacket much like George's and a green woolen hat.

"He's been hit on the head..."

A pool of blood seeped out onto the flagstone floor underneath him.

43

Tuesday, February 13, 1:30 a.m.

"It's Cedric," said Bella, in a voice so low I almost couldn't hear it.

"Freya, Phil—is that you?" Carole called from somewhere inside the castle. "Where are you? I've been searching everywhere."

"She doesn't need to see this," I said to Bella and Sky. "It'll upset her."

Sky nodded and stepped through the back door, swerved around Phil and Cedric's dead body, and ran down the hallway to keep Carole away from the scene. "Carole?" she called as she ran.

Bella stayed frozen on the threshold, her gaze fixed on Cedric sprawled on the boot-room floor. "Who would do this?" she whispered. I swept her into a hug.

"We're going to find out. I'm so sorry." I pulled back, and her head hung down in the space between us. She looked utterly beaten.

"I only met him that one time," she whispered. "All I wanted was . . . All that's happened since I've been here is death, one after the other."

"Come on. Let's get you away from this." As I took her hand, the lights flickered again, and the back door smashed against the wall as snow gusted in through the opening. "Sky?" I called before turning back to Bella. "I know you don't want to be here, and I understand, but we need to stick together. I don't want anyone else getting hurt. If we assume that it was Cedric arriving in the taxi you saw, then it was someone in this castle that murdered him. And I've a bad feeling that they may have planned this all along."

"To kill Cedric?" Her voice was weak and small.

"This castle belonged to Cedric. With him dead, someone is set to inherit... Who knew that Cedric would be arriving tonight?"

It couldn't be India, I thought. She wouldn't have invited more people to the castle if she'd intended to murder Cedric, would she?

Sky hurried back toward us. "Carole's in the drawing room." She scanned Bella, took her by the hand, and led her away.

With Bella, Sky, and Carole safely in the drawing room, I could focus on Cedric. "Find anything?" I asked Phil.

"I assume that someone was waiting behind the back door, and as Cedric walked through, they hit him," he replied.

In the far corner something caught the light. "What's that?" I took a step nearer and saw a pewter candlestick. A corner of its square base was dented, with a small pool of liquid underneath it—blood.

"Phil..."

He looked up, and I nodded toward the corner. Turning, he saw the candlestick and rose to take a closer look. I followed him, relieved to move away from Cedric. For me, it doesn't matter how many dead bodies I've seen—it never gets any easier. And this time, it also meant we were stuck in the castle with a murderer.

Phil didn't touch the weapon. He pulled out his phone and started taking photos. "I would say that this is what was used to kill him."

"Impostor Euan and Cedric were both hit over the head with objects. Alexandra's murder seemed far more planned out, and poison is a more detached death. The murderer just slipped her the mushrooms and waited for her to die at a later date..."

"You think we could be looking for more than one murderer?"

"Um..." We both turned to see Sky standing in the hallway door.

"In the car on the way back here, I searched into who'd visited Cedric in the prison, and there was someone..." Her gazed flicked to Cedric. "And they matched with the passports we found in Alexandra's flat..."

Phil shook his head and stood up, telling her not to say anything more. "Let's keep what we know to ourselves. Shut the door. I'll call Rodgers. It's time all this ended."

"We heard on the radio on the drive back that another storm is due to hit soon. There's a weather warning. Will the police come out in that?" asked Sky.

"Let's hope so. We should go and check on Bella... Tonight, we all stay together. Sleeping in shifts if we have to. Someone doesn't want us looking into all this, and I don't think they're just going to let us walk out of here after what we've seen." He looked down at Cedric. "I think this is why we were shut in the cellar."

I agreed. Phil was FBI and I was a consultant for the FBI; someone who knew that hadn't wanted us around when Cedric arrived. Phil sighed—clearly he saw the same danger that I did. No one would be sleeping tonight.

~

In the drawing room, Carole was standing by the fire with George and Bella. Jazz was playing more quietly now from an old gramophone. Bella's hand was on Carole's arm in a vain attempt to get Carole to sit down on the sofa with her. I smiled, knowing just how hard it was to get Carole to do something she didn't want to do—but Bella's anxiety was written all over her, and I wanted us all to act as if we knew nothing. Feigning ignorance would be our only protection until the police arrived.

When Carole saw Sky and me enter, she turned off the music. "Oliver thought we could all do some dancing, as I was winning at poker, but then I couldn't find you." She looked at me in Bella's coat. "Where've you been? I've been worried. I went upstairs, but . . ." She'd thought that Phil and I were searching Euan's room.

I looked over at George, who was poised and listening to every word.

"When we went to the cellar, the door jammed. Got out just in time to see Bella and Sky arrive and went out to greet them," I said as Carole came hurrying to my side. "Where's everyone else? You look pale. I think we should all retire upstairs. It's late."

"Maybe we should all have a nightcap," said Sky. "But you don't need to stay with us, George, if you're tired."

George settled back in his armchair, letting her know that he wasn't going anywhere.

"What happened?" asked Carole, gripping my arm. "What don't I know?" she whispered.

"We did call for you." The memory of shouting through the locked cellar door came rushing back to me.

"Oh . . . well . . . George thought Jane was shouting about something, so everyone ran to help her, but when we got there, she said she hadn't called out but wasn't feeling well and wanted to stay in bed. It was strange, and I didn't hear it over the music." The look Carole gave me lasted a beat too long, and I realized that she had something she wanted to tell me too. "India and Oliver took Dolores to a bedroom upstairs and said they would also retire for the night."

Phil appeared in the open doorway and leaned against the frame. "I've called . . ." He saw George and clearly didn't want to warn him that he had called the police. "I . . . saw there's been an accident on one of the main roads out of Edinburgh. A tree down somewhere. Sounds like chaos." He was telling us that it would be some time before help arrived.

Probably not before the murderer has the chance to flee.

"I think I'll go to bed." I smiled at Carole, knowing she would follow me, and left the drawing room—venturing back out into the main hall, wondering if we could somehow take away everyone's car keys.

"What's going on?" Carole stalked after me, followed by Sky, with Bella joining us from the corridor.

"Cedric James is dead," Bella whispered.

"He was killed in prison?" asked Carole.

"No . . . he's—" I motioned toward the boot room.

Carole's mouth opened and then closed. "Tell me."

Phil stood behind us, watching the drawing-room door to make sure George didn't overhear our conversation. "I've locked the back door and the door to the boot room to preserve the scene."

Carole shuddered. "This is terrible." Then the truth dawned on her. "The murderer is in the castle."

"I think that's a strong possibility. So no one is sleeping tonight, and we're all going to stay up talking as if nothing is wrong."

Outside the window, the storm was getting even worse. The lights flickered again, and in the moments of darkness, fear struck my heart. Apart from my daughter, Jade, most of the people I cared about were here in the castle.

"We can either hole up in one of the bedrooms or stay up in the drawing room. Does anyone have a preference?"

Phil hurried toward me and then coughed.

George stepped out of the drawing room and cocked his head—he knew something was going on. "I'm going to check on Jane. Good night."

"Good night," we mumbled in reply.

"Back to the drawing room," said Phil. "I think it's better we're on a different floor from the rest of them."

Within a few moments, we were all settled on the sofa and chairs around the fireplace with the flames licking around the fresh logs Carole had thrown on.

"I have something to tell you all . . ." Sky looked over at Bella. "We found passports in the flat." Her voice was a soft murmur and we all leaned forward, except Phil, who kept to the edge of the room near the door.

"And? Don't keep us in suspense, darling," said Carole.

Bella pulled an envelope out of her pocket. "We found these in Alexandra's building. None of them are who they say they are... Look..."

Phil stepped in and plucked them from her grip. "Three passports. Alexandra Grove, Steve Grove, and Ivy Grove." He flipped the photo page toward us.

"And it was Ivy—or India, as we know her—who had been to see Cedric a number of times," said Sky. "As had Steve Grove—or impostor Euan, as we are now calling him. So India has known everything all along. She was in on the fraud. Is Alexandra her mother?"

We took a closer look at the passports.

"No," replied Phil. "It says *Miss* Alexandra Grove, or Alexandra Pattern, as we knew her. So she must be India's aunt and Euan's sister..."

My mind ran through everything I knew and what the police believed. "And why would a sister kill her own brother if they were working together? Why blackmail him, when she was also hiding her identity?" I turned to Sky. "Can you get out that computer of yours? We've all assumed this con was happening behind Cedric's back. But if India and the impostor Euan went to visit him, then he knew all along."

"It's still in the car. I'll go and get it," said Sky, standing. Bella stood as well to go with her—maybe she wasn't immune to friendship after all.

"Let's have another look in the study," I said. I had an idea. Phil, Carole, and I went into the study, and I ran my fingers along the bookshelves until I came to the old Bible I had already noticed.

"What are you looking for?" asked Phil.

"All along, we have been looking for who the dead man really was and not focusing enough on where the real Euan McGovern might be. Thanks to Sky and Bella, we now understand the family relationships of the impostors. But what of the McGovern family?" I pulled out the old Bible. "Back in the day, family Bibles were passed down the generations and . . ." I opened the large, leather-bound volume. ". . . Sometimes there's a family tree written in the front. Like this." I held open the first page and ran my finger down the list of handwritten names going back to Victorian times, or possibly further.

Reading through them, I took in a sharp breath at the same time as Phil said, "Interesting . . . And now we know."

"It was in front of us the whole time." I reached across to pick up the photograph of two boys that sat on the desk.

Sky and Bella appeared in the doorway; Sky had her laptop in hand. "Could you make up an excuse and get everyone to the drawing room?" I said to Phil.

He went to the door, then paused to look back. "I know this is the agency's first case with the FBI, but this is great work. And you found the silver. You'll get the reward."

"But we don't know all of it. There's still a murderer to find. One of Cedric's sons died in the car crash, but the other one is still alive. That's the very last piece of the puzzle. Where is the real Euan McGovern?" I said.

"You think Cedric's second son is here?" asked Sky.

"I haven't quite put it all together, but until we find out, the Boston case can't be closed." I loved the hunt, but just as important was seeing justice for the three people who had been murdered. "Sky—can you hunt down some answers, now that we know the right questions to ask?"

"It's what I do best." She smiled.

"Arthur set out to get Bella the resolution she needed, and I'm not going to stop until I've honored that."

Phil's smile shone at me with something that seemed a lot like pride, and I beamed back.

44

Tuesday, February 13, 2 a.m.

Darkest night blanketed the castle, and the snow had created drifts up the windowsills while the fire crackled and popped against the icy back draft. But with the amount of chatter in the drawing room, it was clear that no one cared about the time or the weather.

Phil had helped Jane down from her room. She looked far better than she had earlier, but Dolores was still telling her that she really should have eaten something.

I stood in front of everyone—Phil leaned against the door, one hand behind his back, where I suspected his gun was hidden. Sky was standing by Bella's side. She had come to Scotland because Carole and I had left her out of the hunt, so she'd decided to insert herself into it—and I was so glad that she had. We wouldn't be leaving her behind next time. She had been instrumental in finding the breadcrumbs we needed to solve this case.

Once, I'd thought that only someone with a deep knowledge of history and the art, antiques, and antiquities world could join the mission Arthur had entrusted to us. But I'd been wrong. Sky loved the chase—that's what drove her, and it drove the rest of us too. Our common ground was not where I'd expected to find it, but it was no less valuable.

The hunt for the truth. If we kept getting cases from the FBI and made enough contacts to take on private clients too, then I was going to have to find another shop assistant so that Sky could work full-time for the Lockwood Agency.

Dolores cleared her throat and ran a hand through her hair. "Are you going to explain why you've pulled us all out of our beds?" Her nose wrinkled as she glanced at the window. "According to the weather forecast the graupel will start coming down hard and fast soon. This snow is going to be heavy all day tomorrow, so I hope no one has any intention of driving."

She said it as if there weren't a dead body laid out on the boot-room floor. Maybe she didn't know.

Oliver went to stand by her chair. "We'll walk you back to your house in the morning, Gran, but I want to make sure the power is reliably on before we leave. There's a generator here."

And a murderer, Carole mouthed to me.

"It would be wise for everyone to stay here until the storm is over," Phil said. He wanted to keep everyone in the castle until the police arrived. "But we got everyone up because there has been a ... development."

"What's that supposed to mean?" demanded Dolores.

Jane shuffled in her seat to get closer to George. I was quite sure that George would have told her everything he knew—that Cedric had been the true laird and owner of Fawside Castle.

"When did Cedric approach you to sell the estate?" I asked George.

His gaze narrowed in on me and his brow furrowed. "When he first got arrested, he phoned me to discuss selling. He was devastated by the death of his son and didn't want this place anymore. I said I would go around and examine the property, then tell him what I thought we could list it for ..." His hand rested on Jane's thigh. "Jane and Christopher were ..."

The truth rippled into me, and I made a guess—trying to make it sound like a statement—keeping my voice as even as possible. "Jane, you said you were in a relationship before Euan with a man who taught you all about Mauchline Ware and Wemyss Ware. Was that man Christopher McGovern? Cedric's son, who was killed in the car crash?"

Jane shifted and pulled her cardigan around herself.

"She's always been here," spat Dolores.

"But that's not what you told us, Dolores, was it?"

She glared at me.

I continued. "That's who you really loved, wasn't it, Jane? And after he died, you knew that the man passing himself off as Euan McGovern was an impostor. You used that information to keep you in the lifestyle you'd become accustomed to. You sent poison-pen letters to impostor Euan to remind him of what you were owed. Did you ever have an . . . intimate relationship with the man everyone knew as Euan? Or was it all for show?"

"Those letters don't prove anything other than that Euan was a fraud. You don't know anything," said Jane and George took her hand and squeezed it. "Christopher was meant to have all of this. Cedric adored him . . . We were all meant to be here together, until . . ."

Sky leaned forward. "Until the crash. I read every newspaper article there was on the case. The impostor was the only survivor of that crash, wasn't he?"

"Christopher was never even meant to go on that job," Jane said. "He never wanted to but he wanted to keep the castle in their family, and that was the only way Cedric had managed to keep it for so many years. We were waiting for Cedric to agree to open it up as a wedding venue, open up the gardens, as a legitimate way of generating income. He was so close to saying yes and retiring . . .

"After Christopher died, there were a couple of years when fake Euan and I didn't talk. He wanted me to move out, so I may have had to send him some reminders of what I knew. But we got over all that. It was long ago. I've no idea where the letters are now. I assumed he had destroyed them. That's the truth. I didn't kill anyone."

The timeline slotted into place. "Steve Grove, the impostor, worked with Cedric, selling his forgeries? And . . . what? . . . Stealing to order on the odd occasion? So, when Christopher McGovern died, Steve stepped in to impersonate the long-lost son, Euan McGovern, and run the castle on Cedric's behalf?"

Jane sighed and nodded. "But that's not all. Just before the Glasgow job, Steve had got wind of Christopher's plan to take over the running of the castle as a proper venue. No more crime, and no more big paydays for Steve if Cedric retired. And then there was the crash, and Christopher died." Her eyes met George's, as if pleading with him, but I didn't know for what reason.

He picked up the story. "At first, Steve, or Euan, as you knew him, moved in just to 'help sort a few things out,' and then he started to take over. Cedric had said Jane could stay as long as she liked . . ."

"He never said *as long as she liked*!" spat India. "She was meant to leave, but she had it too good here . . . No one wanted you here."

"But George convinced her to stay in the castle and make sure the sale went through and show all the prospective buyers around and charm them. Is that right?" I asked. "What did he offer you, Jane? A cut of the commission? Cedric didn't want anyone to know that the castle was up for sale because he knew that impostor Euan would stop it. So you were here to make sure impostor Euan, Alexandra, and India, or should we call you Ivy, didn't get in the way? I'm guessing the commission would be pretty substantial for a property and land this large."

"George had nothing to do with this," Jane said. "It was all Steve and his grand plans. He never cared how he made his money, as long as he had a lot of it. And the rest of his family were the same." Jane jabbed a finger in India's direction.

"We did what we had to do," said India. "And you profited from his contacts, didn't you? *That's* why you never left. He showed you where the stolen wooden boxes and ceramics were stored, and you sold them in America. Made quite a bit of money. Don't act innocent."

She had to be talking about the Wemyss and Mauchline Ware in Arthur's journal. The collections that had been in the back of Jane's car when she crashed.

Jane pointed at Phil. "Can't you arrest India now? If Euan and Alexandra didn't kill each other, then she must have killed them both so she could inherit the fortune they were amassing in their offshore bank accounts. She seems so innocent, but she knew where the money came from the moment she stepped off the plane."

"I was a kid . . ."

I put up a hand to try and calm the situation. "India—or should I call you Ivy?—isn't in line to inherit the castle. She isn't a McGovern." India glared at me but clamped her jaw shut. "Bella and Sky found all your passports at Alexandra's flat."

"The con is up, love! You'd better start packing." Jane smirked at India.

"I'll leave when you do," hissed India. Oliver reached for her hand.

"Then there's no one left to inherit in the wake of Cedric's death, is there? He told me from the very beginning that both of his sons were dead. So there'll have to be a search for long-lost heirs, I suppose," said George.

Bella came to stand next to me and said under her breath, "Who killed them all? You know, don't you?"

I nudged her shoulder, which was as much physical contact as I thought she would tolerate. "It's all going to be all right. Arthur knew we would get to the bottom of it."

"That's ridiculous," said Jane. "Just arrest India, and we can all get some sleep. She was always sneaking about, listening in to what was being said . . . She was in on everything . . ."

"I think you're right about that," I replied, studying India as she curled into Oliver's side. "India really did know everything. And she did what she thought she needed to do to survive." I stepped toward her. "You were close to Arthur Crockleford, weren't you?" India shrugged in reply. "I think Arthur worked this all out, that you and your father were not real McGoverns. I suspect that was because he had traced the *real* Euan McGovern. But it was meeting Bella that really made you worry. You believed Arthur had sent her. And so you told the only person you could trust."

"I didn't tell my father or Aunt Alex that Bella was going to the castle that night . . ." India sat up and glared at me.

"No, I don't think you did. But I think you told Dolores. A housekeeper always knows what's going on. She's been very protective of you, hasn't she?"

"Well, of course I have. She's just a girl," snapped Dolores.

"That's not it." I held up the Bible. "In this Bible is a family tree. You, Dolores, were married to Cedric James McGovern for six years, and during that time you had two boys. There is a photograph in your house of two boys . . . your sons, Euan and Christopher. You implied it was a photo of your grandsons, but that was just to throw us off.

"It was very clever, really . . . all so well planned out. You had free rein of this castle, and you knew Cedric. I believe you spent your time finding out every little secret. One of which was the existence of the Leith flat, its location, and the keys. Inside the flat, you found the paintings, so you had Oliver move them into the attic here. Will the police find his fingerprints on them? It was you who told us where to find them, because you put them there. It must've taken months, or even years.

"Did you know your estranged son, the real Euan McGovern, had had another daughter? What did you think when India showed up saying she was Euan's daughter? Were you worried? Cedric might have told some of you that the real Euan McGovern was dead to him, but Dolores suspected that her son was still alive. He had two children that she knew about, and loved, but there could have been others that she didn't."

The room was holding its collective breath until Bella spoke up. "You knew all along?" She wasn't talking to Dolores. She was pointing at India, and I saw just how desperately she'd wanted to believe she had a sister. "What did your father offer you to change your name and keep quiet?"

"I told you to keep away from my dad. That he wasn't a ... good person." India gripped Oliver's hand so tightly that her knuckles were white. "We were all doing so well. The paintings were selling, and my dad was keeping up his end of the bargain for Cedric. Keeping the place afloat while he was inside. And in exchange, Cedric let him keep the remaining profit of the paintings he sold."

"Why did you go along with it all, when he was so cruel to you?" asked Phil.

"Look, I kept my mouth shut, and I got all the education I needed. I was about to get as far away from my aunt and my dad as I could. But when he died..."

"You stuck around to see if you could somehow inherit. To see if the con would work," I said. "But have you even seen a will? I don't think you have, because there was no need for the solicitor to show you one. Cedric was the owner of the castle, and he was still alive. It wasn't about the inheritance. You just didn't want the police to look too closely at your father's death in case they found out his true identity."

India glared at me.

I nodded at Sky.

"Right, that's my cue, isn't it?" She opened her laptop. "Steve Grove, your father, the impostor, was in a car crash six years ago, just before you came to England. In that crash, Christopher McGovern was killed. Cedric James was driving."

"No, my dad wasn't there. He said he proposed the deal to Cedric after the crash, when it was clear there was no one to look after the castle and keep the other side of the business afloat... My dad knew how the art market worked. And my aunt, and some guy called Chris Prince, could help him move the stuff. Cedric agreed because he was in such a mess over his son's death."

"Yes, that's what confused us at first," said Sky. "But then Freya realized we needed to cast the net wider, because everything came back to Cedric. I searched for who had called the emergency services after the car crash... ran a search on local newspapers. One local paper had a quote from Euan McGovern explaining how he had 'discovered the crash.' Except the *real* Euan wasn't even in the country."

"Sky is quite brilliant at what she does when given the right questions to answer." I held up the family Bible, and India frowned. "I remembered that long ago, people recorded the births of new family members in their family Bibles, and this was the last piece of the puzzle. Euan McGovern's middle name was George."

George started shaking his head. "Oh no. I've nothing to do with this."

"He hasn't." I looked around the room.

"So... what are you saying?" asked Bella.

"Euan George McGovern is living as George McGovern in Queenstown, New Zealand, and Sky has just come off the phone with him. He had a strained relationship with his mother and father, and he cut Cedric off altogether after Christopher died in the crash.

"He also told Sky that his ex-girlfriend left him years ago and moved to England... taking their two small children with her. The last he heard they were living with his mother which he didn't sound happy about." I faced Oliver, who was trying to look confused. "The real Euan

McGovern, who lives in New Zealand, is your father. And *you* will be the heir to Fawside Castle when he dies." Before he could reply, I focused on Dolores. "The two boys in that photo in your cottage are your two sons . . . you made us think that they were your grandchildren. And it worked, until . . ." I held up the Bible. "Your eldest lives on the other side of the world, and your second-born was killed in the car crash while running from the police."

I expected a reaction from Dolores, but she just sat in her fireside armchair and watched the flames. Until at last, she said, "Katy, Euan's ex-girlfriend, showed up at my door with Oliver and his sister, begging for help after flying all the way from New Zealand. She had gone to the castle first, but Cedric had turned her away. Cedric and Euan never got on, probably because Euan was a far more talented painter than his father. I hadn't spoken to my ex-husband, Cedric, for years, and I would've kept it that way until he called to tell me that Christopher had died." Her voice cracked. "At the funeral, I didn't make myself known, but I saw . . . I heard . . . some odd things. Like a man who wasn't my son using his name." She gripped the arms of the chair.

Oliver shook his head and spoke at last. "A couple of months later, Gran asked me to drive her up here again. We found someone calling themselves by my father's name answering the door. He assumed Gran had come for the housekeeping job he had just advertised. So she took the position as his housekeeper. It was the perfect opportunity to get to the bottom if it all."

Dolores stood and placed her hand on Oliver's shoulder to stop him talking. "I came up with a little plan. Oliver's sister hasn't been . . . well. We needed money . . ."

"And what was I?" India's voice cracked as she turned to Oliver.

"Indie, you were a way to get information. What did you think? That you were going to inherit all this?" Dolores chuckled. "The impostor Euan and Alexandra were getting too close to the truth . . .

They'd begun to suspect who Oliver really was. He does look quite like his father. But Oliver and his sister deserve their inheritance, not for Cedric to sell it off and disappear." She glared at Jane and George. "My granddaughter is coming out of the hospital soon; she had a breakdown, and she needs somewhere to rest. When we heard Cedric was getting out... well, everything had to happen."

Tears ebbed down India's cheeks as Oliver stepped away from her and stood with his hand outstretched. "It's time to go, Gran."

Phil pulled out his gun. "I don't think so. Sit back down." He gestured with the gun toward the sofa. "I want to hear the rest of it. Dolores... if you will enlighten us? Because I don't believe that you could have hauled Steve Grove's body out into the garden. Or that you would have had the upper-body strength to hit Bella or Cedric over the head."

Dolores sighed. "I'm old, but I'm not a weakling. I'm a good cook, and I do know a thing or two about mushrooms. Of course, I confess to everything. Hitting that impostor over the head with a candlestick... everything." Oliver was about to open his mouth, but Dolores gripped his arm. "I'll just sit here and wait for the police."

Watching her slowly lower herself back into the chair, I knew that Phil was right; she certainly hadn't done it all on her own. Oliver was the one who had really killed Steve Grove and Cedric and hit Bella over the head—I just hoped that the police had some DNA or fingerprint evidence to prove it.

45

Bella
Tuesday, February 13, 4 a.m.

Oliver and Dolores had been working together, but Dolores wouldn't let Oliver say anything. They sat on chairs at opposite ends of the room with their mouths tightly shut. It annoyed Bella, as she wanted every last detail on why they had attacked her . . . when they were probably family. But she also admired the loyalty they shared. Everyone had given up asking them questions, as Oliver had started to say "No comment" to everything.

There is a certain time of night, just before the break of dawn, that allows icy darkness to seep into your bones. It scored a shiver down Bella's spine as she grabbed a log and threw it onto the fire. It popped and hissed, and she wrapped her arms around herself. Phil picked up her coat from the arm of the sofa and brought it over, placing it around her shoulders. "Thanks," she whispered without a hint of venom in her tone. Warmth spread through her.

Phil retreated to his place in front of the door. His gun was drawn. An irritated itch wanted to trickle down Bella's spine, driving her to leap up and open the door, as she hated being caged in anywhere—but this time it was easy to ignore. This time, she knew that Phil would step aside if she asked—the door wasn't blocked for her. And it was only a little bit grating to accept that she trusted Phil now.

She pulled the coat around herself and acknowledged that she had spent the last hour with her back to Oliver and Dolores. It wasn't lost on her that she would never, in normal circumstances, have ignored two murderers who were only feet away. But the sense of safety she now felt was hard to overlook. And that safety had shockingly been created by an FBI agent, even though her instincts had told her to stay away from him. And to keep her distance from the members of the Lockwood Antique Hunter's Agency, who had absolutely no sense of self-preservation or adequate weapons training. And all of this had almost certainly been handed to her on a platter by her old friend and mentor, Arthur Crockleford.

Clever, Arthur.

He had known that Bella couldn't really find what she was looking for when she searched for her real father. Her real father was in New Zealand, and she had no idea whether he wanted to meet her or not. Her half-brother, Oliver, and his sister had left Euan when they were very young, and according to Dolores they'd had little contact with him since. Euan wasn't going to win any father of the year awards.

But Sky was right—Arthur had given her another option: he had given her the people *he* considered family. Freya and Carole. And they, in turn, had given her Sky; and even Phil. Arthur had known what she needed long before she had seen it for herself.

Bella pulled her knees up to her chest and rested her forehead on them—she was exhausted. A hand touched her shoulder and she looked up, expecting Sky or Carole, but it was Freya sitting down next to her.

"Are you okay?" Freya's voice was low and her brow crinkled with concern.

Bella shrugged. She wasn't. "I'm fine. Guess you should be careful what you wish for, shouldn't you?"

"I don't understand?"

"Turns out my grandfather is a forger who got his own son killed in a car crash, and my grandmother and half-brother are murderers." Her stomach twisted in disappointment.

"But your father is alive and living in New Zealand," said Freya. "Plus, you have us."

They heard Sky laugh and glanced over to see that Carole was telling her some anecdote and refilling her glass of wine. They were both chuckling.

"What are you going to do now?" asked Freya. Before Bella could make something up, she continued, "Come back to Suffolk with us. There's a spare room above the shop. You can stay there until you know what's next, or until the next case comes in. It's totally up to you how you work with us. I was wrong to try and create a role that you needed to fit into, but you're a great value to the agency. We need you . . . in whatever way you want to show up."

Bella focused on the dancing flames again. She couldn't remember the last time someone had said that they needed her. "I'll think about it."

She had never been part of anything, not a friend group or a large family—it would take some getting used to if she were to allow herself to become part of what Freya was building. But she couldn't deny that what Freya and Carole wanted to create called to her. She didn't want a life of always looking over her shoulder and being attacked by . . .

"Which one of you hit me?" she called over to Dolores and Oliver.

"Does it matter?" asked Dolores.

Bella rose and stalked toward them. "Yes."

Oliver's gaze rested on his—their—grandmother, and Bella knew the answer. "Did you know who I was?" she asked Dolores.

The old woman's gray hair was coming free of her plait. "I knew that Euan got a Turkish woman who lived in London pregnant nearly thirty years ago. He was always bad news, so when he left the country with the law on his heels, I thought that little baby was better off without him. But then Arthur Crockleford came around and started asking questions, and I started to wonder where that little girl was. I'm a very good listener, and I knew there was no Emma Page working at the auction house... As soon as I saw you out the window, I could see my son in you." She shook her head. "There was no other option. This here..." She motioned around the drawing room. "This is for the grandchildren that I brought up—Oliver and his sister. It was never meant for you."

Bella wanted to shout at her that she was one of those grandchildren too, but there was no point. Instead, she turned to the facts. "It belongs to the real Euan McGovern while he is still alive," she pointed out, her chest clenched with the pain of betrayal by a family she had never known.

"Well, that all depends on what the will says, doesn't it?" said India. "Cedric told me he disinherited Euan."

Warm hands rested on Bella's shoulders; Sky was standing behind her. "Come sit with us."

Bella retreated to the sofa and slumped in between Sky and Carole, the weight of her situation making her bone-tired.

Carole tapped her knee, bringing her attention back to the sofa. "Sky was telling me about the fourth journal Arthur left." Her voice rasped with tiredness. "Have you seen it?" When Bella shook her head in reply, Carole continued, "You must ask Freya to show you when we get back to Suffolk. Lots of lovely Venetian glass. There might be a link to the annual Venice Carnival Robberies. I love Venice, don't you?" There was an unmistakable twinkle in Carole's eye that made Bella smile. "Sometimes it takes a very skilled mistress of disguise to catch a thief."

A laugh emerged from Bella's lips, and she shook her head. It was as if Arthur knew that everything she had learned, all the skills she had acquired while working in the art and antiques black market, could be put to better use. He was always telling her to choose a different path, and now one had opened up before her. She arched her neck around to study Phil, whose gaze flitted between Dolores and Freya. Could she really work with the FBI? Bella was apt at hiding, and she knew she could walk out of the castle and never be seen by them again. The real question was, did she want to be on her own again?

In the distance, the faint shrill of sirens had everyone on edge—apart from Phil, who straightened his shoulders and looked like he was even more in his element. Bella smirked as Phil opened the drawing-room door. At least Detective Rodgers was going to have to acknowledge that he had been wrong—not just once, in accusing Bella, but twice, in thinking Euan and Alexandra had killed each other. Even so, she didn't feel the need to see him again anytime soon.

She rose to her feet.

"This way," Phil said to Dolores and Oliver, herding them with a twitch of his gun.

Carole grabbed Bella's arm as she was about to leave. "This couldn't have been solved without you. We have the silver, so we get the reward from the insurance company, and we've uncovered where the Boston paintings came from, who painted them and who we believe trafficked them over there. With your share of the reward money, you could visit the real Euan McGovern in New Zealand. I heard Freya and Phil talking, and Euan may be getting a little visit from the local authorities soon, to check he's not still painting forgeries . . . but after that, you could go and experience some New Zealand sunshine. Our winter is their summer. I've heard there's this speedboat that zooms down the river in Queenstown and spins around—I mean, what could be more exciting?"

Bella hummed. Maybe, before she decided on her next course of action, she should finish what she had started and meet her father at last.

"And perhaps you've just inherited a castle." Carole winked at her and turned away to charm Detective Rodgers, who was glaring at Phil and Freya as they tried to explain what was going on and how Cedric had ended up dead in the boot room.

Sky slung an arm around Bella's neck. "So, you're going to drive back with me. Carole thinks we should make Freya and Phil drive back to Suffolk together alone." She placed her head on Bella's shoulder. "Just until you decide what you want to do."

Bella nodded. "Is your car roadworthy for that sort of long drive?"

"What? I take offense at that. I'm dating a mechanic, and he keeps my car well serviced!"

Bella sniggered and nudged her. Then they both burst out laughing.

"Back to Suffolk, then?" asked Sky, trying to catch her breath.

"Sure," replied Bella. Because, surprising as it was, she had to admit there was nowhere she would rather be, nor any other people she'd rather be with.

46

Freya
Thursday, February 15, 4 p.m.

I stood in the kitchen at Crockleford Antiques and waited for the kettle to boil as memories of the drive back ran through my mind.

It had taken us nine hours to drive down to Suffolk. Phil and I had taken Carole's car; Sky, Bella, and Carole had already jumped into Sky's and taken off before we had a chance to discuss driving arrangements.

Along the way, I had pulled into the same service station where Carole and I had stopped on our way to find Bella. More than anything, I was relieved that we had found her and she was safe. I was glad she was coming back with us.

I'd collected our coffees and sat down as Phil leaned across the table. "Are you going to keep ignoring it?"

I looked at him. "What am I ignoring, exactly?" I was trying to keep my voice even and my pulse from racing.

"What's going on here." He motioned between the two of us. "Us."

"I don't . . ." I really didn't want to talk about what was going on, because I didn't know what "us" was. "We're colleagues."

Before Scotland, I think I would have used the word "boss," but that was not the way our first case had played out—Bella had taught me that. I had learned, in standing up for her, that I could be a different type of leader and the Lockwood Antique Hunter's Agency could be a different type of team, one of our own making. We had solved the case in our own way. Sky and Bella might have murky pasts, but they had proved their unconventional methods could be used for good.

"I am incredibly grateful to you for hiring us as consultants, but there are other cases to solve. We're always available to consult for the FBI, but we also have matters of our own to investigate." My mind played through the images of Arthur's fourth journal, with its listing of Venetian glass and other Italian treasures. I copied Phil's earlier gesture, waving a hand between us. "*This* could be complicated, and I have my team relying on me."

Phil tilted his head and smiled slowly. It was the type of smile someone might use to placate a wild horse. "Your team? I'm glad this case has taught you that. It's always been your team, but I'm the sort of person who will step up and take control if no one else will. You've a great group, and I'm glad to be part of it." He reached out and tucked a stray curl behind my ear. I froze and scanned the café, relieved to see that no one was paying attention to us. My cheeks felt warm, and I assumed they were turning red.

"Maybe we should get back on the road," I said.

"We do have time to talk about it."

"Do we?" I really didn't want to face the emotions that were running through me.

"We do. I've booked a room at the Crown for a couple of days, as I'm owed some vacation, and I'd like to spend some time getting to know you better," he said. "And then perhaps you will trust me enough to show me the next journal that Arthur Crockleford left you."

"Oh, there aren't any more. It was just those three." I stumbled over the lie.

"We both know there are more than that." Phil stood and picked up his coffee. "Let's get back on the road."

～

The shop was bubbling with life as I carried the tea tray to the table in front of the bay window. There was a strong scent of furniture polish that reminded me of home, and Carole's husky laugh echoed round the room. Agatha was gleefully directing Phil to move chairs around and making sure everyone was gathered as she reached for a Lalique glass plate—which was far too precious to be used, but I loved that she was putting it in the center of the table. A cake box was opened, and Agatha set out bright pink cupcakes and slices of red velvet cake, along with cucumber sandwiches.

"You all missed Valentine's Day, after all," said Agatha, coming to stand next to me. "How was the drive?" She winked at me and tilted her head in Phil's direction. "Carole told me you were arriving, so I thought I'd arrange a welcome party."

"I'm glad to be home. I'm glad everyone's here." I caught Bella's eye and smiled. On the drive back I had wondered if she would stick around, and I was glad to see that she had.

"As it should be." Agatha sat down next to Bella and started to explain that Simon, her husband, had taken retirement, so she had put him to work in the tearooms, and the old ladies loved him. It just so happened that Agatha loved antiques as well... And I realized that we might have found our new part-time shop assistant.

Carole picked up the teapot to pour as the low winter sun shone through the window. Sky briefly looked up and smiled as I sat down next to her before going back to placing more cakes on her plate.

Phil was opposite Bella, and they were chatting about some thefts in New England as if there had never been any animosity between them.

"Thank you so much, Agatha, for all this. And for looking after the shop. It was really very kind of you." I gave her arm a squeeze.

"Well, we high street shopkeepers have to look after each other. There are too many small businesses closing down. We're the heart of the village, and you and your aunt are part of that."

I beamed at her.

"And I see that everyone is back together again." Agatha nodded toward the table as Sky was telling Phil that he wasn't allowed any more cupcakes while plucking one from his plate. "I know this is still new to you, but you're doing so well. Arthur would be thrilled." She patted my arm. "And I sold quite a few items while you were away. I think I may have missed my calling. Anytime you need someone to look after the place, you let me know." She stood up before I could insist that she stay and pulled on her coat. She gave everyone a wave and was out the door before I could thank her again.

Evening arrived early at this time of year, and the streetlights buzzed to life outside the shop window as I watched Agatha head home.

"I've got all the ingredients for a hot toddy," called Carole, holding up a bottle of Scotch. "I'll get to cocktail-making."

"Just a heads-up," said Sky, catching Bella's eye. "When Carole puts alcohol in something, it's enough to embalm someone."

Carole returned with a tray of mugs and handed them around. She raised her mug and held it up toward the center of the table. "To us."

"To us," we replied in unison, tapping our mugs together.

I saw the happiness on Bella's face as she took us all in, and it made me relax back into my chair. We had solved our first case together, and we were all here in Arthur's shop once again because each of us had chosen to be here.

We were not just colleagues, we were friends—friends with a common goal and a joint love of the hunt. And together, we were stronger than ever.

ACKNOWLEDGMENTS

Being half Scottish—my mother grew up in the Borders town of Galashiels—I spent a good amount of my childhood in Scotland. It was an utter joy to return there while writing this book. I loved every second of it. I hadn't been back in far too long, and the book was the perfect excuse to take a road trip. So, last summer my family and I packed up the car and headed for Scotland: part research, part walk down memory lane, which included a long-overdue catch-up with Riddell Graham and following his great itinerary. It was one of the best family holidays we've ever had—and it only rained for two days! My kids' favorite part of the trip was the cat café in Edinburgh, even though they have two cats at home they ignore.

Some of the villages and buildings in this book were inspired by my research, but this is a work of fiction, so I have changed and adapted both where I needed to.

To my editors—Francesca Pathak at Pan Macmillan, Adrienne Kerr at Simon & Schuster Canada, and Sean deLone at Atria—thank you ever so much for helping this book to shine. Over the past year I've had the pleasure of working with some brilliant publishing teams who have helped my books fly. Thanks to Lucy Hale, Christine Jones, Stuart Dwyer, Claire Evans, Leanne Williams, Alex Coward, Becca Souster, Laura Marlow, Becky Lushey, Josie Turner, Laura Sherlock, James

Annal (for yet another brilliant cover design), Emily Sumner, and the wider team at Pan Macmillan. And thanks to Gena Lanzi, Dayna Johnson, and Morgan Pager at Atria, and to Mackenzie Croft and Cayley Pimental at Simon & Schuster Canada.

To my agents, Samantha Haywood at Transatlantic and James Wills at Watson Little—thank you for jumping in and making sure everything ran smoothly for this book. I'm excited for the future.

I have named many of my friends in past acknowledgments; you know who you are, and I'm still so thankful for all your support. But a big thank-you must go to Kate Wells, Annalise Avery, and Nicola Baker for being in our accountability WhatsApp group. Without this group of hugely talented authors, *Murder at the Castle* would never have been delivered on time. Thanks to Ali Clack for all the coffees, Annette Caseley and K. C. Collinson for booking writing retreats and letting me gatecrash, and Kristin Perrin for joining me on book adventures. Max aka Digital Forensics for being the go-to police procedural expert and Hannah Brennan for giving me ideas how to get around police procedure! And special thanks to the authors who have taken the time to read and give me a blurb.

To book bloggers, influencers, booksellers, and librarians, you have my heartfelt gratitude for all your support.

To my family—thank you for putting up with me endlessly talking about writing and my books. Being an author has always been my dream, and I feel incredibly grateful to be so supported.

And of course, to you, dear reader, thank you for reading.

You can find out more about me and the books at www.clmillerauthor.com.

ABOUT THE AUTHOR

C. L. Miller started working life in publishing as an editorial assistant for her mother, Judith Miller, on the *Miller's Antique Price Guide* and as a researcher for the *Antique Hunter's Guide to Europe*, and then went into hospitality and events. After she had children, she decided to follow her long-held dream of becoming an author and began writing full-time. She was an Undiscovered Voices winner and was showcased in the UV anthology.

C. L. lives in a medieval cottage in Dedham Vale, Suffolk, with her family.